LONG JOURNEY BACK

JEANNE BANDOLINA

Cover design by Damonza.com

Manufactured in the United States of America

LONG JOURNEY BACK is available on Amazon.com in paperback and ebook.
You can email Ms. Bandolina at Godsbest4you@yahoo.com.

This book is dedicated in loving memory to my father.

Donald R. Hunter

United States Navy (WW2 Pacific Front)

1943-1946

Pomona, California Fireman

1960 -1976

*Proceeds from the sale of this novel will be donated to:

Wounded Warrior Project and Gary Sinise Foundation

ACKNOWLEDGMENTS

With the deepest appreciation:

My co-author God, who blessed me with the story.

My mother, who has encouraged me each step of the way.

My beloved family (aunts, cousins, and two sisters-in-law), who have shown me the true meaning of being tenacious and never give up on the dream.

James McCully, who has been a major contributor to the story.

Kyle McNeal (*BirthRights*) for his early coaching and editing assistance.

Greg Gallein, my beloved friend from "down-under," who took the manuscript through the final proofread.

My editor, Nicole Ayers (*Ayers Edits*) who continues to mentor, encourage, and enlighten me on the guidelines of being an author. The gift of her friendship is an added bonus.

LONG JOURNEY BACK

Who shall separate us from the love of Christ?
Shall tribulation, or distress, or persecution,
Or famine, or nakedness, or peril, or sword?
For I am persuaded, that neither death, nor life,
Nor angels, nor principalities, nor powers,
Nor things present, nor things to come,
Nor height, nor depth, nor any other creature,
Shall be able to separate us from the love of God,
Which is in Christ Jesus our Lord.

ROMANS 8:35, 38–39, KJV

✝

CHAPTER ONE

T HE VOICE OF THE air traffic controller came through on Captain Alex Decker's headset. "Galaxy Express three-four-two, you are cleared to four thousand feet. Check your airspeed."

"Roger that," he responded. After descending to the next choke point on their approach to Piedmont Triad International Airport, he adjusted the speed accordingly.

While keeping a vigilant eye out for other aircraft in the area, Alex scanned the cloudless sky, the color known as Carolina blue in this part of the world. The weather today was a pleasant change compared to what he and his first officer, Scott Daniels, had experienced during the past three days. They had encountered blizzards in the north and severe thunderstorms in the south while traveling up and down the eastern corridor.

Topping that challenging sequence of events was what transpired the previous day in Jacksonville, Florida, when an alarm signaled a fire in the right engine during take-off. Daniels shut it down and activated the fire suppression system as Alex pushed the one remaining engine to its limits to gain altitude. First responders and emergency vehicles were in place by the time they circled back to the field. However, they weren't needed, for the two seasoned pilots safely landed the plane. Within the hour, the crew and passengers were on their way to Pittsburgh after transferring to another Galaxy airplane.

The faceless voice of the air traffic controller echoed in Alex's headset. "Maintain present heading for a runway zero-five-left approach. Winds zero-two-zero at six knots. You have gate twenty-eight on the north concourse."

"Roger that," Alex replied. Just then, a hand gripped his right shoulder, the heat from it radiating through the fabric of his shirt. Startled, he spun around.

A man in a police uniform stood right behind him. "Captain, change concourses." The tone in the officer's voice was demanding, and the fingers on Alex's shoulder dug into the flesh beneath his shirt. "Request a gate on the south concourse."

"You can't be in the cockpit during landing," Alex said sharply, his face forming a scowl.

"You say something?" Scott asked, his eyes transfixed on the instrument panel in front of him.

Alex glanced at his copilot, then back over his right shoulder. The man was gone. "I . . . Never mind." Focusing on landing the plane, he heard the man's baritone voice once again.

"Everyone on this plane is in danger!" The words boomed in Alex's ears. "Do it *now* before it's too late!"

Adrenaline pumped through his veins as gut instinct—acquired during his years of military service—kicked in. Though Alex had learned to follow an order once given, this didn't make any sense. And he would later question what compelled him to switch to VHF2 on the radio control panel, which he connected with operations. "This is Galaxy Express three-four-two, Captain Decker requesting a gate on the south concourse."

Scott glanced over; his surprised expression regarding the last-minute change didn't go unnoticed, and Alex held up a hand to dissuade any questions.

"Roger that, you have gate forty-five, south concourse," the operations controller replied. "I'll inform the tower."

Alex reconnected with VHF1—the uplink to the tower—and the air traffic controller's voice crackled in his ear. "Galaxy Express three-four-two, we have you on visual."

He positioned the plane on the glide path. "Okay, Scott. Flaps down, gear down, arm the speed brake."

The radar altimeter announced their altitude: 1000 feet, 500 feet, 100 feet, 50 feet. Alex flared back on the controls just as the wheels connected with the runway and experienced the familiar jolt.

"Nice job, Captain," Scott said with a smile as they exited the runway and proceeded to the terminal. "A greaser."

"Makes a big difference when the weather isn't tossing us around." Though Alex's voice remained calm, his mind was racing.

Alex was on his feet as soon as they arrived at the gate. Reaching for his hat and jacket, he said, "Sorry about the last-ditch change in gates, Scott. I need to speak to the chief pilot prior to going back out."

He opened the cockpit door and spotted the senior flight attendant addressing the passengers as they deplaned.

"Sally, you gave a police officer access to the cockpit while on approach without prior authorization. That's not acceptable. I need to speak to him right now. Where is he?"

Her brow furrowed in confusion. "I don't understand your question. I can assure you that no one entered it during the entire flight."

Unconvinced by her response, Alex studied the passengers' faces as they exited through the front door. The mysterious visitor didn't come into view, and he surmised the man had already deplaned.

Stepping into the jetway, he maneuvered around the disembarking passengers and made his way into the terminal. He searched up and down the semi-busy concourse and came up empty. With no other option available, he swiped his badge through the ID scanner at a nearby door and descended toward operations.

Even though it was Saturday, the chief pilot would be in his office. Captain Robert Jacobson was not merely Alex's boss and former commanding officer but also his best friend. Maybe Robert could help him make some sense of what happened in the cockpit.

"Boss in?" Alex called out when he reached operations.

Not waiting for an answer, he proceeded down the long hallway and came to an abrupt stop at the entrance to the chief pilot's office. The young policeman, who was in the cockpit earlier, now stood in front of Robert's desk.

CHAPTER TWO

THE CHIEF PILOT, HUNCHED over the desk, raised his head. "Alex? What're you doing here? I thought—" His gaze shifted to the police officer. "I'm sorry. I didn't hear you come in. Can I help you?"

The man in uniform never had a chance to respond. An explosion from outside the building shook the windows in the hallway. "No!" he yelled and pushed past Alex as he dashed from the room.

A second blast—louder than the first one—caused the hallway windows to explode inward, sending shards of glass flying into the office. Alex dropped to the floor, shielding his head with his arms as debris rained down. Robert dove underneath his desk. As soon as it grew quiet, they were up on their feet and out the door with Alex taking the lead.

They joined the policeman and the growing crowd outside operations and stared in disbelief as plumes of black smoke spiraled up from the midsection of the north concourse. Red, yellow, and orange flames licked up the side of the building and danced along its roof. Toxic air containing invisible residue from melting plastic, metal, and burning jet fuel made Alex's eyes water and left a rancid taste in his mouth.

A loud *whoosh* caught everyone's attention as the jetway at gate twenty-eight erupted into an inferno. A female agent—visible in the tunnels opening—stood waiting for an inbound aircraft. The flames overtook her; screaming, she fell ten feet to the ground below.

Alex momentarily recalled another hellish catastrophe when his wingman's plane crashed while landing on board an aircraft carrier. Sickening screams emanating from those trapped inside the building across from them drew him back to the present.

Addressing the operations supervisor, Robert shouted to be heard over the sirens from approaching first responders. "Jack, how many aircraft do we have on the ground?"

The paunchy middle-aged man—his face drained of color—reluctantly drew his attention away from the burning concourse on the other side of the tarmac. "Nine. Five here on the south concourse, four on the north."

Senses already in overload, Alex registered an inbound Galaxy aircraft, which had stopped a short distance from the jetway in flames. People escaping the burning building were about to cross its path. He gripped the supervisor's forearm in a vice hold, his voice booming, "Radio the captain to shut down those engines! Someone's going to get sucked into one!"

The supervisor sprinted towards operations. In no time, the aircraft's engines grew quiet as a tug showed up and towed it out of harm's way. Upon returning, he informed them that TSA had closed the airport. "We're on lockdown."

Even with the growing cacophony of sirens and turmoil, Alex heard the policeman, who stood beside him, speaking to himself. "Oh my god. I'm so sorry, Caroline."

Alex pivoted on the balls of his feet to confront the man, but the officer was no longer there.

The chief pilot grabbed his arm, redirecting his attention. "Where's your plane?"

"Right here"—Alex pointed over his shoulder—"We were scheduled to go right back out."

"Who's your first officer?"

"Scott Daniels."

"Have him stay with the aircraft. You're with me."

Alex acknowledged the mandate then addressed two Galaxy ground-service employees standing behind him. "Which direction did the policeman go?"

Their confused expressions spoke volumes. Alex restated the question. "The uniformed officer that was standing here with me, did you see which way he went?"

Perplexed, they hesitated; the taller one finally said, "I'm sorry, Captain. We didn't notice any policeman with you."

He wanted to yell in frustration, *not again!* Pushing past the two men, he elbowed his way through the packed group of Galaxy employees, his eyes taking in each person as he passed. When he broke free, he collided with a ramp-service employee, nearly knocking the man to the ground. The employee regained his balance and limped over to a tow-tug. Glancing back at Alex, their eyes briefly met before he climbed up and drove away.

Alex spotted his first officer on the ramp near the tail section of their plane and gave up the search for the policeman. Scott was bent over with vomit splattered at his feet. He straightened as Alex approached, his color ashen and his breathing erratic. "I was doing a ground check of the plane when I heard the first explosion." He shuddered. "The second one happened, all those people . . . the glass blew, and they came flying out, engulfed in a huge ball of fire."

Facing that direction, Alex counted six bodies on the ground beneath the blown-out windows at gate twenty-eight. First responders had arrived, but they were too late. The corpses continued to burn. The pungent smell of burning flesh—even at this distance—made bile rise in his throat.

Pushing all other concerns aside, including the policeman, he focused on the next course of action. "Scott, we're in lockdown. I need you to stay with the aircraft until further notice. Keep the main door closed and unauthorized people out. I'll be with Robert. Call me on my cell phone if you need me."

CHAPTER THREE

ALEX AND ROBERT DIRECTED those fleeing the fire to an access door in the south concourse. As soon as everyone was safely inside, they helped distribute bottles of water and blankets while paramedics administered first aid. When more ambulances arrived, Alex and Robert assisted in loading the many injured onto gurneys, who were then transported to a local hospital. After giving their statements and contact information to the authorities, they continued helping ground-service personnel in dealing with the distraught passengers who remained behind.

As the evening finally wound down, the two men made their way back to the chief pilot's office. Alex was stripped to the bone, emotionally and physically. There was no escaping the lingering smell of smoke, for it penetrated everything. Soot and sweat coated his uniform and skin. The acrid taste of residue remained on his tongue, even though he had scoured it twice with an unused toothbrush Robert retrieved from a desk drawer.

He knew he should mention the policeman to Robert. After all, the man was in this room earlier. Or was he? Alex was beginning to question whether the man really existed since he was the only one who saw him.

As his uncertainty grew, he realized what he needed to do was to go home, decompress, and regain a sense of balance in his life. Maybe then he could discern the reality of what had happened in the cockpit and afterward, though, at the moment, he doubted he had the energy to get out of the chair.

The chief pilot sat nearby, eyes closed with his feet resting on top of the desk and a cold cup of coffee nestled on his lap.

Alex checked his watch: 11:09 p.m. "Need me to hang around any longer, boss?"

"No, you go. I'm right behind you."

Alex tentatively rose as Robert stirred and lifted his head. "Why don't you come home with me? It would save you the hour drive to your place."

Stretching to work out the kinks in his back, Alex yawned. "Thanks for the offer, but I want to sleep in my bed tonight."

Robert sat up, lowering his feet to the floor. "The Feds have scheduled a meeting for management at eight a.m. at the Airport Marriott. I want you there as my second pair of eyes and ears."

"Okay."

On his way to the main terminal, curiosity compelled him to bypass it and continue to the north concourse, where he encountered crime scene tape blocking further access. The smell of noxious fumes caused his throat to constrict, and his eyes watered even at this distance. Stepping back, a series of coughs assailed him. Images of the fire further clouded his vision as phantom screams and sirens echoed in his brain. As the coughing subsided, he pushed the unwanted thoughts back into the dark recesses of his mind and detected movement at the far end of the corridor. Floodlights illuminated the concourse and the tarmac outside. Various investigative teams were working through the night to piece together the timeline leading up to and after the fire.

"I'd hate to have your job. Been there, done that, and it isn't fun."

The FAA had made a televised announcement earlier in the evening as to the cause of the explosion. Two drug enforcement agents—disguised as Galaxy Express ground-service personnel—apprehended a known drug trafficker arriving on Flight 820 from Atlanta. The felon grabbed the DEA agent's holstered gun while being escorted down the jetway stairs to an awaiting van. A struggle ensued, and the weapon discharged. The bullet punctured a tanker truck's fuel hose connected to the aircraft.

Friction from the bullet's impact ignited the fumes, whereby the fire traveled simultaneously down the hose of the tanker and along the plane's fuel lines in the wing. The truck blew up first, then the airplane. The force of the explosions and the subsequent fire tore through the midsection of the north concourse.

Alex was relieved to learn the accident wasn't due to a deranged idiot seeking revenge by killing innocent people. Just the same, friends and families of the victims would be struggling to cope with the horror of what had happened.

And what about the police officer? Was the man real or an illusion? Alex battled with those questions and his perception of reality as he drove home, south, through the dark countryside.

SUNDAY, APRIL 15
LEE COUNTY, NORTH CAROLINA

He believed a good night's sleep would give him the rest he needed but was proven wrong as nightmares from his past life resurfaced.

Intense heat scalded his skin and sent shivers of pain throughout his body. He tried to take a breath, but poisonous fumes filled his lungs and threw him into a coughing fit. Everywhere he looked, the fire blocked his escape. Sarah, his wife, called out to him. She was beyond his reach. How could he save her if he couldn't find her? The unthinkable was happening. Panic clouded his judgment, and he remained frozen in place.

"Alex, where are you? It hurts. Hurry!" Her voice tore at his heart.

The dream changed. He was on an aircraft carrier flight deck. Jet

fuel from a F/A-18 Super Hornet, which had crashed upon landing,
fed the inferno. It shouldn't have happened. A crosswind caught the
left-wing of the Navy jet five feet from touchdown, causing it to
dip to the left and cartwheel across the deck. Pilots and flight-deck
crewmen scattered to escape chunks of hot flying debris as the air-
craft broke apart. In desperation, Alex tried to reach his wingman,
Chris Reynolds, trapped in the plane as flames licked at his ankles.
Crewmen kept pulling him back.

"No! Let me go. Let me go!"

The dream faded, and he sensed a presence in the room.
Blood pulsated in his ears as his heart hammered against his
chest. He kept his eyelids closed and focused on his breathing
until his heart rate slowed. Opening his eyes, he discovered the
room veiled in dark shadows and no one in it other than himself.

"What in the world?" He was convinced someone stood next
to the bed, staring down at him as he slept. Switching on the
light, he glanced at the clock: 3:33 a.m.

Now fully awake, he put on sweatpants and a jersey and
went for a run to clear his mind of the haunting images. Soon
the quiet rhythm of his Nikes on the dewy grass soothed his
jangled nerves. The spring night air was invigorating, and the run
charged him with adrenaline. Regrettably, it failed to dismiss the
previous day's events. The face of the policeman kept resurfacing.
The man's intense green eyes, commanding voice, and the heat
from his hand on Alex's shoulder were as real now as when the
officer first appeared in the cockpit.

Alex jogged up and down his private runway until the cres-
cent moon dropped low on the western horizon. While walking
the final two laps to cool down, he decided to check on Amelia.

He stepped through the side door of the small hangar and
flicked on the ceiling lights. The polished red exterior of a vintage
Stearman WWII biplane sparkled like stars in the sky. "Hello,
girl. Miss me?"

A 1941 Staggerwing Beechcraft sat next to it in the second

bay. Alex had purchased it three months ago for a rock-bottom price due to the fact it needed a complete overhaul. He welcomed the challenge, for he loved working on antique airplanes. When finished, buyers seldom quibbled over the asking price due to their pristine condition.

He had refurbished and sold numerous antique biplanes through the years, but he would never sell his first and favorite airplane, the Stearman named Amelia. Placing a hand on the fuselage's cold, smooth exterior, he felt euphoric energy pumping through his veins. He had intended to take her up for a spin today. Unfortunately, yesterday's events had changed those plans.

As the sun crested the eastern horizon a short time later, Alex traveled north along the two-lane country road while making his way back to the Piedmont Triad International Airport.

CHAPTER FOUR

O N ANY GIVEN DAY, airline personnel packed Copal's Grill due to its proximity to the airport. It was open 24/7 and offered down-home southern cooking— not-so-healthy but delicious. Today, due to the airport's closure, the place was virtually empty except for a handful of regulars.

Alex occupied his usual table with his back to the wall, a habit acquired during his time in the service. The plump waitress with mousy brown hair streaked with gray placed a cup of coffee, orange juice, and a glass of water on the table in front of him. "Mornin', Capt'n. The usual? Scrambled eggs, sliced tomato, and dry wheat toast?"

"You read my mind, Ina Lynn." He heard her chuckle softly as she scurried toward the kitchen.

Working through a week's worth of mail, he sorted each piece into various piles on the table. Ina re-emerged from the kitchen and topped off his coffee, "Can I give you some of my bills?"

Alex tossed a credit card statement onto a growing stack. "Sure, no problem. Better yet; we'll swap out."

Ina's smile faded, and her tone lost its playful banter. "Airport's closed. You ain't goin' to work, are you?"

"No, there's a meeting I need to attend."

"It's too awful," she said in a choked voice. "I wish them talkin' heads on TV would shut up."

"Couldn't agree more."

An attractive, petite woman, dressed in a dark blue suit and silk blouse, entered the restaurant while they were talking and sat at the table to his left. A stylish haircut framed her face and enhanced her striking features. Alex nodded a silent greeting to her, and she responded likewise.

"Good mornin', ma'am," Ina Lynn said as she handed the woman a menu. "Today's specials are on the front. May I gets you some coffee?"

"Yes, make it large with an extra shot of caffeine. For that matter, bring me the whole pot."

FAA? Home Land Security? Undercover agent? Nah, she's too attractive to go unnoticed.

As the ladies concluded their verbal exchange, the front door opened, and three rowdy young men entered the restaurant. The pungent odor of sweat mixed with alcohol assaulted Alex's senses as they passed by his table. He checked the time: 7:05 a.m. "Oh, brother," he mumbled to himself.

The leader wore torn jeans, a plaid shirt, and a black leather jacket. His two companions mirrored his choice of wardrobe and body language. Their loud voices bounced off the walls of the restaurant as they settled into a nearby table. "Yo, Ina Lynn, bring us some grub. You got some hungry men on your hands."

The waitress emerged from the kitchen, balancing two breakfast platters of food in one hand, and a coffee pot in the other. She topped off Alex's cup and placed one of the plates in front of him. "Hold your horses, boys. I gotta serve some other folks first."

Noticing the woman in the power suit, the ringleader said, "Well, look what we've got here. Ain't you a pretty thing!"

Alex groaned under his breath and glanced in their direction. It was apparent the young man had left his brains in the booze bottle. Ignoring him, the woman continued reading something on her iPad.

"Hey, sweet cheeks. You ain't from round here. You like to party? We could show you a good time."

Alex started to intervene but stopped when their eyes connected. "I've got this," she mouthed.

The troublemaker slid his chair over next to the woman and placed an arm around her shoulders. "I bet you've never been with a good ol' southern boy. You've no idea what you've been missin'."

Staying attentive to the scene as it unfolded, Alex reached for his coffee cup and noticed the breakfast platter in front of him. It consisted of runny eggs, sausage, bacon, and grits *swimming* in melted butter. Ina had delivered the wrong order. The food's greasy smell—together with the excessive amounts of coffee he had consumed—soured his stomach. He fought the urge to vomit.

Addressing the ill-mannered young man, the woman set the iPad down. "You need to go back to your table." Her voice was stern, as if reprimanding a spoiled child.

Ignoring her request, he moved closer and placed a hand on her upper thigh. The woman recoiled when the idiot leaned in and whispered something in her ear. Extracting herself from his clutches, she got to her feet, grabbed Alex's plate of food, and slammed it into the punk's face. With her free hand, she reached into his jacket and withdrew a gun.

While snatching Alex's plate, she inadvertently bumped his arm. Hot liquid from the coffee cup splashed onto his neck and poured down his shirt. He sprang to his feet in reflex, knocking over the table and scattering the mail across the floor. Ignoring the mishap, his eyes remained locked on the woman, awaiting her next move.

Gooey eggs and grits dripped down the young assailant's nose, cheeks, and chin onto his shirt. He spat out, "You b—"

She shoved the table into him with her thigh, and it caught him in the chest, cutting off his words. Next, she checked the gun's safety and dropped it into her bag along with the iPad. "Hands where I can see them. That goes for your two friends." All three complied.

Registering pain, Alex sucked in a breath through clenched teeth and glanced down at his once-clean white dress shirt. "Oh, boy."

She offered him an apologetic smile as she pulled out her cell phone.

Bubba, the owner, emerged from the kitchen. He towered over the woman by eight inches and two hundred pounds. "Rudy, what've you done? I've told you time and again you boys can't come in here after you've been out drinkin' all night. Your pappy's gonna pitch a fit." .

A rustling noise at the far table caught everyone's attention. One of Rudy's friends slid his left hand beneath the table.

The pretty woman slid back a corner of her jacket and displayed a gold shield attached to the waistband of her skirt. "Don't even think about it, puppy. Put it back."

The young man complied as the woman dialed 911. "This is Special Agent Rodriguez. I'm at Copal's Grill next to the airport. I've got three young men who appear to be drunk and unruly. One of them brought a concealed weapon into a public restaurant. Hold on a second."

She eyed her assailant. "Rudy, do you have a license to carry this gun?" He diverted his eyes and didn't reply. "I thought not."

Glancing at Alex, she asked, "Do you want paramedics to check those burns?"

He held up the palm of his hand. "Not needed; I'm good."

Ending the call, she got the attention of the waitress, who hovered nearby. "Ina Lynn?"

"Yes, ma'am." Distraught, the waitress's eyes were the size of golf balls as she took in the scene.

The agent pointed to Alex. "I spilled a cup of your delicious coffee down the front of this gentleman's shirt. Can you lend him a hand?"

Alex sidestepped the scattered envelopes and papers on the floor. "Come on, Ina Lynn, show me where the first-aid kit is in the kitchen. I'll pick up the mail afterward."

Reminiscent of the previous day, sirens rang in the distance as they left the dining room. He hoped this morning's adventures weren't a prelude to the rest of his day.

CHAPTER FIVE

PIEDMONT TRIAD INTERNATIONAL AIRPORT
GREENSBORO, NORTH CAROLINA

THE DIGITAL CLOCK ON the front console read 7:55 a.m. as Alex drove into the Marriot parking lot. Exiting from the truck, he pulled on a sports jacket in a futile attempt to mask the XXL T-shirt Bubba had loaned him.

Robert was waiting for him in the lobby. "You're late. Let's go." Finally, noticing the T-shirt, the chief pilot paused. "Why are you wearing that? Never mind. Just stay out of sight."

Once they reached the conference room, Robert joined the Galaxy management team in front as Alex settled into a seat near the back. He smiled when he spotted the dark-haired person in the front row; it was the spirited woman from the restaurant.

Hank Townsend, chairman of the Airport Authority Board, approached the podium and introduced himself. "I want to thank each of you for coming. The board members and I wish to express our sympathy for the loss of the employees from Galaxy Express Airlines and Landmark Aviation. I'll now hand this meeting over to the FBI, who'll be managing the investigation."

A stocky, broad-shouldered man in a dark business suit moved to the podium. "Good morning. I'm FBI Special Agent Richman. As you're aware, at three thirty-three p.m. yesterday, a Landmark Aviation fuel truck and a Galaxy Express airplane caught fire. It immediately spread to gates twenty-seven and twenty-eight on the north concourse."

Though the FBI agent was rehashing yesterday's televised news feed, an added tidbit caught Alex's attention. *3:33? Isn't that the same time I awoke this morning?*

Feeling a hand on his right shoulder, he looked behind him. No one was there, which only validated that his nerves were on edge due to the previous day's events and further compounded by the lack of sleep.

Agent Richman continued, "The inbound passengers on Flight Eight Twenty Seven and three of the four crew members deplaned prior to the fire starting. One crew member, nine Galaxy ground personnel, and eight civilians didn't survive. Forty-eight people were taken to the hospital and treated for burns, shock, and injuries."

He paused to take a sip of water, then added, "The airport is currently closed to all commercial airlines, except for the air-freight companies, which resumed service this morning. Our goal is to reopen the airport with limited service by this time tomorrow morning."

Murmurs echoed through the audience. Richman held up his hand to silence them. "The north concourse sustained considerable damage, and Galaxy Express Airlines has lost the use of seven gates. It's a significant number since this airport is a regional hub for them." He scanned his notes. "In the meantime, passengers are being rerouted through the Raleigh and Charlotte Airports. FBI Special Agent Rodriguez, who's sitting in the front row, is the lead for this investigation."

As the meeting drew to a close, Alex exited the building to get some fresh air. In no time at all, Robert and Agent Rodriguez came through the front entrance doors, and he joined them. As the chief pilot made introductions, Rodriguez studied the bright orange T-shirt beneath his jacket that read *COPAL'S GRILL* with

Bubba's Breakfast and Bar-B-Que printed below it. She raised her head, and their eyes met. "You again!"

In response to Robert's puzzled expression, Alex explained. "We met over coffee this morning."

"I asked Agent Rodriquez if the FBI could release our grounded airplanes as soon as possible," Robert said. "They're needed elsewhere,"

Addressing his concerns, Rodriguez said, "I won't guarantee anything at this point, although I'll see what I can do."

"Alex, I want you to stick around," Robert added. "You'll ferry one of the planes to Atlanta once I get the green light. I'll have a copilot on standby ready to go with you."

"Understood. I'll get a hotel room here."

"Let me help with that," Rodriguez said as she typed on her iPhone. "There. I just booked one for you and put it on the government's tab."

He grinned. "Saa'weet. I also need my travel bags, which include my flight manuals. I left them on the plane I brought in yesterday."

"I'll have them delivered to you within the hour."

A short time later, Alex lay on the hotel bed, propped up against the pillows. He placed a damp towel on the tender skin of his chest and neck. The relief was short-lived, for there was a knock at the door.

The room-service order arrived along with his travel bags. He tipped the bellman, placed the food tray on the bed, and removed the plate cover. The aroma of a baked potato and ribeye steak made his mouth water. Even though it was still early, he was ready for a decent meal.

Surfing the television channels, he wasn't surprised the local stations remained focused on the fire at the airport. He selected an old movie while savoring the last bit of steak and leaned back on the pillows.

He awoke with a start, momentarily disoriented by his

surroundings. The afternoon sun filtered through the window sheers enveloping the room in diffused light. As his mind cleared, he relaxed.

It was a mistake to fall asleep with the television still on. Someone was always blowing someone or something up. Alex reached for the remote and shut it off. "I've had enough things exploding in my life."

He got up and changed into khaki pants and a black knit shirt. His mind remained filled with apprehension and questions. Alex needed answers, and the place to start was at the airport.

CHAPTER SIX

THE TSA AGENT AT the airport's security checkpoint motioned for Alex to pass through the X-ray scanner. "Sorry for the delay, Captain. With the airport closed, I needed to check with some folks prior to giving you access."

"No problem." He passed through the security scanner and walked toward the bank of windows that overlooked the tarmac between the two concourses. The airport seemed deserted except for a bustling of activity at the midsection of the north concourse.

Alex stared at the charred remains of the jetway where his inbound airplane was initially slated to park. If it weren't for the police officer showing up in the cockpit, his plane would be a skeleton of its former self and melted into the asphalt.

Moving on, he approached the north concourse entrance and encountered a temporary wall that was put up during the night. Ducking beneath crime scene tape, he reached to open the access door, and he heard someone approaching from behind.

"Where are you going, Captain?" Agent Rodriguez slipped beneath the yellow tape and joined him.

Surprised, he greeted her with a sheepish grin. "I'm no different than the idiots on the freeway passing an accident. We have to take a peek."

"Sorry, I can't let you do that. Besides, your boss is looking for you."

Alex's cell phone rang, and Robert's name was on the caller ID screen. "You psychic?"

With a lighthearted chuckle, she gestured dismissively with her hand. "On the way here, I informed Captain Jacobson we're releasing the grounded Galaxy airplanes first thing in the morning. It's time to strap on your flight goggles and parachute."

He lifted the phone to his ear as Rodriguez started toward the main terminal. "Give me a second, boss." Alex lowered the phone and called out to her. "How did you know I was here if you're not psychic?"

Turning and walking backward, she said, "TSA called me, and I asked them to delay in letting you go through so I'd have time to get here. I had a hunch that you would come this way."

Alex nodded. "You're good."

"That's what they tell me. Travel safe," the agent said, then spun around and vanished around a corner.

He spoke into the phone. "I'm back. What's up?"

The tone in Robert's voice carried an air of authority. "The Feds will be releasing our aircraft first thing in the morning. You and First Officer Chip Murphy will ferry one to Atlanta. Wheels up at zero five-thirty. It's the same plane you brought in yesterday, fueled and ready to go."

Making his way back to the hotel, Alex mentally went through a checklist. "Anything else?"

"When you get to Atlanta, report in for temporary duty with crew scheduling. I've already notified them."

Back in the hotel room, Alex ordered a grilled chicken salad and spent the evening skimming through vintage airplane magazines he had brought from home. At nine, he repacked his overnight bag and flicked off the light after placing a request for a wake-up call.

The dreams came in waves as he drifted off. An angelic voice called out to him; her words were hard to make out. *What are you saying? I don't understand.*

Alex awoke with a start. The green glow from the digital clock sitting on the nightstand read 3:33 a.m. Closing his eyes, he beckoned sleep to return and found the effort useless. The images of those escaping the burning north concourse played over and over in his mind. He reflected on the woman's voice in his nightmares. He knew it wasn't his wife, Sarah, so who was it? And what was she trying to tell him?

MONDAY, APRIL 16

Shades of pink, fuchsia, and soft tangerine painted the Monday morning predawn sky as Alex banked the Galaxy Express aircraft south. Once they landed in Atlanta, he and the first officer reported to crew scheduling.

The haunting nightmares continued to invade his dreams at night as he spent the week crisscrossing the country. By the time the weekend approached, he was mentally and physically exhausted.

While on a layover in Denver Saturday night, he made up his mind to go down to the bar and have a drink on the premise it might help him sleep. The place was packed, and a four-piece band played a familiar song from the '80s. Sliding onto a recently vacated barstool, Alex had a sudden sense of foreboding in the pit of his stomach. Coming here was a bad idea. Four years, five months, and eighteen days had passed since his last drink.

Alex was in the midst of changing his mind when the bartender shouted, "What'll it be, buddy?"

"Budweiser."

The young man wiped off the countertop and laid down a coaster. "Coming right up."

Surveying the room, Alex noticed the bar held a cross-section of people—all ages, sizes, shapes, and skin colors. The music wasn't obnoxiously loud, and the band carried a good tune.

The bartender sat three beers down in front of him and grinned.

"I ordered a single beer," he snapped, his voice harsh in his ears.

Ignoring the rude inflection, the young man pointed to a nearby table. "Those three ladies each bought you a round."

He glanced in their direction, and a blonde, redhead, and brunette greeted him with a welcoming smile. Even in this light, Alex could tell they were probably in their mid-twenties and beautiful.

"This must be your lucky night," the young bartender said.

"I'm forty, so at my age, it's more of a miracle."

Grabbing the beers, he approached their table. "I appreciate the gesture, ladies. Unfortunately, I have a wife and five kids waiting for me at home." With a wink, he added, "Maybe in another life."

In the elevator, he questioned his judgment and sanity, not only at declining the company of three lovely women but for ordering the beer. Troublesome reminders of rehab ran through his mind and how he had nearly destroyed his life after losing Sarah. Alex had made a commitment to himself and Robert—no more drinking—and had worked hard at keeping that promise. Even so, he recognized the signs indicating that he was teetering at the edge of an abyss.

He paused upstairs in the hallway before pressing the access keycard against the scanner for his room and read the number on the door: 333. Upon entering, he went straight for the mini-refrigerator stocked with beverages and snacks available for purchase. Alex withdrew a can of beer, popped the tab, and placed it on the cabinet in front of the television. He added a couple of mini vodka bottles to the lineup, his preferred chaser in the old days. His cravings escalated the instant his senses caught a whiff of their alluring smell. Sitting on the edge of the bed, he stared at the containers of poison in front of him. That's how he labeled them these days. Drain cleaner or alcohol, in his mind, they weren't much different.

Alex tried to recall how many times the number three had shown up during the past seven days. On Wednesday, while on a layover in Memphis, he had ordered a grilled chicken sandwich and a smoothie at McDonald's. Back in his hotel room, he discovered the bag contained three Big Macs instead of his original order.

Reviewing the past week's travel itinerary, he recalled that his hotel room's location each night had been on the third floor, including the one at the Airport Marriott on the first day. To top it off, he consistently awoke at 3:33 a.m. He closed his eyes and attempted to clear his mind. *It's all a coincidence, nothing more.*

He got up and carried the beer can and vodka bottles into the bathroom, where he dumped their contents down the toilet. "I don't know about tomorrow, but tonight you have no power over me."

CHAPTER SEVEN

ALEX HAD BEEN RELIEVED when his temporary duty assignment ended the previous evening. He caught the last flight out of Atlanta to Greensboro and was back home by midnight.

Exhausted, he sat at the kitchen table, gripping a coffee cup, and willed the digital clock on the microwave to speed up. At eight o'clock, he dialed the number of the therapist who worked with him following rehab.

"I'm sorry, Captain Decker," the receptionist said. "Dr. Zimmerman is out of town and won't be back for another week."

Disconnecting, he pitched his phone into the trash and paced about the kitchen. "It's a good thing I'm not suicidal!"

He considered driving to the VA hospital in Fayetteville. On the other hand, that could open a can of worms he didn't want to expose to the light ever again. Thus far, he had succeeded in keeping the PTSD and drinking at bay. The question being, for how much longer?

Retrieving the cell phone, he called his AA sponsor at his office. The receptionist answered, listened to his request, and placed him on hold.

In no time, she came back on the line. "You're in luck, Captain. A patient had a last-minute cancellation, and Dr. Newman said he would see you at eleven."

RALEIGH, NORTH CAROLINA

Alex was on familiar turf as he stepped through the door leading to Dr. Newman's private office. Sunlight filtered through a large bay window at the opposite end of the room, sending shards of rainbow colors dancing across the wood flooring. It took a moment for his eyes to adjust and notice the doctor motioning for him to take a seat on the couch.

The doctor took a seat across from him in a wingback leather chair, and wasting no time, got right to it. "I haven't heard from you in a couple of weeks. How are you doing?"

Alex's mouth went dry as he fidgeted nervously with his cuticles. "I—I don't know. Not so good, I guess."

"Have you relapsed?" the doctor asked, his voice grave.

"No!" Unable to meet the man's eyes, Alex let out a long sigh, flexed his fingers, and settled back in the chair. The ticking of an antique grandfather clock on the far wall filled the momentary void that followed. "It's about the fire at the airport." His voice was hushed at first, then grew in volume as he continued. "It shouldn't have happened!"

Unaffected by the sudden outburst, the doctor asked, "Were you there?" Not getting a response, his friend pushed forward. "I can only imagine what you're going through right now. Have you discussed any of this with Robert?"

Alex didn't reply. Instead, he shifted uncomfortably in his seat and stared down at the floor between his feet.

"I'm sure the airport authorities are offering crisis counseling to those who witnessed the tragedy. Have you considered reaching out to them or one of your company's therapists?"

Alex felt the room was closing in around him as his breathing became labored. Rising, he walked to the bay window, creating a space between them. With his back to the doctor, he said, "I came to you rather than going to Robert or the corporate shrinks because they'll think I'm nuts. I won't let anything jeopardize my pilot's license. You know flying is my life!"

"Yes, I do."

Alex spun around to face the doctor. "I believe those people could've been saved. The policeman tried to warn us. If we just had had more time." Raking his hands through his hair, he added, "And that woman who keeps haunting my dreams. What does she want?" The tone in his last words resonated with frustration and anger.

The doctor's brow furrowed in confusion and worry. "What are you talking about?"

Ignoring his friend, Alex headed to the door. "I gotta go."

"Wait!" Dr. Newman jumped up, reflexively reaching out with his hand. "Don't leave. I promise I'll help you sort through this."

Alex paused at the door with his hand on the knob. His next words came out in a choked voice. "No one should've died. Not Sarah, or my wingman, Chris, or any of those people at the airport." Then he was gone.

∞

While mentally sifting through what had just transpired, Dr. Newman walked over to his desk. As a pediatrician, he wasn't professionally qualified to deal with PTSD, but his friend needed help.

Reaching for the desk phone, he buzzed his receptionist. "Julie, ask Dr. Fletcher if he has any free time today. I need to speak to him as soon as possible."

He sat down and typed Alex's name on the search screen of his laptop. Reading through the list of options, he didn't see his friend's name pop up in connection to the airport fire. He did find a few entries related to Captain Decker's military service history and his current career with the airlines. Farther down on the page, it noted the pivotal moment when the two men had become interconnected. It was the obit for Alex's wife, Sarah Decker, who had passed away five years earlier.

Dr. Newman narrowed the search to the airport fire nine days earlier, which produced multiple entries. He read through the first one; there was no mention of his friend. One name on the list of casualties did catch the doctor's attention: Flight Attendant Caroline Bishop.

Bishop was a prominent name in the Raleigh area, and he questioned if there was a connection. He planned to probe more into the tragic incident later; however, his immediate concern was his friend's emotional stability.

CHAPTER EIGHT

PIEDMONT TRIAD INTERNATIONAL AIRPORT
GREENSBORO AIRPORT, NORTH CAROLINA

ALEX LEANED AGAINST THE sunbaked brick building outside Flight Operations, its warmth soothing the tension between his shoulder blades. Thoughts of the earlier visit with his AA sponsor faded as an airplane taxied to a nearby gate. The airport was operating as well as could be expected under the circumstances. Plastic tarps and temporary barricades blocked gate twenty-six from view, and the acrid stench of the fire no longer lingered in the air. In compensation for the loss of gates, he spotted two buses transporting passengers from the main terminal to Galaxy Express aircraft remotely parked out in midfield. Alex made a mental note to give Special Agent Rodriguez two-thumbs-up if he ran into her.

Inhaling the familiar fumes of jet fuel, he smiled. It wouldn't surprise him if his blood contained the same petroleum mixture. The momentary reverie was short-lived as he returned to the task at hand and glanced at his watch: 1:05 p.m. He had been told Robert was at a lunch meeting when he first arrived. Assuming the chief pilot was back by now, Alex opened an exterior door gaining access to the hallway, which led to his friend's office.

"Hey, Alex, good to have you ba . . ." The chief pilot's words faltered as he studied his friend. "You don't look good! Are you coming down with something?"

"Glad to see you too, boss," Alex said, ignoring his friend's worried expression. "From what I noticed, they're moving right along with repairs to the damaged concourse."

"Yes. Matter-of-fact, they've amended the date our gates will be ready for use." The chief pilot motioned for Alex to take a seat. "How was the temporary duty?"

"Three babes tried to pick me up in Denver Saturday night." He omitted the part that he was in a bar.

"Wow, good for you! How'd that turn out? You don't have to give me a full briefing; an overview will do."

"I bailed. I'm old enough to be their father. I'm sure they had no problem finding my replacement."

"You never know." Robert tossed a stack of papers onto a growing pile. "You may have given them a lesson on the value of being with a more mature man."

"Moving on . . ." Alex rested his elbows on the armrests of the chair and laced his fingers together. "Do you remember the policeman who was here in your office last Saturday? It was right before everything went crazy."

Squinting, Robert bit his lower lip as he tried to recall the person.

"Think hard; it's important. The man was here in front of your desk when I walked in."

The sound of airplane jets taxiing to and fro filtered in from outside as the chief pilot considered the question. "Nothing comes to mind right now. Why do you ask? Who was he?"

Alex untangled his fingers and sat forward. "That's what I'm here to find out."

"I'm not following. Where are you going with this?"

"I believe the officer knew something bad was about to happen," he said, emphasizing each word.

Robert sat up in his chair as his brows darted toward a receding hairline. "What gives you that idea?"

"Because I think that's why he came to talk to you. I also overheard him say something as the three of us were standing outside watching the fire."

"What was it?"

"He said, 'I'm sorry, Caroline.'"

The chief pilot's tone was demanding as it rose in pitch. "Who's Caroline? And what happened to him?"

"I don't know. That's why I'm here. I need to find him. I have questions regarding what happened that afternoon, and I've no doubt he has the answers."

Robert's eyes were unyielding. "What else?"

He wasn't surprised by the question, for his friend could always sense when Alex was holding back. "The same man was on my inbound airplane." Pausing, he exhaled slowly then pushed on. "He came into the cockpit while we were on approach and demanded I request a different gate, which I did. If I hadn't, we would've parked at gate twenty-seven."

The significance of Alex's words hit home, and Robert sucked in a sharp breath. "Did your first officer see him?"

"No. And when I turned around, the man was gone. I checked with the senior flight attendant and the gate agent as soon as we arrived. No one spotted him leaving the plane or in the gate area. I came downstairs to talk to you about it, and I found him here in your office. As I mentioned, he was right next to me on the ramp and disappeared before I could question him. I asked two employees who were behind us where the officer went, and they stated that they hadn't noticed him." Alex remained quiet, letting the chief pilot absorb this last bit of information. He didn't have to wait long.

"Why didn't you say anything at the time?"

Locking eyes with his friend, Alex said, "To be honest, I started to question if he truly existed since no one else saw him except me. So back to my original question, do you remember him?"

Robert let out a long, slow breath. "Truthfully, I can't say one way or the other. I'm still mentally sifting through that day."

A knock on the door interrupted them. Jack, the operations supervisor, poked his head inside. "That FBI lady wants to talk to both of you. She's waiting in the conference room down the hall. She must've known you were here, Captain, because she included you in the request."

Robert got to his feet. "Inform Agent Rodriguez that we'll be right there." He closed the door, then pivoted to face Alex. "That's quite an assumption you've made that this mysterious policeman knew something was going to happen, especially since you have no proof or witnesses to his existence. I wish I could believe you. However, the fire has left its mark on you. You look like hell. I'm going to ground you until we get to the bottom of this."

Alex sprang from the chair. "No! I don't need time off. I need answers."

Negating his friend's verbal onslaught with a wave of his hand, Robert said, "Don't argue with me. The anxiety attacks have resurfaced, haven't they?"

Alex diverted his eyes.

"I thought so. Are you drinking?"

"No! Do you have to go there?"

Robert held up his hands in front of him. "Okay. Okay. But you have to admit; it's quite a story. We'll continue this discussion later. For now, pull yourself together, and don't say anything about this to anyone, especially the FBI agent."

CHAPTER NINE

R ODRIGUEZ GLANCED UP FROM her iPad as the two of them entered the conference room. "Good, the ops supervisor located both of you." The FBI agent gestured for Alex and Robert to take a seat and spent the next few minutes updating them on the investigation.

"That's about it," she said in conclusion.

They stood to leave; she wasn't finished. "Captain Decker, if you could spare the time, I'd like to talk to you alone, please?"

"Sure, no problem." Alex's stomach was in knots as he retook his seat. Robert left the room and closed the door behind him, but not before giving his friend a cautionary glance.

Rodriguez read something on the iPad then got down to it. "Captain Decker, I was—"

"It's Alex. I'm a captain when I'm in the cockpit."

She smiled and continued. "Alex, you've been with Galaxy a little over eight years, correct?"

"Yes, ma'am. Is there a Mr. Special Agent Rodriguez?"

"Excuse me?"

"You're not wearing any wedding rings?" he said, intending to keep her talking and less focused on him.

"That's a bit personal, Captain." She paused, then lifted a gold chain from beneath her silk blouse that contained a diamond engagement ring, a wedding band, and a gold cross.

"Nice. Why aren't the rings on your hand?"

"In my line of work," she slipped them back in place, "it's safer to keep them close to my heart."

"What does Mr. Rodriguez do?"

"We're off-topic," she said, her voice clipped. "Let's get back to it, shall we?"

"Come on. You know everything about me by now," Alex said, giving her a warm, inviting smile.

"All right. My husband is a professor at Georgetown University."

"A professor! How old is he?"

"Enough!" She started to laugh and caught herself. "Alex, I need to ask you a question. You requested a sudden gate change while on approach. Why?"

"We were scheduled to go back out within the hour. I needed to talk to Robert, so I requested a gate closer to operations." He was surprised at how self-assured he came across despite the fact his heart was racing.

"I find it odd that you waited until you were nearly on the ground to request the gate change. I'll let it go for now, for I need to address something else. We've come across a peculiar situation, and I hoped you might shed some light on it. Thirty-four seconds of data are missing from the cockpit voice recorder while you were on approach. Do you have any clue how that could have happened?"

Gray shadows framed his peripheral vision as he tried to focus on her words, and the ringing in his ears drowned out her voice. His throat constricted, and he found it difficult to breathe as his hands and arms, depleted of oxygen, tingled and grew numb.

Rodriguez was at his side. Sliding his chair away from the table, she pushed his head down between his knees. She grabbed an empty takeout bag from a nearby trash can and placed it over his nose and mouth. "Breathe into this. I'll be right back."

In what felt like no time at all, Alex heard Robert's voice as his friend knelt next to him. "Hang in there, buddy. Take it slow. You'll be okay."

He wasn't aware of time passing. However, as the tightness in his chest subsided, he straightened and sucked in a lungful of air. His voice was weak as he spoke. "Can we go outside? I'm feeling claustrophobic in here."

They helped him to his feet and exited the building through an adjacent door. Leaning back against the building for support, he said, "Agent Rodriguez, update Robert regarding the missing data on the black box. As soon as she's finished, Robert, you recount what I shared with you about the policeman."

As if the last words drained what remained of his energy, he slid down to the ground and rested his forehead on his bent knees. When Rodriguez and Robert finished talking, Alex opened his eyes. The agent strode back and forth as she spoke to someone on her cell phone. "Thanks, Pete. I'm on my way."

Alex rose to his feet as Rodriguez disconnected the call and approached him. "The policeman, can you describe him to me? What color was the uniform? Was he wearing a name tag? If so, did it say lieutenant? Captain?" The tone of her voice emphasized her intent. No more games—she wanted the truth.

He held up a hand. "Give me a moment. Everything happened so fast." He closed his eyes and struggled to quiet his mind while concentrating on her questions. "He was white with auburn-colored hair parted on the left side and dark-green eyes. The uniform shirt was blue. I didn't catch the name printed on the insignia bar pinned to the pocket. However, I did notice the patch on his shirtsleeve. It was red and blue with yellow lettering." His eyes flew open. "Capital City Police, Raleigh, North Carolina, was embossed on it."

CHAPTER TEN

THE ELEVATOR OPENED ON ground level. Alex, Robert, and Agent Rodriguez exited and proceeded down the long corridor passing the TSA offices, a division of Homeland Security. When they reached the door leading to the temporary FBI command center, a tall, stocky man in an FBI jacket exited, and Rodriguez made introductions.

"Welcome to our little piece of Heaven," Special Agent Jeff Dunn said as he held the door open for them.

With Rodriguez taking the lead, they maneuvered through a maze of bland-colored cubicles occupied by a handful of FBI staff, some on the phone and others busy typing reports on a computer. Toward the back, they entered a small, dimly lit conference room.

A freckle-faced man in his early thirties with sandy-colored hair sat in front of a bank of flat-screen monitors mounted on the wall. His fingertips paused on the laptop keyboard. "Hey, Rod. Who are your friends?"

"Pete, these two gentlemen work for Galaxy Airlines. Captain Robert Jacobson is the chief pilot for the crew base, and this is Captain Alex Decker. I brought them down here because I have something I wanted to show Captain Decker."

Rodriguez extracted a manila folder from a stack on a nearby table, withdrew a photograph, and handed it to Alex. "This is a picture of Flight Attendant Caroline Bishop, who perished in the fire. Any chance you knew her?"

Studying the photo, he hesitated before answering. "No, I don't recall meeting her, and the name isn't familiar to me. It's possible she was part of a cabin crew I worked with in the past, yet nothing comes to mind at this point. Where was she based?"

"New York. She was twenty-eight and joined the airline right after college. I'm aware that cockpit crew work with flight attendants from a variety of bases on any given day. Considering that, you two might've crossed paths somewhere along the way, and that would help explain the visitor to the cockpit."

Alex was perplexed by her comment, and it must've shown in his face.

"Give it another try, and let me know if anything comes to mind. Take your time."

He heard a cell phone ring in the background and the hum of people talking in the outer office area and blocked it all out. Mentally he ran through the gamut of cabin crew he remembered working with over the years, but the young woman wasn't among them. Although the more he studied the photograph, he thought they must've met in the past. There was something vaguely familiar about her.

"Did you notice her eyes? They're a unique shade of green, wouldn't you say?"

He examined the colored photograph closer and stared in disbelief. The facial features of the phantom policeman were nearly identical to the flight attendant. They could've been twins.

Rodriguez keyed in a password on her iPad. "Earlier, I was reading about Caroline's brother, Marcus Bishop, who was a policeman with the City of Raleigh. Last year, a teenage boy, whom Marcus was mentoring, shot and killed him. The young man was tried as an adult and is serving a life sentence at the prison in Bennettsville, South Carolina." She held the iPad up so Alex could view what was on the screen. "This is a picture of Marcus."

The hair on the back of Alex's neck bristled as a chill ran up his spine. The small windowless room was closing in on him, and he struggled to catch his breath. "It's him, the man who was in my cockpit—the same one that was in Robert's office. How's that possible?" Not waiting for a response, he thrust the iPad and Caroline's picture at Rodriguez and walked out.

In the hallway, Agent Dunn stood at the elevators, talking to someone. The agent glanced his way, and Alex turned in the opposite direction to avoid an encounter. At the end of the hall, his legs gave way; he slid down the wall to the floor. Robert, Rodriguez, Agent Dunn, and Pete arrived, forming a semicircle around him. "Can't—catch—breathe," he said in a choked voice.

"I'll call the paramedics." Agent Dunn spoke with authority.

Alex held up his index finger, signaling them to give him a minute, at which point Rodriguez addressed her two team members. "Let's give the captain some privacy. Jeff, you and Pete go back to work,"

"Are you sure, Rod?" Pete said. "He's white as a sheet."

"Go. Captain Jacobson and I'll stay with him."

The chief pilot remained close at hand as Rodriguez lowered herself to the floor next to Alex. In time, the pounding in his ears eased up. Though his chest still felt tight, he could breathe easier. He sensed the agent's eyes on him as he flexed his fingers and stretched his neck and shoulders, thus coaxing the oxygen-enhanced blood to bring life back into his limbs.

"Are you normally prone to visits from ghosts?" she asked.

"No," he said with a half-hearted chuckle. "There were moments I believed I sensed my wife's presence after she passed. I finally realized it was only wishful thinking."

Narrowing her eyes, she continued to study him as if he were under a microscope. "Can you offer any explanation for the missing data on the black box?"

"I haven't a clue," he said, shaking his head.

"You understand there is no recording of your conversation with the mysterious policeman? Is there anything you've omitted?"

"No, I've recounted everything as it happened." His response failed to appease her, and the agent's eyes remained locked on his. Not giving her a chance to press the issue, he stood and reached out to help her up. "Let's go. You're going to give me an uncensored account of what happened that day."

Alex and Rodriguez were in a heated debate by the time they re-entered the small conference room with Robert trailing behind.

"I'm not leaving!" Alex said, his voice echoing off the room's four walls.

"I beg to differ," she stated firmly. "As weird as it sounds, you believe you saw the ghost of Caroline's brother on two occasions leading up to and right after the fire started. Besides, there's the issue of the missing data from the black box. However, they've nothing to do with the focus of our investigation at this time."

She withdrew a business card from her pants pocket and handed it to Alex. "Call me if you remember something that might be beneficial. As for now, we're done here."

Moving to the door, Alex shut it with a loud thud and defiantly positioned himself in front of it with his arms crossed. Though feeling drained due to the back-to-back anxiety attacks, he believed Agent Rodriguez wasn't entirely upfront with him. "What really happened that day?"

Robert collapsed into a nearby chair. "May as well give it up, Agent Rodriguez. That man has a stubborn streak which runs wider than the Grand Canyon."

Incensed, she closed the distance between them. "I won't be bullied. This is my investigation, and you are no longer needed here, Captain."

Locking eyes with her, he said, "You aren't going to get rid of me that easily. I've no doubt you've run a background check on me. And your research revealed that Robert had me assist the NCIS special agent, Mack McGovern, onboard our aircraft carrier during my recuperation after being captured in Afghanistan. While working with Mack, I elected to leave the Navy and work for NCIS out of their San Diego office. For that reason, this type of thing is not new to me."

"You're right," she snapped. "You're not telling me anything I didn't already know, yet you gave it up within a year. That's when Robert resigned his commission, left the Navy, and started working for the airline. At this point, your friend somehow talked you into walking away from a six-figure income with NCIS and living four blocks from the beach in Coronado. You and your wife relocated to this area, and you began your career with Galaxy Airlines. Good for you. That brings me back to the fact that—"

Refusing to let Rodriguez dwell on his limited investigative experience, Alex interrupted her. "I was good at what I did then, and I can help you now."

Throwing up her hands, she vocalized her frustration. "Ahhhh!"

"Don't say I didn't warn you," Robert said with a smile.

After some deliberation, she said, "I have a conference call scheduled with my boss in a few minutes. Come back in an hour."

CHAPTER ELEVEN

E RE-ENTERED THE TEMPORARY FBI offices forty-five minutes later with Robert in tow. Alex's friend insisted on tagging along to make sure he didn't end up in jail before the day was over. "I'm surprised you didn't padlock the door after I left," Alex said, flashing her a crooked smile.

"Trust me, I considered it," Rodriguez replied. "At the same time, I decided your assistance might prove beneficial."

"Do you want me to leave?" Robert asked.

"No, you can stay. While you were gone, I ran a current security background check on both of you, and, not surprising, you each have impeccable track records. That being said, I trust what you two witness here will not leave this room."

She instructed Pete to run the video recordings from the various security cameras displaying Flight Eight Twenty Seven's arrival on the monitors. "Calibrate them so they're in sync with each other."

Pete's fingers danced across the keyboard as if it were a baby grand piano, and five of the monitors mounted on the wall in front of them came to life. Pointing to the middle one, he said, "The images from the camera at gate twenty-seven shows the ramp area. The others are from different cameras installed along the outside of the building."

Alex and Robert moved in closer as ground personnel

prepared for the airplane's arrival. As the aircraft came into view, a ramp-service employee directed it into the gate area. The AC cable was hooked up to the plane's underbelly, and the jetway was positioned in front of the passenger-access door.

A Galaxy passenger van drove up, and a ground-service rep climbed out. He sprinted up the external jetway stairs two at a time as another employee exited the driver's side of the van and positioned himself at the bottom of the stairs. Alex recalled that the news identified the two men as undercover DEA agents who were there to apprehend a well-known drug courier from the inbound flight.

The undercover agent re-emerged, and they watched as he forcibly dragged a short, wiry man with thick pepper-gray hair down the stairs toward the waiting van.

Clutching a leather shoulder bag to his chest, the man twisted left and right in a futile attempt to break free from the agent's grip. Red-faced, he was angrily spewing inaudible words in his assailant's direction.

The undercover agent said something, and the man stopped abruptly, then glanced up toward the concourse building. He released the bag, letting it tumble down the stairs, end over end, and spun around. Breaking free, he wrestled for control of a gun the agent held.

Alex involuntary flinched when the fuel truck blew up, and the center monitor went blank. Meanwhile, the other monitors displayed the growing fire until the second explosion destroyed those cameras.

Pete switched off the monitors, and the screens darkened.

Alex was the first to dispel the silence that followed. "The agent had his gun drawn. That's different than what they reported in the news."

Rodriguez didn't respond, and he pressed the point. "Come on. There's more to this than what we led the public to believe."

Facing Alex, she said, "The two men in Galaxy uniforms weren't undercover agents."

"What are you saying?"

Reaching into a folder, she removed black-and-white photographs of the two men and handed them to Alex. "They're mercenaries with a long history of working with the wrong people at the right price. For quite some time, they've been on our watch list – that is until dropping out of sight over a year ago."

Alex gestured to the monitors. "Then why did you announce it was a DEA bust?"

"Our first goal was to inform the public that this wasn't an act of terrorism. In truth, we needed time to investigate what happened while keeping it out of the public eye and off someone else's radar. Unfortunately, we're still in the dark as to why those men wanted to snatch the passenger off the flight."

"Unbelievable!" Robert said, his voice cutting through the air.

"Why didn't they pick him up as he left the airport?" Alex interjected.

"Good question; maybe someone was waiting for him out front, and they didn't want to chance it. There's one more thing," Rodriguez added. "We haven't been able to identify the passenger. He was traveling with false documents, and we haven't found him in our facial-recognition database or with DNA testing of his remains."

As she continued, Alex replayed the video recordings in his mind. Tuning her out, he sat down in the chair next to Pete. "Play them again for me, please."

Rodriguez and Robert heard the request and stepped in behind the two men. As the screens came to life, she leaned closer to the chief pilot. "What's going on?"

"I'm not sure; I wager we'll soon find out."

After the second run-through, Alex flexed his shoulders and

stretched his neck as the bones in his spine popped and released. "One more time, Pete."

The videos continued until the split second, when the passenger glanced up. "Stop it right there, zoom in, and give me a clear view of our mystery man."

Alex sat back and closed his eyes, willing his disjointed thoughts to unscramble. *What am I missing?*

He sat up. "Pan out, show me the whole airplane from this view. That's it. Stop! There! Do you see it? There's someone at the window right in front of the wing."

All eyes were on the middle monitor.

"I don't notice anything," Robert said.

Alex nudged Pete's arm. "Zoom in closer."

Pete's fingers repeatedly pressed a button on the keyboard, and the airplane's window filled the center screen. He clicked to enhance the picture, and an image materialized. "Wow! Good catch, Captain. I missed it due to the glare on the window."

"It's her!" Robert exclaimed. "It's the policeman's sister."

CHAPTER TWELVE

G IVING HIMSELF SPACE TO process this new revelation, Alex rose and paced back and forth as he sifted through the internal dialogue that flooded his mind. *Is it Caroline's voice I hear in my dreams? If it is, what is she trying to tell me?*

"Captain, are you all right?" Rodriguez asked.

Her words cut through the voice in his head, and he stopped in his tracks. "Why was she the only crew member that perished on the airplane? What happened to the passengers and the rest of the crew?"

"From what we've ascertained from the security cameras and interviews with the crew, everyone had exited the plane prior to the explosion. For some unknown reason, Caroline and the mysterious passenger lingered behind."

Alex reclaimed his seat, his attention on the monitors. "Pete, give me a view of the flight attendant and passenger on the same monitor, split-screen. Sync the two videos to run together in a slow time-lapse."

Other than the hum from the electrical equipment, all was quiet as they stared at the middle monitor.

Leaning forward, he said, "Stop right there. Back it up a few frames and zoom in closer on each of their faces. Good. Now go forward slowly, one frame at a time. Stop!"

The flight attendant and the passenger simultaneously

glanced in the direction of the terminal building, and Alex felt as if their eyes were on him, piercing his soul. "What are the two of you staring at?" he said under his breath. Then his heart rate sped up with excitement. "Someone is watching from inside the building!"

"What gives you that impression?" Robert asked.

"They're both looking at the terminal." Alex pointed at the monitor. "Somebody is at the window in the gate area, and your mysterious passenger recognized him. Pete, bring up the video that shows the inside of the terminal at gate twenty-seven on a different screen."

The new recording gave them an unobstructed view of the gate's waiting area. Pete zoomed in. "You're right. Someone's at the window."

A man—dressed in an oversized jacket, baggy pants, and a baseball hat—stood at the window, which offered an unobstructed view of the ramp area.

Per Rodriguez's request, Pete ran all three video recordings concurrently, overlapping the time sequence.

They watched as the passenger and his escort descended the stairs and stopped midway, prior to the man at the window walking away. At that moment, the passenger hurled himself at his assailant, and they fought for control of the gun. In a blink of an eye, a ball of fire ripped through the gate area, and the screen went blank.

"Who is he?" Robert said, his voice growing with excitement. "Was he killed in the blast?"

Rodriguez motioned for Pete to dump everything and bring up the video from the concourse corridor adjacent to gate twenty-seven.

"I'm on it."

Speaking more to himself than the others, Alex said, "Three. The number three. Of course! There was a third man involved with the abduction of the passenger. It's the man in the window.

That must be what Caroline or her brother, Marcus, have been trying to tell me."

"What are you talking about?" Robert asked, his brow furrowed in confusion.

Waving off his friend, Alex reflected on this new revelation. *Now I understand the significance of the number three showing up continuously since the fire.*

When he finally spoke, he ignored Robert's question. "The man in the window knew the airport layout and the location of all the security cameras. Did you notice he makes a point not to show his face? I doubt we'll get a good view of him going through TSA security either. That's if he came in that way."

Food arrived, and the small room filled with the mixed aromas of French fries, onion, and hamburger. Pausing in between bites, they viewed the next video recording as the man in the window exited the gate area and passed in front of a bookstore. The gate and concourse behind him erupted into flames. He flew through the air, arms and legs flailing, and landed face-down on the floor. His jacket was on fire; he rolled over and over to extinguish it. A woman, her clothing ablaze, collapsed nearby.

Chaos followed as people scattered in all directions in a desperate attempt to escape the advancing blaze. The video had no sound, yet Alex didn't need it. Mouths gaped in silent screams as one by one the fire overtook them.

With the second explosion, the bookstore erupted into a raging inferno. A heavyset gentleman—enveloped in flames—ran out of the shop, tripped on the fallen woman, and landed on top of her. They got the impression their mystery man was unharmed from the ordeal when he sprang to his feet and darted in the direction of the main terminal.

Rodriguez put down her half-eaten hamburger. "I've lost my appetite."

"He escaped the fire, and he's still wearing that stupid baseball hat," Pete said around a mouth full of food. "How's that possible?"

Those who survived the explosions were running toward the main terminal. The man was briefly blocked from view in the stampede. They caught a glimpse of him as he cut left and departed through an emergency exit door.

Alex tossed his unfinished meal into the trash and asked Pete to get him a view of the ramp and tarmac outside gates twenty through twenty-four.

The latest video feed displayed airline personnel and passengers spilling out of the emergency exit onto the ramp. Some paused and glanced back at the burning building. The rest ran toward the middle of the tarmac between the north and south concourses. Those who stopped to gawk at the nightmare unfold at gate twenty-six witnessed the agent plummeting from the jetway, consumed in flames.

Pete reran the video. "He never came out."

"Yes, he did." Alex pointed. "That's him."

"He's in a Galaxy uniform," Robert said in disbelief. "He changed clothes. Where and how?"

"Apparently, he slipped beneath the stairwell and changed into the uniform," Alex said. "He must've had it hidden beneath his other clothes."

The video started, and Pete zoomed in on the man in the ground-service uniform as he made his way across the ramp. His face remained shadowed by a different hat. This one had a Galaxy logo imprinted on it.

Alex shifted in his chair to get a closer view. "I lay odds our guy was in uniform when he gained access to the airport earlier. He changed into street clothes prior to entering the concourse and probably planned to switch back prior to leaving the property the same way he came in. The fire changed everything. He needed to get out of there before TSA locked everything down, and the police showed up."

Pete pressed pause; the man's silhouette remained on the

screen, his head turned away from the camera. "How did you determine it was the same guy, Captain?"

"He was limping as he ran through the concourse, and so is this guy. It seems he did sustain an injury."

Rodriguez addressed Pete. "He's on the fringes of the crowd of people running toward the south concourse. Get us there."

A new video feed produced the view of the ramp in front of gates forty-one through forty-seven. Pete continued tracking the man on the middle monitor as he crossed the tarmac and blended into the growing cluster of ground personnel and civilians who were witnessing the fire. At that point, he disappeared from view. "Where'd he go?" Pete said with an edge of irritation.

"He's in the background, working his way through the crowd," Alex said as he directed their attention to the middle of the monitor.

Alex and Robert were in the foreground; his inbound aircraft was visible behind them.

Sucking in his breath, Robert exclaimed, "He's right behind us!"

As expected, the phantom police officer, Marcus Bishop, wasn't visible on the screen.

Alex had a sense of déjà vu as they tracked their man until he climbed up into a tow-tug and drove away. It proved warranted as Pete replayed the last scene, and he witnessed himself colliding with the fugitive.

The tension in the room became palpable.

Cutting through the silence, Robert voiced what was on everyone's mind. "Who is this guy, and where'd he go?"

Alex closed his eyes and recalled his encounter with the man. "Did you notice I collided with the guy briefly as he headed to the tug?" In unison, they looked at him. "I forgot about it until now. I don't recall specific facial features. I do remember that he was Caucasian and about my height. Mostly, I remember the limp."

Rodriguez sat forward with excitement in her seat. "You got a glimpse of him! What else do you remember?"

Opening his eyes, Alex shook his head in frustration. "Sorry. That's all."

"Give it a few minutes. You may remember something else. In the meantime, let's track this bozo until he leaves the property. Hopefully, we'll get a clear image of him and the license plate number from his getaway car, probably stolen from the employee lot. We'll check those security cameras also."

While the others reviewed more videos, Alex replayed the confrontation in his mind, which was sketchy at best. Nothing else came to light.

They lost sight of the man for good when he reached the hangar area. Backtracking, they found where the three men drove onto the airport property in a stolen Galaxy passenger van. Using fake ID badges, they gained access to a security gate near the freight hangars.

Once the final video ended, Pete spoke up. "He had to still be somewhere on the property. There's no way he left the airport without first running into TSA or local police."

Deflated, Rodriguez sat back in her chair. "I agree. Pete, I want you to do a second run-through of all the videos tomorrow and check for what we may have missed."

Robert got to his feet. "I've got to go. I have a wife and kids at home waiting for me. Not saying it hasn't been an interesting day." He checked his watch. "Nine o'clock! I'm in the doghouse for sure."

The others followed suit, stood, and stretched out the kinks.

Confronting Alex, Robert said, "This doesn't change things. Consider yourself grounded for now. Go home and get some rest. We'll talk tomorrow."

Alex started to argue the point when Rodriguez interceded. "Captain Jacobson, I was hoping I could solicit Captain Decker's help. He made a worthwhile contribution to the investigation today. Maybe he could shed more light on it as we go forward."

Robert shrugged. "Okay, by me."

"What do you say, flyboy? Ready to work for the government again?"

"Do I have a choice, Madam Super-agent?"

"Careful. I may change my mind and send you packing."

He smiled. "I don't think so."

CHAPTER THIRTEEN

Rodriguez greeted Alex as he approached. "So you decided to show up. Good, let's get to work."

"What's on the agenda for today?" he asked as they headed towards the north concourse.

Handing him a TSA ID badge, she said, "The first thing is to give you a walkthrough of the damaged gates."

He attached the badge to the neck lanyard containing his Galaxy ID. "It's official. I'm back to being a gofer for the government."

"Yep."

The faint lingering smell of smoke and charred residue invaded his senses as they made their way down the lengthy concourse and approached gates twenty-seven and twenty-eight. The two areas sat across from each other and were identical in their devastation.

Scaffolding lined both sides of the concourse. Numerous piles of burned debris sat next to shrink-wrapped pylons stacked with new building supplies. The walls and flooring were stripped bare everywhere except for the two gates. Crime scene tape deterred access to those areas.

He studied the damaged metal trusses overhead. Ceiling tiles that initially covered the support beams now bore the effect of intense heat from the fire. If it weren't for the tarp that covered the roof, the blue sky would be visible. Rebar supports lined up like parading soldiers in place of the wall that had separated gate twenty-seven from the bookstore.

Alex held up the yellow tape for Rodriguez to pass under and joined her as they made their way to the windows overlooking the ramp at gate twenty-seven. Their shoes crunched on broken glass and debris, leaving footprints in the ashy film that coated the flooring. Dangling melted wires hung from the ceiling above an indistinguishable black form that had been the check-in desk. The jetway access door, blown from its hinges, lay blackened and blistered on the floor. Thick dark-gray discoloration—a by-product of low-lying toxic gases—trailed up a nearby wall.

Sheets of clear plastic covered the missing windows. Rodriguez pushed one aside, giving them a clear view. Alex sucked in a breath as he took in the charred remains of the Embraer E175 airplane; its fuselage melted into the asphalt. The aircraft's tail section sat on a flatbed truck nearby, and an assortment of indistinguishable items was tagged and lying on the ground below them. The scenes he observed the previous day on the monitors were one-dimensional and gave him a sense of detachment. Now, watching the investigative team painstakingly sift through the ashes, it became real.

Lingering toxic fumes gave him a sinus headache. He pinched the crown of his nose with his fingertips and briefly massaged his temples, which offered some relief.

As the pain dissipated, he focused on the wing area. *How many times did I see Caroline's face in the window yesterday?*

Shifting his attention, he said, "I've witnessed firsthand what can happen when an airplane catches fire fed by jet fuel. Still, I don't think I'll ever get used to it."

Nodding in agreement, Rodriguez said, "I want you to sit with Pete today and review all airport video recordings from the week leading up to the fire. Maybe our unidentified third man was on the airport property beforehand, and you can get a clear image of his face."

She absently pushed a strand of hair caught in the breeze behind her ear. "I'll get you copies of the personnel files of all Galaxy employees stationed here. I'll include what we have on every civilian killed or injured plus the two mer—"

Her words faded as a firm hand gripped his right shoulder. Before he could turn to see who it was, a man in a maroon jacket and a baseball cap materialized on his left where Rodriguez previously stood. He couldn't see the stranger's face, for it was cast in shadows.

Scanning the gate area, Alex was shocked to find everything exactly as it was prior to the fire. An agent was behind the check-in desk talking to a customer, and others milled around the gate area and concourse. He caught sight of the airplane and inhaled sharply. It glistened in the sunlight, completely intact.

As the mercenary proceeded down the jetway steps with the mysterious passenger, the man beside Alex laughed. Searching the window in front of the wing, Alex couldn't see Caroline, though he knew she was there. He banged on the large window-pane with his fists, feeling its cold, hard surface with each impact. "Run, Caroline. Get out of there!"

The man in the baggy jacket ambled away just as the two on the jetway launched into a battle for control of the gun.

Pressure from the hand on Alex's shoulder dissipated as the window in front of him dissolved into thin air. He pitched forward with arms flailing. Rodriguez grabbed hold of his shirt with both hands and jerked him backward. Regaining his balance, Alex bent forward with hands on his knees, breathing heavily.

"What just happened?" The alarm in Rodriguez's tone was unmistakable. "One minute, you were fine, and in the next, you were taking a nosedive out the missing window."

"I saw something—a vision," he said in between taking large gulps of air.

She laid a hand on his back between the shoulder blades. "Come with me." Taking his arm, she guided him to a stack of sheetrock, where he sat down. Her face was awash with skepticism as she sat down beside him.

Taking a labored breath, he said, "It was the man in the baseball cap. He stood in your place. I watched everything unfold in real-time as it happened. What's most disturbing is that I couldn't make out his facial features." He exhaled in frustration and rubbed his neck. "I'm not crazy," Alex said with conviction.

"Hmm, I'm beginning to wonder," she said, glancing sideways at him. "The visions and ghost sightings, you've never experienced them until now?"

"No! I can honestly say I've never been through anything like this in the past."

"When we get back downstairs, I want you to write down everything you remember about it. Leave out nothing. The smallest detail may help in some way."

"I can do that."

Seeing that Alex felt better, Rodriguez stood. "Until you figure out what's going on, I suggest you stay away from open windows."

Alex rose to his feet. "No argument there."

Rodriguez's eyes bore into him. "Are you seeing anyone regarding the anxiety attacks and the visions?"

"Matter of fact," he stated with a sheepish grin, "I met with someone yesterday morning before I showed up here. I have to admit, it didn't go well."

"Really? What a surprise," Rodriguez interjected with a slight smile then grew serious. "Logic dictates that I shouldn't involve you any further in this investigation, but my gut is telling me otherwise. For that reason, I'm going to ask, do you want to continue helping us? I'm giving you an opportunity to bail out."

He didn't hesitate. "As I stated earlier, I need answers, and so do you. I'm in."

CHAPTER FOURTEEN

LEE COUNTY, NORTH CAROLINA

As THE SUN DROPPED behind the trees in the west, Alex swung off the well-maintained country road onto the long narrow lane leading to his house. Parking in front of the single-story weathered structure, he shut off the engine and scrutinized his domain.

The covered front porch, which ran the length of the house, and back deck were new due to the fact it had been a hazardous undertaking to walk on either one. The exterior's paint was peeling and bleached out, and the roof, which needed replacing, was coated in green moss and pine needles. It didn't leak yet, and the plumbing worked. The stone fireplace was a bonus, for the place could get quite drafty during the winter months. The microwave continued to warm his leftovers, so he was in good shape.

The grassy private runway and the hangar that housed his two antique airplanes were a different matter. Both were new and in pristine condition. Alex longed to take Amelia up for a spin; unfortunately, the evening was fast approaching.

Climbing out of the truck, he ascended the stairs two at a time and entered the house. Depositing his keys and wallet on a small table in the foyer, he walked into the living room. It was sparsely furnished with a worn couch and a battered coffee table littered with empty water bottles, a pizza box, and airplane magazines.

An eight-by-ten picture frame was the only item that occupied the large oak mantel over the fireplace. It contained a candid shot of a beautiful blue-eyed brunette dancing in a puddle, a ray of sunlight capturing her smile.

"Hello, darling. I hope you had a good day. Wait until you hear about mine."

In the kitchen, he reached into the refrigerator for a bottle of water and heard a car drive up out front. Retracing his steps, he walked out onto the front porch just as Dr. Newman climbed out of a new red BMW Roadster convertible.

"Good evening. Am I interrupting anything?"

"Not at all." With a wave of his hand, Alex gestured for the doctor to come on up.

Settling into one of the ladder-back rockers on the porch, Dr. Newman said, "I promise I won't stay long. I was just wondering if you came up with a solution regarding your concerns yesterday."

Alex remained standing. "Good question. I'll get you a drink while I come up with a suitable response? Bottle of water or soda?"

"Water would be great."

Re-emerging from the house, he handed his friend the drink and lowered himself into the seat next to him. They gazed out across the driveway toward the woods while rocking back and forth, each man preoccupied with his own thoughts.

Breaking the silence, Alex said, "Nice pair of wheels. Business must be good."

"It's a birthday gift from Melony."

"That's not fair. All I get from your wife is a home-cooked meal and a cake."

The rocking chairs' rhythmic sound, mixed with the mating calls of the cicadas, penetrated the silence that followed.

Alex exhaled. "You're not going to say anything until I answer your question, are you?"

When Dr. Newman didn't respond, Alex said, "Yes, in a roundabout way, so you're free to go now."

"Okay." The doctor got to his feet.

"Oh, sit down. Does the silent treatment work with your wife?"

"Not usually. Most of the time, it's the other way around." Swatting at a pesky mosquito, the doctor said, "You've enlightened me in the past with stories about the early years when you performed in the air shows. I got to thinking after you left yesterday that you've never mentioned what made you consider becoming a pilot in the first place?"

Handing the doctor a can of mosquito spray that was within arm's reach, he said, "You want to delve into it now?"

"Sure, why not."

He was relieved his friend put the earlier visit behind them. Just the same, Alex considered the doc's request. He didn't like visiting the past, for too many demons lurked in its shadows. On the flip side, he did cherish his childhood memories prior to the world sucking him into its stormy arena. "I was on my way to play baseball with friends at a local park when I heard an airplane approaching. It wasn't a jet. It had a different sound."

∞

Shielding his eyes from the sun, Alex watched a red biplane bank to the right and continue south. The enchanting image lingered in his mind long after it had faded from view. The following Saturday, he rode his bike out to the private airfield on the edge of town.

Standing beside a hangar, he watched various small aircraft take off, circle the field, and land. Bouncing on his feet with excitement, he tried to imagine what it would be like to fly among the clouds. The desire was so compelling that he soon found himself inside the airport's small office.

A man about his father's age stood behind the counter. "May I help you, son?"

Assorted pictures of vintage biplanes adorned the walls, and Alex pointed to one. "I want to learn to fly one of those airplanes, sir,"

"A World War Two Stearman. You have excellent taste. What's your name?"

"Alexander, but everybody calls me Alex."

"How old are you?"

"Twelve, but I'll be thirteen next month!"

"Glad to meet you, Alex." The man's eyes twinkled as he shook Alex's hand. "I'm Mr. Burroughs; most folks call me Bear. Do you have the money for lessons?"

Alex's shoulders sagged, and he believed the dream unattainable until he heard the man's next words. "I thought not; I have an idea. You could come to work for me, and I'd credit your time to pay for the lessons. I've been considering hiring a part-timer to help out around here, and I believe you're the right man for the job, that's if you're serious about learning to fly."

"I am, sir! There's no doubt in my mind."

"Good. I expect you to keep up with your chores at home and school work. A good pilot needs education."

"Yes, sir." They shook hands to solidify the verbal contract.

Handing Alex his business card, Bear said, "Call me when you're available to work, and I'll put you on the schedule."

"I'll do that, sir. Thank you."

Alex couldn't wait to share the good news with his parents and raced home on his bike; however, his enthusiasm waned as he drew closer. What if they wouldn't let him take flying lessons even if he promised to pay for them himself?

At dinner that evening, everyone was talking except Alex. His brother and sister were arguing, as usual; they called it debating. His parents—ignoring the others at the table—conversed among themselves.

Taking a big breath, he made his announcement. "I'm going to take flying lessons."

The room grew silent, and Alex watched as the words caught his mother's attention. "No need to shout, dear. Hold on, what did you say?"

They waited for his response, and Alex dug down deep for his man-voice and repeated his declaration. "I've accepted a part-time job at the private airfield. The money I earn will pay for my flying lessons." The look on their faces was comical. Alex wanted to laugh but didn't dare.

His father was the next one to speak. "Alex, that's a terrific idea. I believe you'd make an excellent pilot."

Wide-eyed, Alex stared in disbelief with his mouth agape. His siblings and his mother stared at his father as if the man had lost his mind.

The topic of discussion was closed when Alex's father picked up the conversation with his wife from where they'd left off. "Did you mention something about having dinner Saturday night with the Edwards?"

CHAPTER FIFTEEN

"YOU STILL WITH ME?" Alex said, giving his friend a wary smile.

"Yep." The doctor gave the impression he was invested in the story as he continued rocking back and forth. "What was it like, your first airplane ride?"

"Wow." Alex shrugged. "That says it all."

Gesturing for him to continue, Dr. Newman said, "Fill in the blanks for me."

Alex leaned back in the rocker and studied the covered porch's beadboard ceiling. "It was a cold November day, and Dad gave me a ride to work. Bear told my father that he should stick around; he had a surprise for me.

"I was helping Bear's son, Tim, work on a yellow vintage biplane, and Bear wanted to take it up for a spin. We parked the plane in front of the office after towing it over from the hangar."

∞

Alex ran to his dad. "Look at that, Pop! Isn't she a beaut? I'm going to buy one like it as soon as I get my pilot's license." Glancing up, Alex noticed tears in his father's eyes. "What's wrong?"

"Nothing, son. It's only my allergies."

"Okay, Alex," Bear said. "Let's go."

He was confused. "Go where?"

"For a ride." Bear climbed up into the plane.

"I didn't realize I'd earned enough credits for a lesson, sir."

"Actually, you have, but we'll leave that for another day. Get up here, boy."

Alex scrambled up into the front of the two-seater biplane and buckled up. Bear yelled from the back, "Don't touch anything. You hear me? Just sit back and enjoy yourself."

His heart was racing as the engine revved, and the propeller whined. Senses on high alert, every inch of his body experienced the vibration of the plane as they taxied onto the runway, and before he realized it, they were airborne.

Cold wind chafed his face; he paid it no mind. All the past Christmases and birthdays combined into one couldn't equal this moment. Alex scanned the panel of gauges and made up his mind that he would learn everything about an airplane from the inside out. He also promised himself that he would own a biplane one day like this one and name it Amelia in honor of the female aviator he had read about recently.

Bear eased back on the throttle, and the rhythmic sound of the aircraft's engine changed as they dropped down onto the runway. Alex wasn't ready to quit. It was at that moment his passion for flying took hold. He would be back in the air soon because it was where he belonged.

∞

Nodding his approval, Dr. Newman said, "I agree. You're a lucky man, my friend. Not everyone gets the opportunity to achieve their heart's desire."

"We're both blessed in that way." Alex rose and advanced to the edge of the porch. At the railing, he turned to face his friend. His mood changed, and the lines around his eyes—attributed to the sleepless nights—deepened with concern.

"What's going on, Alex?"

"It's been some time, but my anxiety attacks have returned.

I'm grounded until I get them under control. The doctor I was working with after rehab is out of town, and I'm required to see someone. Got any suggestions?"

His friend stood and joined Alex at the railing. "You met Dr. Fletcher at the house during our Christmas party last December. Fletcher and I share office space. He works with veterans, and I believe he'll be able to help you."

Alex gazed out across the yard. "Okay."

"You'll need to make an appointment with him. In the meantime, I'll ask Dr. Fletcher to call in a mild anti-anxiety prescription for you in the morning."

He shook his head. "No drugs. I told you what I think about that stuff. Alcohol addiction was hard enough to overcome."

"Okay. You'll need to discuss your reservations with Dr. Fletcher when you meet with him. In the meantime, I'll make a list of homeopathic options for you."

"I'll call your office first thing in the morning to make the appointment and get the list."

"Sounds good."

Evening shadows deepened as the day gave way to twilight, and cold dampness descended upon them. Alex walked his friend to the car. "Since you taunted me with your new wheels, what if next visit I show you my latest fixer-upper with wings?"

"Great idea. How about Sunday? I'll bring my family?"

His friend's suggestion caught Alex unprepared, for he hadn't entertained guests since his wife's death. Realizing it had been too long, he yielded to the request with moderate misgivings. "Okay. Sunday, sure. I'll put some burgers and steaks on the grill, and we'll make an afternoon of it."

"We'll look forward to it."

With hands resting in his back pockets, Alex followed his friend's car with his eyes until it reached the highway. "Oh, boy. Doc's bringing the wife and girls for a cookout on Sunday. That'll bring on an anxiety attack for sure."

CHAPTER SIXTEEN

I N THE DREAM, ALEX stood next to Caroline in the aisle of the airplane. He considered it odd that she was oblivious to his presence.

She addressed a gentleman sitting at the window seat on the right. The man appeared to be in his late fifties or early sixties. His clothing was disheveled as if he had traveled a great distance, and his hands rested on a leather shoulder bag lying on his lap.

"Sir, we're at the gate," Caroline said with a smile. "Everyone has deplaned."

Not hearing her, the man continued to stare out the window, watching the ground crew unload the luggage from the belly of the aircraft.

Caroline spoke again; this time, she got the stranger's attention.

"Oh . . . thank you," he said. Stepping into the aisle, he paused to meet her eyes. "You're as lovely as your mother when she was your age."

Perplexed, her brow creased. "Excuse me?"

"I'm sorry. Forgive my ramblings. I meant to say that you remind me of someone I had a crush on back in the day. She was very special, as you are, I'm sure."

"What a nice thing to say, thank you. Are you going to be all right? Do you need assistance?"

"No, I'll be fine. It's been a long trip." His words were laden with exhaustion and a heavy Eastern European accent.

Trailing the man as he made his way to the front exit, she paused and retrieved some discarded trash out of a seatback pocket. The rest of the crew had disembarked earlier, and Caroline planned to join them once she finished searching the cabin for forgotten items and collected her things. As she continued up the aisle, she spotted a child's book wedged between the seat and the wall on her left. She bent down to get it, and something outside the window caught her attention.

Leaning in, Alex glanced over Caroline's shoulder and noticed a Galaxy employee escorting the older gentleman down the external stairs. He assumed the employee must've been waiting for the man in the jetway.

As the two men descended, the passenger glanced up toward the terminal windows that overlooked the tarmac. Caroline followed his gaze, as did Alex. Someone was at the window watching what was transpiring on the jetway.

Alex squinted against the sunlight that poured through the airplane window, which made it difficult to make out the man's features. The stranger moved away from the window, and Alex's attention was drawn back to the two men on the stairs. The passenger must've recognized the man in the window, for without warning, he twisted out of his escort's grip, released the leather shoulder bag, and grabbed a gun the employee had concealed beneath his jacket.

As the two men struggled for control of the weapon, Alex said, "Run, Caroline! Run!"

"Security! I need to call security," Caroline said more to herself.

They sprinted toward the front of the plane, Alex trailing behind her. When they reached the cabin divider, an explosion shook the aircraft. Caroline grabbed a seat back to steady herself and whirled around. Her eyes went wide with terror as a ball of flame raced up the aisle.

Alex reached for Caroline in an attempt to shield her, and his hands came away empty. Caroline raised her arms to protect her face as the searing heat and fire engulfed her.

∞

Alex emerged from the nightmare, drenched in sweat. The smell of burning flesh filled his senses as searing pain ravaged his body. In the dream, he witnessed everything Caroline had experienced in those final moments.

He tried to run, but his legs became entangled with the sheets, and he ended up tumbling out of bed. Still half asleep, he thrashed about in the darkness, slapping at his limbs in an attempt to extinguish the imaginary fire that was consuming him.

Fully awake now, he groped for the lamp on the nightstand. His heart pounded in his chest as he examined his arms, chest, and legs in the dim light. There wasn't a mark on him, yet the skin was flushed and hot to the touch. The fire existed in the dream. Despite that, his throat felt scorched and blistered. He shivered as bile rose to his throat; dashing to the bathroom, he vomited into the toilet. When his stomach gave its last heave, he clambered into the bathtub and turned on the shower, letting cold water wash over his fevered body.

CHAPTER SEVENTEEN

RODRIGUEZ CAUGHT UP WITH Alex in the breakroom Wednesday morning. "You don't look so good this morning. You have a rough night?"

"You could say that; I'll be alright."

"Before you get rolling on the day, I wanted to let you know there's a memorial service scheduled for Caroline Bishop tomorrow afternoon. Her funeral was last week while you were gone. It was a private graveside service with immediate family and close friends in attendance. This one is open to the public. I figured you might want to go."

He ruminated over her words. "Are you asking or telling?"

"It's up to you. If you do go, I'd like you to attend both the service and the reception at the parents' home afterward."

He nodded. "Where's it being held?"

"At a lovely old church in downtown Raleigh. She grew up in North Carolina."

"Caroline from the Carolinas. Sounds like a country-and-western song," Alex said, failing to make light of the unsettling news. "Okay, I'll go."

THURSDAY, APRIL 26
RALEIGH, NORTH CAROLINA

During the first half of the day, Alex passed the time running errands in the state's capital. His first stop was the North Carolina Energy and Environmental Agency. Reps from the gas and power companies had contacted him numerous times since he had bought his property. They were interested in leasing a portion of it for drilling. He was currently researching the pros and cons of fracking before deciding one way or the other.

The earlier activities had kept his mind preoccupied. Now that he sat parked across the street from the historic Edenton Street Methodist Church, he was consumed with trepidation. His stomach was in knots, and a nervous sheen coated his skin, despite the spring air drifting in through the open windows of the truck. The last time he had attended church was for his wife's funeral. The year before, he blew off his niece's wedding, and his sister still hadn't forgiven him.

The service was scheduled to start in thirty minutes, which allowed him to observe the attendees as they filed into the place of worship. Alex scanned the crowd in the hope of spotting someone that might fit the physical characteristics of their mystery man in the airport video recordings. He had no such luck.

A limousine motorcade arrived, and the governor of North Carolina and his wife exited the second vehicle. Before entering the church, they shook hands with several top-ranking businessmen, women, and community leaders Alex recognized. *Who are the Bishops that they should warrant such noteworthy friends?*

∞

The traditional memorial service lasted just under an hour; however, to Alex, it seemed to go on forever. Following the benediction, the ushers escorted Caroline's family from the sanctuary.

He remained seated as the others around him filed out. His eyes drifted along the stained glass windows that ran down both sides of the church depicting the life of Christ. A kaleidoscope of memories flooded his mind as his eyes settled on the vibrantly colored window above the dais. It reminded him of the chapel where he and Sarah were married.

The final piece the organist selected happened to be one Alex had requested for Sarah's memorial service. When it concluded, the silence that followed magnified his sense of loss.

Glancing up, he noticed the ornate ceiling supported by wooden crossbeams, and at the same time, recalled the mangled trusses at the Greensboro Airport. Caroline's image framed in the airplane window came to mind but was immediately replaced by Sarah's.

He recalled holding his wife's thin, frail hand as he sat beside her in the hospital bed. She had dark circles under her eyes, and her once beautiful face was ashen and gaunt. With what strength she had left, she lightly squeezed his hand, smiled, then closed her eyes, and was gone. The memory of it consumed Alex, and seeing red, he sprang to his feet with clenched fists. "I'm here, and the roof hasn't fallen. On the other hand, it might once I say my piece."

His tone was venomous as he spat out the words barely above a whisper. "There are those who believe you are a forgiving, compassionate God. You've probably forgiven me more times than I can imagine. However, I'll never forgive you for letting Sarah die! Never!"

∞

Waiting for his resentment to subside, Alex stood off to the side in the church's foyer as the last of the mourners made their way through the receiving line. He recognized the flight attendant and the two pilots who were speaking to Mr. and Mrs. Bishop as the same ones that worked on Caroline's inbound flight.

He stepped forward and approached the first person in line. A young woman with steel-blue eyes, honey-colored hair, and graceful features extended her hand. "Thank you for coming." Her voice had a silky air to it, sweet and gentle. "How did you know Caroline? Was she a friend?"

"No, I'm here on behalf of Galaxy Airlines. I'm so sorry for your loss."

"Thank you," she replied in a subdued voice.

Alex introduced himself and asked, "Are you Caroline's sister?" Unbeknownst to the pretty woman, he already knew the answer, having read Marcus's file. She was engaged to Caroline's brother, Marcus, until he got killed.

"No. I'm Susanne Taylor, a close friend of the family." She turned to Caroline's mother. "Barbara, I'd like to introduce you to Captain Decker. He works for Galaxy Airlines."

Mrs. Bishop placed her warm hand in his. "Thank you for coming."

"May I offer my deepest sympathy? It's obvious that your daughter was a special person."

Caroline's mother faltered slightly, then regained her composure. "We're having a reception in our home. The address is on the back of the program. I hope you can come."

He acknowledged the invitation and continued through the receiving line, offering his condolences to Jim Bishop and the rest of the family members.

Back in the truck, he rested his forehead on the steering wheel and closed his eyes. *What am I doing here? This is crazy.*

CHAPTER EIGHTEEN

THE BISHOPS' HISTORIC HOME was located in Raleigh's quaint section in the heart of Cameron Park. Alex made his way around the people socializing on the covered porch that ran the house's width and entered through the open front door. To his right, the living room overflowed with the same dignitaries he noticed at the church service.

In a far corner, Susanne Taylor was engaged in conversation with the mayor of Raleigh and a state senator. Jim and Barbara Bishop were nearby talking to the governor and his wife.

A lavish array of food dominated the large mahogany table in the formal dining room. Alex had no appetite, and he wasn't in the mood for superficial interaction with strangers. Working his way past the grazing mourners, he continued in the direction of the hallway when a portly young man in glasses approached him.

"You better grab something before the good stuff's gone." The man with an acne-scarred face held a plate laden with chicken wings and sliders.

"Thanks, I'll pass," Alex said as he sidestepped him.

While searching for a bathroom, he came upon two framed lithograph prints by Charles Hubbell on display in the hallway. Alex recognized the artist's work. The first one was of Lindbergh's vintage airplane—the Spirit of Saint Louis—and the other one depicted Captain Eddie Rickenbacker's SPAD 13 and five German biplanes engaged in battle during WWI.

A door stood ajar across the hall from the pictures. Believing it led to a bathroom, Alex pushed it open. Scanning the room, he saw two high-back upholstered chairs were positioned in front of an antique fireplace, and a mahogany desk sat against one of the walls. The cozy setting of the room drew him in.

Closing the door, he advanced to the center of the room, where daylight—streaming in through an octagon-shaped window—created symmetrical designs on the thickly carpeted floor. Alex took his time moving about the place. A variety of landscape paintings adorned the pale green walls, all by the same artist, Caroline Bishop. The colors, shapes, and light in each rendition represented Mother Nature at her best.

The door opened and closed, and a familiar perfume accompanied the woman as she joined him. Though she was older than Caroline, the similarities were uncanny.

"Mrs. Bishop, I'm so sorry. I didn't mean to intrude upon your private quarters. I was searching for the restroom."

"No need to apologize." Waving a hand that encompassed the room, she said, "This is my favorite place in the house."

"I can see why." Gesturing to the paintings on one wall, he added, "Each one of these instills a sense of peace and light. Your daughter was gifted."

"Thank you. Today's been overwhelming. I need to take a break and catch my breath. Please stay and keep me company, Captain." She sat in one of two chairs in front of the fireplace and motioned Alex to join her. "As I recall, you work for Galaxy Airlines. Is that how you met my daughter?"

"No, unfortunately, I never had the pleasure of meeting her." He sensed she longed to hear more, but what he had to offer at this point would seem crazy, if not far-fetched. Moving on to safer ground, he said, "From what I've witnessed, you and your husband have many friends. What a blessing. I recognized a few of the people. Are the rest business associates of your husband?"

"Some are, not everyone. Jim's an independent consultant, a problem solver dealing with the international import and export of goods. If you have a need, he'll deliver. That's the company's new slogan. After all these years, I'm beginning to sound like him." She smiled. It failed to hide the depth of sadness in her eyes.

"Do you work with him?"

"No. He runs things past me from time to time when he needs a fresh perspective. I'm the consultant's consultant." She chuckled softly, which led Alex to surmise it was a self-appointed title that she enjoyed. "My real job was raising the children."

"How did you meet him?" Alex asked.

"Jim worked as an intern for my father in Charleston and stayed on after graduation. Daddy acquired fine furnishings and high-end art from around the world for a select clientele, and Jim managed the shipments. My dear husband was so focused on his career; he didn't notice me at first. Not easily dissuaded, I finally won him over.

"Five years later, Jim left the company and went out on his own. My father was furious and believed Jim had betrayed him. It didn't help once I informed him that I'd accepted Jim's marriage proposal. Daddy disowned me, which was a foolish gesture. I wasn't going to let go of the man I loved. We relocated here to be near his parents, who have since passed. My husband's a kind man with a good heart. I'm blessed."

Alex was curious. "Did you also work for your father prior to getting married?"

"No." Tears filled her eyes, and she reached for the tissue box. "I fear I'm the reason Caroline is dead," she choked out with a sob.

Alex jolted upright in his chair. "What?"

Dabbing at the tears, she said, "I'm sorry. What I meant to say was I'm the reason Caroline became a flight attendant."

She bowed her head, veiling the tears that fell beneath the tissue.

He heard muffled voices coming from the outer rooms as he waited.

Collecting herself, she continued, "I worked for Eastern Air Lines before I married Jim. It was back in the days when the customers were wined and dined from takeoff to touchdown. Caroline followed in my footsteps. The desire was there since her childhood, and she loved it."

A framed picture on the table between them caught his attention. "Is that a photo of Caroline?"

"Yes, and my son, Marcus. He passed away last year."

A single tear trailed down her cheek as she rested a hand on the silver frame, and Alex's heart felt as if a ton of bricks slammed into his chest. He had read the detailed report regarding the shooting of Caroline's brother, Marcus, which included photos of the crime scene. *Me and my big mouth. I'm such an idiot.*

"Mrs. Bishop." She lifted her chin, and watery eyes met his. "I can't imagine what you and your husband are having to deal with right now. I'm so, so sorry."

Unable to respond, she shifted her gaze to Caroline's photograph with her brother.

Giving her the opportunity to collect herself, Alex stood and approached the fireplace, where he studied a collection of framed pictures of various children—different ages and skin coloring—sitting on the mantel. "Who are these little ones?"

Barbara dried her eyes and rose to join him. "They're our foster children, eight total. Each child has an impairment or disability. We cared for them until they were adopted. Marcus and Caroline were a big help."

He noticed her mood brightened somewhat as she spoke, and he was glad he had inquired about the children. Though he knew very little about them, he sensed the Bishops were good people and considered it unfair that they'd lost both of their grown children due to tragic circumstances.

Looking up at him, she said, "I'm sorry. I'm the one doing all the talking. I never asked about you. Are you married? Do you have children?"

In that instant, Alex's pleasant smile dissipated, and the atmosphere in the room changed.

Reaching out, she rested a gentle hand on his arm. "I'm sorry. I wasn't aware that you'd lost someone too. The one blessing that brings comfort is knowing that they're with God."

A sarcastic grunt escaped from Alex's throat, and he couldn't meet her eyes.

"You're still angry. That's okay. It's part of the grieving process. Give it time. Remember, God is always with us. Even though we may choose to shut him out, He never abandons us."

Withdrawing from her, he said, "I'm sorry, I need to go." Pausing at the door, he said, "The perfume you're wearing is a familiar scent. I'm not able to place it."

In reflex, she fingered the gold chain holding a cross at her neck. "It was Caroline's favorite. She bought it for me in New York."

A memory came forth in which he had taken Sarah to New York to celebrate their first anniversary. She had discovered the perfume in a little shop in SoHo and wore it on special occasions. Sadly, the bottle broke during one of their military moves, and he never found a replacement.

Barbara interrupted Alex's musings. "It's called—"

He finished for her, "Toujours Vôtre." *Forever Yours, how ironic. If only it were true.*

∞

A tall, well-dressed man in his late fifties stood on the porch, his eyes never leaving Alex as he crossed the street and climbed into the Chevy Silverado. The pudgy younger man, who'd spoken to Alex earlier, stepped up next to him. "Isn't that—?"

"Yes," the older man interrupted.

"Small world. Wonder how he knows the Bishops."

"From what I gathered, he works for Galaxy Airlines. Maybe he flew with Caroline."

Scratching his pimply-scarred cheek, the chubby man smiled to himself. *I wonder what my big brother will do when he learns his nemesis is in the vicinity. I may have to stir that hornets' nest.*

The older man glared down at his companion with dark, menacing eyes. "You shouldn't have come today. It was stupid."

"No worries," the young man said, his words laced with arrogance. "There's no one here who could recognize me."

CHAPTER NINETEEN

HALFWAY THROUGH THE MORNING, Rodriguez's boss paid a surprise visit. Alex became aware of the FBI district director's presence when a voice bellowed from behind him, "Who's that?"

"*Dragon Boss* is back in town," Pete said, barely audible. "Be warned, Captain. He breathes fire." They were doing another run-through of the various airport security videos when they were interrupted.

Alex rose to greet Special Agent Richman, whose sizeable frame filled the doorway. "Captain Decker, sir. It's a pleasure to meet you."

The senior agent remained skeptical as they shook hands. "Captain? Captain of what?"

"Alex's helping with the investigation," Rodriguez said as she entered the room. "He's a pilot with Galaxy Airlines and ex-military."

"What branch?"

"US Navy, sir. Ten years."

Richman's attention was on the various monitors as he moved farther into the room. Addressing Alex without looking at him, he said, "Did you do any investigative work while in the service?"

"Yes, and I worked with NCIS for a year once I got out."

Arching one eyebrow, the director said, "Maybe you'll be of some help after all."

Rodriguez stepped up next to Alex. "The captain is the one who discovered a third person was involved in the attempted abduction of our mysterious passenger. On the video, he spotted the man in the crowd as everyone ran from the burning building."

"Good," Richman said, nodding his approval. Moving towards the door, he said, "I'm on a flight back to Washington in an hour. Show me what you've got, Rod."

Without another word, Agent Rodriguez and Dragon Boss left the tech lab.

Alex retook his seat. "Fire-breathing?"

"Definitely," Pete said, his attention to the monitors.

The minutes dragged on, and Alex checked his watch for the umpteenth time. Being tied to a desk all day was inhumane as far as he was concerned. The small windowless room made him feel claustrophobic and added to his sense of boredom and restlessness. He stood, stretched, and let Pete know that he was going for a walk.

Out in the hallway, he ran into Special Agent Jeff Dunn waiting for the elevator. Earlier in the week, they'd chatted in-depth and discovered they shared common ground in their military histories. Agent Dunn, an ex-marine, served one tour in Iraq and two tours in Afghanistan.

Mystified, Alex shared what was on his mind. "I don't get how you and the other agents do it? All that training and experience, and here you are digging through ashes and filling out endless reports."

"It covers my alimony and child-support payments each month. Besides, I like to think I make a difference." Agent Dunn's eyes remained transfixed on the elevator doors as if willing them to open. "I was practicing my peripheral-vision exercises as you walked up. You have a food stain on the front of your shirt, and you're wearing brown shoes. What color are mine?"

Resisting the urge to glance down to confirm what he already knew, he said, "Black."

"You're catching on. The FBI good book says, 'Know thyself and what the other guy is wearing,' or something like that."

"I admire your discipline. I'm not good at sitting around. Even in the service, it drove me crazy. Put me where the action is, or better yet, put me in an airplane."

"Now, I understand why Rodriguez refers to you as Cowboy. You like to go in with guns blazing."

Shrugging, he smiled. "Looks like your boss has me pegged. She's something else."

Agent Dunn's eyes narrowed as he studied his new friend. "Be careful, Captain. She has a husband hanging out in the wings."

"That's what I understand. Rodriguez said he's a professor at Georgetown, and they met in college. Lucky guy."

The elevator doors opened, and they entered.

Pressing the bottom button for the main terminal, Dunn added, "By the way, I'm out of here."

Alex spun around. "What's going on?"

"A failed bank robbery escalated into a shootout and kidnapping in Lynchburg, Virginia. It's not good. The robbers split up and crossed the state line with a hostage. The team is being airlifted out."

"What about this investigation?" Alex snapped.

"Sorry to say, it's old news. As you know, we've dismantled and moved the airplane to a secure off-site warehouse. A skeleton crew of agents will remain behind with those from the FAA. Everyone is relocating to the off-site location tomorrow. Pete and Rod are remaining behind for now. It'll be months before this project winds down."

The agent's words further dampened Alex's mood. "Watch your back, Jeff."

"That's the plan."

They reached the terminal and parted ways. Alex noticed three Galaxy pilots as they cleared TSA. Two of them waved at him and continued on their way. The third pilot, First Officer Scott Daniels, broke away and joined him.

Pointing to the Homeland Security badge that hung on the lanyard around Alex's neck, Scott asked, "What's that?"

"I'm moonlighting to pay for my airplane addiction."

"Good for you." Scott's voice grew pensive. "I wanted to thank you for your support on the day of the fire. I was a mess."

"Don't be so hard on yourself. What you experienced would distress anyone."

Focusing on the floor tiles at his feet, Scott said, "I called my wife on my cell phone while waiting on the airplane. She said that she wasn't worried because God was with me."

"That's something my wife, Sarah, would have said back in the day."

"Anyway, I felt better after I talked to her. It could've been worse. I'm thankful you requested a different gate."

"I guess God was keeping an eye on both of us," Alex said with moderate conviction.

Scott nodded in agreement. "I have to run. I'm glad I ran into you. Take care."

As his coworker headed toward Flight Operations in the south concourse, Alex recalled that Sarah believed God always had a plan. "If we don't know what it is," she would tell him, "then we have to be patient. He will let us know when the time is right." *I hope it's soon. I need my life back.*

CHAPTER TWENTY

ALEX HEARD A RUSTLING noise in the underbrush nearby as he proceeded along the path that led to the hangar. Spinning around, he scanned the nearby woods. His skin grew clammy, and beads of sweat formed on his upper lip. In a flash, haunting images erupted in his brain of the night he was captured by the Taliban.

He couldn't remember the last time he had experienced flashbacks of this sort, and it caught him by surprise. His nerves were admittedly on edge these days, and he was glad he had made the appointment with Dr. Newman's associate for the upcoming week.

Once his mind returned to the present and his heart no longer pounded in his chest, he stepped through the hangar's side door. Alex's neighbor, Sam, called down from the electric lift. "Good, you're back. Can you hand me the straight peen hammer and the diagonal pliers?"

He retrieved the tools from under the fuselage of the Beechcraft and passed them up to his friend. "Need any help?"

"No, I'm good. Nine hundred and ninety-nine more parts to replace, and she'll be good to go."

"Don't remind me." Bending down, Alex tightened one of the lug nuts, which held a new wheel cover in place. "I was crazy to buy this bucket of bolts."

"Don't worry. We'll have it in the air—someday." His neighbor loved refurbishing old cars. However, Sam stumbled upon a new passion when Alex introduced him to antique airplanes.

"All done here," Sam said as he lowered the lift and stepped off. "It's time for lunch."

As if on cue, Sam's wife, Wendy, came through the door carrying a picnic basket. "You two hungry? I made sandwiches from the bread I baked this morning."

"You read my mind," Sam said with a grin.

Alex placed his tools on the workbench. "Let's eat on the back deck."

∞

He exited the house with cold beverages in hand as Wendy slid onto the picnic bench next to her husband. He settled in across from them and eyed the array of food—potato salad, fresh fruit, and an overstuffed deli sandwich—artistically arranged on the plate in front of him. "Wendy, you're a gem. If you weren't married—."

Her sweet laughter lingered in the spring air. "I keep telling you someone special is going to show up in your life one of these days. You wait and see."

Alex's eyes drifted beyond the hangar to a meadow filled with yellow dandelions. *I've already had someone special.*

Once they finished the picnic lunch, Sam and Wendy went home, and Alex continued working on the Beechcraft. Soon he realized that he missed his neighbor's congenial companionship and the man's help.

"Marcus, if you're there, make yourself useful and hand me the straight peen hammer?" he said in jest. "It should be in the toolbox." He continued working, his attention focused on the wheel cover, when he heard something hit the cement floor. Glancing to his right, he discovered the requested tool lying within arm's reach.

Shaking his head in disbelief, he said, "Not funny." He reached for the hammer and didn't say another word the rest of the afternoon.

∞

A gentle breeze rustled the treetops as Alex opened one of the hangar bay doors. "Amelia, it's time to take you for a spin. I promise I'll behave—no barnstorming."

The setting sun painted the white billowing clouds pink and orange as the red antique biplane moved gracefully across the sky. In the open cockpit, a cool breeze brushed his skin, filling him with a sense of peace, and he let out a heartfelt sigh.

All too soon, the day came to an end, and it was time to go back. Alex made one final pass over Sam and Wendy's house and banked to the east toward his place. As the last rays of sunlight dissolved into the grayish hues of dusk, he guided the plane onto the runway. After putting it in the hangar, he sat on the porch, blanketed in darkness. His tranquil musings were interrupted by an uncomfortable feeling that someone was watching him. For the second time that day, he went on full alert. He rose and advanced to the railing.

A three-quarter moon dusted the runway and the woods beyond in an ethereal light. He heard twigs break and the crunching of leaves on the ground. Someone was there. Adrenaline pumped through his veins as the muscles in his arms and legs tensed in preparation for fight or flight.

Five deer scampered out of the woods and started grazing on the grassy runway. Alex didn't hear any more sounds coming from that direction. Even so, he couldn't shake the ominous feeling someone was out there.

CHAPTER TWENTY-ONE

Alex breathed in the savory aroma of grilled hamburgers and hotdogs as he transferred the meat to a platter. "Anybody hungry?" His question fell on deaf ears as the adults seated at the picnic table continued to converse. The four young girls, who occupied a card table, giggled intermittently amid non-stop chatter, causing Alex to smile.

At his request, Robert and his family had joined in the cookout with Dr. Newman, his wife, and two daughters. Since rehab, the doctor had become a cornerstone in Alex's life as his sponsor. Consequently, the two families became friends while attending various events in support of Alex.

The weather was accommodating with forecasted clear skies. A warm breeze rippled the oversized umbrella's fabric that shaded them from the sun. He made a mental note to have a permanent cover added to the back deck.

Once the meal was over and the tables cleared, Alex gave his guests a viewing of his latest project. The girls gushed with enthusiasm when they laid eyes on the new biplane. At his encouragement, they climbed into the front and back cockpit seats of the Beechcraft and pretended to fly off to Never-Never Land.

Dr. Newman's wife, Melanie, kept a watchful eye on them as she fidgeted with a gold pendant necklace. "Be careful, girls."

"No need to worry," Robert said. "They can't damage anything. Besides, the plane doesn't have an engine."

Two energetic young boys darted out of the woods and ran to Alex, calling out his name. Wendy and Sam emerged from the path that connected their two properties. Sam waved as he approached. "I hope we're not intruding. We were at the treehouse, and my grandsons heard your voice."

Giving each boy a high five, Alex said, "Not at all."

Sam's grandson, Logan, took notice of the small gathering. "We have enough to play baseball. Would it be okay?"

Robert's youngest, Jessica, jumped up and down with excitement. "Boys against girls?"

"You're on," Alex said, tousling the top of the boy's head with his fingers. "If you'll grab the gym bag of equipment, I'll mark the bases while you're gone. Take your brother, Jake, with you, and he can bring the bats. They're in the house by the front door."

As the sun journeyed across the western sky, laughter and shouts of excitement filled the air. Bases loaded, Jessica stepped up to the plate. Swinging at the first ball pitched, she hit it solid, and it flew through the air. "I did it! I did it!"

"Run, Jessica! Run," the grownups shouted.

"You're losing your touch, ol' man," Alex said in a teasing tone. "I'm going to trade you for Jessica."

"My bad," Robert replied with a shrug from the pitcher's mound.

Alex tugged on the bill of his Pirates baseball cap and watched the ball sail into the woods. "You going to get it?"

His friend laughed. "It's your baseball. You go."

"I got this," Sam called out from first base. "Jake, Logan, I'll give each of you fifty cents if you go get the ball." Watching his grandsons dart in and out of the trees, he said, "We should sit this one out. It might take a while."

"I've got more baseballs in the bag," Alex said as Jessica—rejoicing over the home run—sprinted to second base.

"No, let them go," Sam said, retrieving the batting helmet Jessica dropped when she rounded first base. "Besides, the girls were winning by a landslide prior to Jessica hitting the home-run. Let's grab a cold drink and wait in the shade."

By the time the two boys came back, Jessica's sister, Kayla, had convinced their mother it was time for dessert. Sam and his family were invited to partake.

"Someone trashed our treehouse," Logan announced as he skipped alongside Alex and his grandfather while making their way back to the house.

Alex caught Sam's eye. "What's he talking about?"

"Earlier today, we came across empty beer cans in the tree-house and cigarette butts scattered about the grounds. I'm sure it was teenagers. We'll clean up the mess on our way back home."

"Don't bother," Alex said. "I'll take care of it. It's been a big day, and there's no doubt the boys are tired." He was convinced teenagers weren't the ones hanging in the woods and wanted to check it out for himself.

As he stood on the porch later, waving goodbye to his guests, the iPhone in his back pocket rang. "Forget something?" he said, assuming it was Robert or Dr. Newman.

"Not that I'm aware of," Rodriguez responded. "Then again, I've been having trouble keeping track of my brain lately. Notice one floating around?"

His sense of euphoria vanished. "It's Sunday! I'm—on—a—break, remember?"

"True; nevertheless, it makes my day when I jerk your chain. Pack your bags. We're leaving for DC at daybreak. Something's come up, and I'm taking you with me."

"I quit." The words gave Alex a momentary sense of relief and pleasure.

"Everybody proclaims that on Sunday night." Laughing, she added, "You'll get over it. I'll pick you up at seven a.m."

"I'm serious!" he said with growing frustration. He had had enough of sitting in front of the monitors all week, scanning endless videos. "I'm not cut out for this work. You have tons of Feds who are better suited for the job. Take one of them to DC."

"You're right. I do have people far better qualified to handle this investigation," Rodriguez said. "On the other hand, you have one thing they don't."

"What's that?"

"Think about it. The real question is, how did you know Caroline was at the airplane window? Was that only a hunch?" Rodriguez asked, her tone serious. "And what about the third man? You figured that one out pretty fast. Are you *that* good, or is it the intel you're getting from your spirit guide, Marcus? To put it another way, I'm not letting you off the hook until this case is solved. So suck it up, cowboy."

His annoyance dissipated as he admitted to himself, he couldn't walk away now. "Okay, you win. Wouldn't it be easier if we met at the airport?"

"We're not flying. I hate airplanes. I drove down from DC. You'll be at the wheel on our drive north while I work on my laptop. It's a five-hour trip by car, four if we don't stop to eat or use the bathroom. Sweet dreams," she said, and the line went dead.

∞

At 9:30 p.m., Alex switched off all the lights in the house except for the one on the bedside table. If anyone were watching, they would assume he was reading prior to turning in.

He changed into black pants and a dark long-sleeve shirt and applied green and black camouflage paint to his face. From there, he proceeded down the hallway to the back bedroom, which he used as an office and mini gym. On the far wall, he removed a small section of wood paneling and opened the wall safe. He extracted top-of-the-line night-vision goggles and a Smith and Wesson M&P 9mm, which he placed in a Galco holster at his ankle. He then slipped out a back window concealed by overgrown shrubbery.

For the next two hours, Alex combed the woods using the night optics. He encountered deer, wild turkeys, a fox, possum, and raccoons—but no humans. He did find mashed-down underbrush at the edge of the woods near the house and fresh footprints in the dirt.

After confirming the outbuildings and hanger were locked, he made his way to the treehouse. He removed the NVGs and slipped on plastic gloves. Searching the area using a headlamp, Alex came across more footprints that matched the others. As he tossed beer cans and cigarette butts into sterile plastic bags, he speculated on who his uninvited visitors had been the previous night and couldn't come up with anything that could justify it.

CHAPTER TWENTY-TWO

T HE FOURTH FLOOR IN the Hoover building consisted of a maze of cubes and small offices where IT specialists and analysts monitored individuals involved with money laundering, misappropriation of funds, and potential terrorist attacks. When Pete joined Rodriguez's team, a small conference room had been retrofitted into an office, which he shared with two field agents. The cramped benign-colored space contained three desks, one pushed up against each wall, which afforded minimal space for anything else, including humans. Luckily, due to fieldwork, Pete and his teammates were seldom in residence at the same time.

Alex sat at one of the unoccupied desks, reviewing yesterday's investigative report submitted by the Greensboro team, which offered nothing new.

Sitting at the desk opposite Alex, Pete sighed in frustration. "I know what you're going to ask, and I told you to let it go."

"Is reading minds part of your job description or merely a hobby?"

"I'm out of here." The cramped space was getting on both their nerves. Snatching up his laptop, Pete stood to leave. "I'm not able to get anything accomplished with you underfoot."

Rodriguez had been in an ill-tempered, hostile mood ever since Tuesday. Alex had kept bugging Pete regarding the reason for Rodriguez's meltdown. That was not what was on his mind right now.

Glancing up from the laptop, Alex addressed the IT technician's back as the younger man headed for the door. "Do you have any idea what your boss has against flying? I invited her to take a ride in my plane, and she responded as if I'd offered her rat poison."

That got the younger man's attention. Retracing his steps, Pete sat down next to Alex and placed his laptop between them. After logging back in, he said, "The answer to your question is on YouTube."

"YouTube?"

Pete selected the video of Captain Sully landing the US Airways airplane in the Hudson River on January 15, 2009. As the passengers began evacuating through the window exits, Pete zoomed in on the left-wing. "Focus on the woman helping the others climb into the rescue boat. Is there something familiar about her?"

"It's Rodriguez!"

Closing the browser, Pete said, "Rod was on her way to Columbia via Charlotte. She didn't make it that day. She did the next—by car. Now she drives to a site rather than flying whenever possible."

"It makes sense. An experience like that could make the most seasoned traveler skittish."

Pete agreed with a slight nod and added, "There's more to the story. She was fresh out of training and among the first responders to the Pentagon on 9/11. Right afterward, Richman assigned her to the FBI team investigating the Pentagon and Stonycreek sites. She takes every airplane incident personally."

∞

From the time they had arrived in DC on Monday, Alex had remained tied to his desk in the decaying J. Edgar Hoover FBI Building. Lunchtime provided him the one opportunity to escape.

The building's location on Pennsylvania Avenue offered numerous points of interest within walking distance. On Wednesday, he had explored the International Spy Museum. Captivated by the array of "Bond" type paraphernalia, he presented Agent Rodriguez with an extensive wish list upon his return.

"In case you haven't noticed, cowboy, it's the twenty-first century," she said in a snarky tone while reading the handwritten note. "These are from the dinosaur age."

Today he stood in the middle of the US Navy Memorial Plaza, where he had attended two services during his time in the Navy. The first one honored his wingman, Chris, and the other one was for his father. Sarah sat beside him during both ceremonies.

His father resigned his commission at thirty-five when he met and fell in love with Alex's mother. They were married a few months later. Alex recalled the dream he had the night prior to his father passing away. In it, his dad said, "I'm going back out to sea. Don't worry about me. Take care of your mother, and tell her I've always loved her. I'm proud of you, son." The day following the memorial service, they scattered the old sailor's ashes at sea.

Realizing he had missed the standard Sunday call with his mother, Alex reached for his cell phone. His thumb was about to press the send button when he caught sight of a man in a warm-up suit jogging past the *Lone Sailor* statue. The stranger had short-cropped dark hair, broad shoulders, and an athletic build. Alex recalled noticing the same person on two other occasions. The first time was Tuesday morning; dressed in a business suit, he was in the lobby of the Marriott where Alex was staying. The second time Alex spotted him was in the gift shop of the Spy Museum on Wednesday. On that occasion, he was wearing a baseball hat, tan khaki pants, and a black golf shirt.

   With his eyes conveniently concealed behind sunglasses, Alex pretended to study one of the base-relief etchings while observing the man. Before rounding the corner of the building, the stranger glanced his way. Alex had an inkling that it wasn't a coincidence. He pocketed the cell phone and walked briskly to the street corner. He searched the multitude of people on both sides of the main thoroughfare; the stranger had disappeared.

CHAPTER TWENTY-THREE

Alex barged into Agent Rodriguez's office. "Are you having me followed?"

Ignoring him, she continued reading something on her computer. Dark circles under her eyes punctuated the worried look on her face. "Idiots. They're all a bunch of idiots."

He couldn't make out what was on the monitor, and a sense of foreboding besieged him. Moving closer, he placed his hand on her shoulder. "What's wrong?"

A moment passed before she registered his presence and glanced up. "Good, you're here. I'm sending you home."

"I'm not going anywhere until I know what's going on here. You're obviously upset."

Avoiding the confrontation, she pressed on. "Did you talk to the psychiatrist your sponsor recommended?"

"Yes. Dr. Fletcher and I Face-Timed on Monday and yesterday. He wants to meet with me in person next time."

"Another reason for you to go home." She glanced at her watch. "Ask my admin to book you on the next flight out."

His voice was agitated as he spoke. "I'm not leaving until—."

Cutting him off, she said, "I'm in the middle of something here, and . . . Wait a second! Did you say someone was following you?"

"It was nothing, never mind."

Returning her attention to the computer screen, she

dismissively waved him off. "I'll catch up with you in Greensboro. Go on home."

Alex left in search of Pete and found him in their shared, cramped corner office. "I want to know why your boss is so upset, and you're going to fill me in right now."

At first, Pete didn't respond; instead, he typed something on his laptop and turned it toward Alex. "I'm going to the breakroom. Want anything?"

"No, and you're not going anywhere until you tell me what is going on."

The door to the office was open. So as not to be overheard, in a quiet voice, Pete said, "Once you read what's on the screen, don't mention it to anyone, especially to Rod. Not a word. Got it?"

Surprised, Alex nodded in acknowledgment as Pete walked out.

Alex read the first entry on the search screen. NEW YORK TIMES: *Professor Carl Mitchell of Georgetown University Vanished Monday Evening While in Route to an IT Conference in New York City.* He recognized the connection. The missing professor and Rodriguez's husband were one and the same. There was no mention of his wife or that he was married to an FBI agent. Most likely, the Feds wanted to keep that tidbit out of the news.

As he clicked the mouse and read the latest news update, he shook his head in disbelief. The professor and his abductors had disappeared, leaving no trail or clue to their whereabouts.

RALEIGH, NC
6:24 P.M.

Dr. Newman glanced over at his friend, who sat in the passenger seat of the BMW. "Alex, you're a million miles away."

Redirecting his attention from the passenger window, Alex said, "Excuse me?"

"You were talking and wandered off midsentence."

Alex shrugged. "Oh, sorry. There's too much going on right now. Did I thank you for picking me up at the airport?"

The doctor changed lanes and passed an eighteen-wheeler. "Yes, and you tried to come up with a lame excuse about why you couldn't accept my dinner invitation for tomorrow night. So, where did you drift off to?"

"You're a good driver."

"Wrong answer; I'll let it slide for now."

They drove south out of town and pulled up in front of Alex's house less than an hour later. Dr. Newman shut off the engine and eyed his friend. "Earlier, you started to ask me a question and changed your mind. What was it?"

Alex caught sight of the hangar through the front window as he carefully considered his next words. The investigation, Rodriguez, and her kidnapped husband plagued his mind, yet one nagging idea came forth above the rest. "I wanted your perspective on something regarding the military."

"Since I've never served, Dr. Fletcher may be better suited to answer your question since he works with vets. Apart from that, input from a civilian might shed a different light on the subject."

Alex nervously shifted in his seat. "Okay, here goes. What if all those who have died during hostile conflicts through the centuries had survived? No doubt, many of those individuals carried within them the potential to improve society through science, the arts, music, literature, and technology. If history were rewritten, maybe the cure for cancer and heart disease would no longer be an issue. And what about the towns, museums, libraries, and historical buildings that were bombed, burned, or ransacked, leaving lives in ruin in their wake? And let's not forget the civilians who lost their lives because they were in the wrong place at the wrong time. It's all such a waste, wouldn't you agree?"

At first, the doctor didn't respond. Finally, in a quiet voice, he said, "Are you second-guessing the role you've played in our country's military history?"

"Geez, Doc! This isn't about me. I wanted your opinion, not time-out on the shrink's couch."

Neither spoke. The cheerful chatter of birds in nearby trees did little to alleviate the tension in the car.

Finally, the doctor asked, "Did something happen while you were in DC?"

The top was down on the convertible, and Alex delayed responding by focusing on the scattered clouds drifting overhead. There was no doubt the visit to the Navy's Memorial Plaza had added to his melancholy. Still, he didn't want to go into it right now and redirected the conversation. "This car is something else, Doc. Are you going to let me take it for a spin sometime? I bet it handles sweet on the road."

"Sure, anytime."

Alex was glad his friend didn't press the point and opened the door to get out. Hesitating, he said, "I asked our last president the same question, though I worded it a little differently."

The doctor's eyes widened in surprise. "Really?"

"Back in the day, I was involved in a covert op," Alex said, his voice hoarse. "People had to die for it to be successful. None of our men got killed, only those fighting for a cause they ardently believed in and a handful of civilians. I received a medal and a handshake from the President in the privacy of the Oval Office. Seizing the opportunity, I asked him if he thought there was any hope we, as human beings, could ever get off this crazy merry-go-round. I noted that history keeps repeating itself, and we don't evolve. Generation after generation, humans continue to engage in conflict and war."

"What did he say?"

"Hope." To paraphrase the President, he said, "it's human nature to hope and dream for a better future. The glue that binds it together is faith.' He instructed me not to give up on faith, hope, and the dream. He said, in truth, that's why he and I answered the call to serve."

"Wow, what a moment."

"Inform Melanie to set an extra plate. See you tomorrow night, Doc."

"Sleep well, my friend."

"I wish I could," Alex uttered as he climbed the porch steps and entered the house.

CHAPTER TWENTY-FOUR

FRIDAY, MAY 4
LEE COUNTY, NORTH CAROLINA

THE NEXT MORNING ALEX drove to Walmart in Silver City and bought a burner phone. Sitting in the parking lot, he dialed a number, punched in a numerical code after the beep, and hung up. In no time at all, the expected call came through.

"Your location, Captain?" a clipped voice on the other end said.

"My place, forty minutes."

Thirty-five minutes later, after smashing the SIM card and tossing the phone, he pulled up in front of his house. A young man in a captain's Army uniform stood next to a black military-issue sedan. "Captain Decker?"

Alex nodded in reply.

Holding out his hand palm-up, the officer said, "I need some identification, sir."

Withdrawing his driver's license, Galaxy ID, and TSA security badges, Alex passed them over.

The officer compared the information with that on the screen of his SAT phone and handed Alex a small package along with the credentials. Without saying another word, he climbed back in the sedan and drove off.

Alex tore through the wrapping and extracted a secure satellite phone, not unlike the ones the FBI agents use. It rang in his hand as he sat down on the top step leading to the porch.

A voice from the past came through on the line. "Alex, my boy. I'm delighted to hear from you. How may I be of service?"

"Thanks for taking my call, General. I have a request if it's not too much to ask. Professor Mitchell went missing Monday night while in transit to a conference in New York City. Would you check into it for me?"

The general hesitated before he spoke. "You know the professor?"

"No, sir. I know his wife, Special Agent Rodriguez." Alex recapped the events following the airplane fire at the Greensboro Airport and how the FBI agent had drafted him to help with the investigation. He deemed it best not to mention the apparition sightings and the haunting dreams. "I learned about it yesterday. She doesn't know that I found out, and I intend to keep it that way for now. She's close-lipped about the whole thing and wound tight as a tiger ready to devour whoever comes within range."

His friend grew notably sober as he addressed the seriousness of the situation. "I'm not surprised. I have the pleasure of personally knowing both Carl and his little spitfire of a wife, Maria. Professor Mitchell's expertise in the field of Information Technology is unparalleled, but his specialty is drone technological development. He is on the faculty at Georgetown University and the US Army War College in Carlisle, Pennsylvania. We had a secret-service agent assigned to him five years ago. A security camera showed them both entering a limo at the airport in New York; however, they never reached the hotel. The FBI is working on the assumption it's a kidnapping. Since no one has contacted Maria regarding a ransom, money doesn't seem to be the motive."

"I want to help," Alex said with conviction.

General Pritchard paused momentarily to absorb this latest proclamation. "Alex, my boy, you're smitten with the lady."

He sprang to his feet. "No, I—for crying out loud, don't read more into it! The reason I called you was for an update on the situation and to determine if I can be of help."

"Calm down. My intent isn't to make light of the situation. As chairperson of the Joint Chiefs of Staff, I can speak for the President and the rest of the advisory board in saying we are very concerned. Keep the phone with you. I'll call you if I hear anything."

Alex raked his fingers through his hair. He had hoped for something more concrete but was left sitting on the sidelines. "Thank you, sir."

"No problem," his friend said. "I told you, after what you did for my son in Afghanistan, if you need anything, call me. That offer still stands."

Disconnecting the call, Alex recalled the mission that had dealt him a set of lousy circumstances, followed by one lucky break.

During a nighttime operation over hostile territories in northern Afghanistan, a land-to-air missile took out his plane. He was still waiting for the Navy to bill him for the F/A-18 Hornet he had lost. Maybe they'd deferred the debt since he had ended up captured after successfully bailing out of the aircraft.

During the same mission, Navy SEAL Team Four, led by Lieutenant Brian Wilcox, was sent in to extract four Marines held as prisoners in the same village where Alex was detained immediately after being captured. The SEALs rescued Alex along with the Marines, which included General Pritchard's son. During their escape, Captain Pritchard and a SEAL became pinned down by a shooter.

Alex extracted an AK-47 from a dead Taliban rebel and dove behind a low mud-brick wall with the SEAL team leader squeezed in beside him. They both opened fire on the shooter located in the mud-brick house across from them. Alex got the feel of the gun by spraying the building's exterior wall next to an open door. When the shooter gave his position away by returning fire, Alex lined up the sight aperture and fired. Before the man hit the ground, Alex was on the move in the wake of Lieutenant Wilcox, who was two steps in front of him. They reached the two fallen comrades and ascertained that both had been wounded but were alive.

Ignoring the pain from his cracked ribs, Alex hoisted Captain Pritchard onto his shoulder. The lieutenant did the same with the wounded SEAL, and they made their way toward an awaiting Black Hawk helicopter located in an open courtyard. The chopper lifted into the night as they piled in beside the rest of the SEAL team and the rescued Marines.

∞

The grandfather clock in the living room chimed six as Alex coated the last piece of meatloaf with mashed potatoes and shoveled it into his mouth, savoring the taste. "That meal was outstanding."

Melanie Newman picked up his empty plate and refreshed his coffee. "I hope you left room for dessert. We'll have it on the back deck later."

The large dining-room windows offered a stunning view of the spacious backyard. Blooming dogwood trees peppered the green landscape. Their discarded spring flowers floated to the ground, creating a carpet of white petals.

Alex added cream and sugar to his coffee and glanced out the window. "Your azalea gardens are beautiful this year."

"I'm thankful an ice storm didn't come through during the past week or two and freeze everything like it did last year."

Lucy, Newman's nine-year-old daughter, fidgeted in her seat. "Mommy, can we go to the barn now? I've been waiting all day to show Mr. Alex the new baby kittens. And Kayla and I need to feed the horses."

He smiled at the energetic girl. "Have you named the kittens?"

"Of course. Would you like to take one home?" Her blues eyes danced with expectation.

"What an excellent idea," the doctor said, laughing. "You should take two."

Everyone helped to clear the table, after which they made their way to the stables just beyond the gardens. As they drew near, Alex heard quick footsteps approaching on the gravel path behind him. "Hi, folks. Hope I'm not intruding."

Spinning around, he watched as Rodriguez approached, dressed in jeans, a New England Patriots jersey, and sunglasses. "What're you doing here?" he blurted out before he could catch himself.

"I guess that means you didn't miss me," she said, adding a playful smile.

Dr. Newman placed an arm around his wife's shoulders. "She's a pretty lady, Alex. Are you going to introduce us?"

He made introductions, explaining that Rodriguez was the FBI agent he spoke of during dinner.

A horse whinnied, and everyone turned as Lucy entered the corral on a black gelding. "Mr. Alex, did Daddy tell you Midnight and I won two first-place ribbons last week at the horse show in Stafford?"

"No, he didn't; good for you."

Kayla trailed behind her younger sister on foot with a brown chestnut gelding in tow. Rodriguez ducked through the railing into the corral and gave the animal a wide berth as she ran a hand along its neck and flank. "He's beautiful. What's his name?"

"Thor," Kayla said, beaming. "I've had him since he was a colt. He's five now."

Lucy dismounted and approached Rodriguez. "Hello. I don't think we've met. Are you Mr. Alex's girlfriend?"

Rodriguez gave a throaty chuckle. "No, I'm not."

"Would you like to be? He's very nice."

The agent smiled in agreement and gave Alex a side glance. "Yes, he is, but I'm married. You could be his girlfriend, though."

Lucy scrunched up her nose; the absurdity of such a thing was repulsive. "I'm too young. Besides, Daddy said I couldn't have any boyfriends until I finish college. I'll be very old by that time. I hope I'll still be able to find someone."

Rodriguez's attempt to suppress a laugh failed. "I don't believe you'll have any problem in that area."

While the girls exercised the horses, Alex leaned close to Rodriguez and whispered, "For the record, I don't like surprises."

She glanced at him through rose-tinted sunglasses, which failed to conceal the exhaustion reflected in her eyes. "Aren't you the party pooper?"

Alex and Rodriguez called it a night after dessert and coffee. A full moon crested in the east, and the chirping sound of crickets filled the night air as they walked to her car. She hesitated prior to getting in. "Nice family."

Leaning against the front bumper, he said, "I'm sure you didn't show up for just dessert and coffee. What's up?"

"I need you to meet me in Raleigh tomorrow morning at the Wells Fargo branch in Jim Bishop's neighborhood. I'll text you the address. Eight o'clock sharp."

"You're not going to give me a clue as to what's going on?"

She opened the door and slid into the driver's seat. "I'll explain in the morning once I finalize everything." Noting the ball of fur purring in Alex's arms, she added, "What are you going to do with a cat?"

"Teach it to fetch baseballs, of course."

"So you say." She started the engine. "See you in the morning."

He moved clear of the sedan as she backed out of the driveway. He waited until the car's taillights disappeared around a bend in the road. *What does Marcus and Caroline's father have to do with any of this?*

CHAPTER TWENTY-FIVE

A STORM PASSED THROUGH DURING the night, and the streets remained wet, even though the early-morning sun was out, and the temperature was already in the high seventies. Alex pulled into the Wells Fargo lot and parked. Exiting the truck, he dodged a large puddle as he joined Rodriguez, who stood next to a black FBI surveillance van.

"Morning, boss."

She glanced up from her iPad and motioned him to follow her. Stepping into the van, she introduced him to a man wearing rimless glasses and an FBI windbreaker. "Agent Hernandez is our team expert regarding surveillance."

The agent handed him a flesh-colored wireless earbud, and Rodriguez settled into a nearby chair as the two men tested the electronic listening device.

Gazing down at her, Alex said, "So why am I here?"

She finished taking a sip of water from a Fiji bottle, then began to explain. "Jim Bishop routinely visits the Starbucks across the street on Saturday mornings. After ordering coffee, he takes a table next to the front window. In the past, Marcus or Caroline would join him from time to time. Today it's going to be you."

"So, what's the purpose of this casual encounter that you've skillfully orchestrated?" He was irritated at being used as a pawn in a game that he didn't understand, and it was evident in his tone.

"I'll explain why we're doing this afterward. For now, I want you to get Bishop to talk about his exporting business. Sometimes people will open up to strangers and divulge things they wouldn't share with a close friend or spouse. Go with the flow of conversation and see where it takes you."

Checking the listening device in his ear to make sure it was securely in place, he said, "Where're you going to be?"

"Parked out front on the street. We'll be able to pick up your dialogue from there."

Alex frowned and met Rodriguez's eyes. "The Bishops have been through so much. Do we have to do this?"

She started to answer when something on one of the surveillance monitors caught her attention.

"Time to go. He's entering the building."

∞

"Mr. Bishop?" The man turned away from the window, and Alex was taken aback by the depth of sorrow reflected in his eyes. His face was thin, and his shoulders slumped as if weighed down by the burdens of the world. "I thought it was you. We met at Caroline's funeral. I'm Captain Alex Decker."

Bishop didn't respond.

"May I join you?" Not waiting for a response, Alex slid into the chair across from him.

"I'm sorry," Jim Bishop mumbled, his brows knitted in confusion. "Did you say we've met before?"

Alex repeated his previous introduction.

Bishop didn't respond, and Alex continued, "I'm so sorry for your loss. I sympathize with what you're going through. I lost my wife, Sarah, to cancer a few years ago, and I still miss her every day."

Staring into his coffee as the dark liquid grew cold, Bishop spoke in a muffled voice. "It never really goes away, does it? The pain of loss, especially if they're young, is unbearable." Lifting his head, he met Alex's eyes. "It was three weeks ago today . . . the fire. I'm a man who solves problems and makes things happen, but I'm not able to fix this." His voice cracked as he delivered the final words.

Deciding to give Bishop a moment of solitude to deal with his grief, Alex reached for the man's coffee cup and returned with a fresh one.

Bishop cleared his throat. "Thank you."

Shifting to a different topic, Alex said, "When I was at your house, I noticed two lithograph prints in the hallway of antique airplanes. They're fantastic renditions."

Bishop's mouth curved into a tentative smile. "*The Spirit of Saint Louis Nonstop Refueling* print is from 1942. *A Double for Rickenbacker* is from 1947. They are both original prints. In high school, I saved up and bought them for my grandfather." Staring out the window, he grew silent as his sad eyes reflected a past yearning.

"My grandfather carted me to airshows when I was a kid." Meeting Alex's eyes, he said, "What a thrill it was to witness those daredevils dancing across the sky. Once my son was old enough, we included Marcus in our outings." He grew somber, and his voice was barely above a whisper. "My grandmother gave the prints to me after my grandfather passed. Good memories."

Alex nodded in agreement. "I was one of those daredevils working the circuit during high school and college until I enlisted in the Navy. Now I refurbish antique biplanes."

A comfortable conversation ensued as they exchanged childhood memories of airshows, forgotten pranks, and aspirations.

Soon they were on a first-name basis. *Rodriguez was right;* he mused. *People do open up to strangers when given the opportunity.*

On an impulse, Alex asked, "Have you ever been up in a biplane?"

A wistful smile touched Bishop's lips, and his expression softened. "No. Just in my imagination when I was allowed to sit in the cockpit of one."

"In that case, how about going for a ride with me sometime?"

Alex could tell he had sparked the man's interest. Before his companion could answer, Bishop's cell phone rang. Glancing at the screen, he said, "I need to take this call. I'll be right back."

Bishop lifted the phone to his ear and went outside. Upon returning, he apologized. "That was my brother-in-law. With him, I never know if it might be important or not. You were saying?"

The place was getting noisy, and Alex leaned in close to be heard. "I own a WWII Stearman biplane." He thumbed through various pictures of the planes he had refurbished over the years on his cell phone, after which he extracted a commercial pilot's license and slid it across the table.

"Do you still do the crazy stunts?"

"No, I'm more sensible these days," Alex said with a light-hearted snort. "I intend to take my plane for a spin this morning. Would you like to join me, that is, if you don't have other plans?"

Bishop's eyes narrowed as he considered the offer. "Is it close by?"

"I live thirty-five minutes south, near Sanford. The plane is there. You could follow me or ride with me, and I'll bring you back afterward."

The man's spirits brightened, and his shoulders no longer sagged. "I'll need to run it by my wife first."

"Of course."

Glancing out the window, Bishop said, "My brother-in-law just arrived. There's something he wanted to discuss with me. It shouldn't take long."

He rose to leave, then hesitated. "I'm seriously considering your invitation. I'll be right back."

Alex refreshed his coffee and retook his seat at the window in time to observe the two men in a heated debate. The brother-in-law was taller than Bishop and younger, possibly in his late fifties. Emphasizing a point, he punctuated the air with his finger. Bishop stood his ground and shook his head.

The brother-in-law's features and outburst triggered something from Alex's past, and he experienced déjà vu. He recalled meeting the man at Caroline's memorial service; however, that wasn't it. The drama concluded with the brother-in-law throwing his arms up and storming off.

Bishop returned to his seat. "I've decided to accept your invitation. I walked here from my house. To save time, I think I'll ride with you as long as we are back by three o'clock. I'll need to check with my wife first."

"Understood."

While taking a final sip of coffee, Alex heard a woman's voice as she addressed Bishop. "Good morning. I was hoping you would be here today."

Jim glanced up. "Susanne! What a pleasant surprise."

The man seated at the table behind them stood to leave and collided with the pretty woman, causing her to bump Alex's shoulder. Before he could react, the contents of the coffee cup spilled down the front of his shirt. He leaped to his feet as the hot liquid reached the skin beneath the fabric. *Not again!*

"Oh my!" she exclaimed. "Are you all right?"

Alex held up his hand, palm out. "It's okay. Jim, give me a few minutes. I'll be right back."

Luckily, the men's room was unoccupied. Locking the door, he slipped off his shirt and used wet paper towels to soothe the red, blistered skin. "What is it with me, pretty women, and hot coffee?" he hissed between clenched teeth.

Someone knocked on the door.

"Occupied, go away!"

"Alex, it's me, Jim Bishop. Are you all right? Do you need anything? "

He opened the door ajar. "If you could bring me the gym bag and first-aid kit from the back seat of my truck, I'd appreciate it." He handed over his keys. "It's the black Silverado parked right out front."

As he waited, he heard Rodriguez's voice in the earbud. "You all right?"

"I'll survive, although I think I'm going to give up coffee."

She laughed. "Did you recognize your assailant?"

"Yes, it's Marcus's fiancée."

Alex emerged soon after in a Steelers jersey after applying burn cream and downing a couple of ibuprofen.

Susanne had departed, and Bishop stood alone next to the truck. "Maybe we should postpone this for another time," he said as Alex approached.

"No way. It's going to be a beautiful morning. Let's go—Amelia awaits."

Bishop's expression was one of confusion. "Who's Amelia?"

CHAPTER TWENTY-SIX

BEFORE BACKING OUT OF the parking space, Alex glanced in the rearview mirror to make sure no cars were behind them. To his astonishment, Caroline Bishop's beautiful green eyes met his gaze. He stared in disbelief at her reflection as she gifted him with a radiant smile. At that moment, he experienced a depth of love, compassion, and grace that was beyond measure. All his anger and resentment toward God melted away in that instant.

Caroline looked at her father, who sat in the front passenger seat. A worried frown creased her brow, and the smile vanished.

Alex gave Bishop a side glance in the hopes that he detected his daughter's presence. Obviously unaware of what was happening, the man's eyes remained focused on the front window.

When he looked in the mirror again, Caroline's image was gone, yet he still sensed her presence.

Bishop stirred. "We're not moving. Is anything wrong?"

"No. I was waiting for the person behind me to get out of the way so I can see to back up," Alex said, smiling at the rearview mirror.

Upon exiting the Starbucks parking lot, he spotted the FBI van as it merged into traffic behind them.

LEE COUNTY, NORTH CAROLINA

Alex rejoined Bishop in the living room after changing clothes and applying more burn cream to his chest. His guest stood in front of the fireplace, studying Sarah's picture. "Your wife?"

"Yes."

"She was lovely. She had such a sweet smile."

"Thank you. So does . . . did Caroline," Alex responded, correcting himself midsentence.

"We're both lucky men," Bishop said with a flicker of sadness in his eyes.

"I'm ready to go," Alex announced and handed Bishop a bottle of sunscreen. "Best to coat your face, neck, and ears. The wind and sun will fry you like bacon up there. I also have a UV jacket for you to use and protective flight goggles."

Twenty minutes later, as they approached the end of the grassy runway, Alex lifted Amelia into the air. Visibility was ideal in the wake of the early-morning rain. Though the spring air was brisk, the sun's warmth penetrated their clothing.

The dogwood trees in full bloom bore a resemblance to cotton balls nestled against the emerald-green countryside below. Occasional farmhouses peppered newly plowed fields of red dirt.

Alex banked the plane left toward the mountains. Traveling south, they followed the Blue Ridge Parkway, and the hardwood and pine trees grew thicker as they approached Pisgah National Forest. On the outskirts of Asheville, Alex made a midair U-turn, and they headed back toward his place.

By early afternoon, they were back on the ground and sitting in the wooden rockers on the front porch. Both men were quiet, lost in thought, and savoring the exhilarating experience.

Bishop spoke first. "That was amazing. Thank you."

"Anytime you want another go at it, give me a call."

"I might take you up on it," Bishop said with a hint of playfulness.

Alex hated to interrupt the tranquil moment, but he needed to pick up the conversation where they'd left off during the drive here. "Jim, what type of challenges do you encounter in dealing with the different regulations when shipping to the various countries?"

"Luckily, the companies I contract with oversee most of it. However, I pay close attention if it pertains to hazardous materials."

Alex reached for a cold bottle of water from the small cooler he had brought from the kitchen and handed it to Bishop, then withdrew one for himself. "Do you ever contract shipments for the military?"

"No, there are too many regulations in dealing with the government, any government. All my clients are in the private sector. For example, today, I have six containers of surgical instruments leaving out of Charleston for Brussels. My client manufactures them here in Greensboro. I also have another customer in China who has a shipment of cinnamon inbound to the States, which is arriving in Miami tomorrow. I'm on the phone most days brokering shipments for clients around the world."

The image of Bishop's brother-in-law bubbled up in his mind. "I don't mean to pry; I couldn't help noticing the confrontation you had with your brother-in-law earlier today."

"Blake is a piece of work." Irritation overshadowed Bishop's words. "He's a challenge at best and downright bullheaded at other times. My brother-in-law deals primarily with shipping farm equipment and supplies to third-world countries. The customer base he deals with is very different from mine. Nevertheless, by combining our freight from time to time, I'm able to negotiate a significant discount with the transportation companies."

"How long have you had this arrangement?"

After taking a sip of water, Bishop answered. "Too long, I'm afraid. Evidently, he's done quite well for himself. He and my sister have a nice home right outside of Charleston in a gated golf community. Ironically, my wife gave up the high society style of living to be with me, and my sister—who fancies herself deserving of life among the rich and plenty—flaunts it."

Bishop glanced at his watch. "We should go."

During the ride back to Raleigh, Bishop shared that he was also working with the new president of Côte d'Ivoire to help rebuild the country's infrastructure following a decade of military coups and civil unrest. "Six months ago, President Jabari engaged me to work with foreign suppliers who would be providing the products and equipment necessary to build new factories, homes, and highways. At present, they don't have the resources within their country."

At the red light, Alex shifted in his seat to look at Bishop. "You're involved in all that?"

"Yes. President Jabari's goal is to bring his country into the twenty-first century while providing schools, housing, and employment for his people. I negotiate the shipment of the building supplies and equipment from the US and other countries to Côte d'Ivoire. It's a huge undertaking, yet one I find personally rewarding."

Reflecting on his military career and personal successes, Alex surmised that they were minuscule compared to this man's current endeavors.

"I have to admit," Bishop continued, "I believe everything I've done in my life has led me to this opportunity. I'm honored to help the president fulfill his dream."

Alex was left spellbound and speechless as the light changed, and they continued to Raleigh.

"Would you drop me off at the Oakwood Cemetery instead of my house, please?" Bishop asked. "When I called my wife earlier today, we agreed to meet there. We plan to spend the rest of the day with Caroline and Marcus."

Thirty minutes later, Alex drove through the massive stone archway leading to the historic cemetery and followed Bishop's directions to the gravesites. He stopped the truck, and Bishop reached for the door handle. Pausing, in a choked voice, he said, "Sometimes we pray for God's intervention in our lives, and we believe it's to no avail. I finally figured out, when we need it most, God sends someone to help us make it through whatever we're dealing with at any given time. I believe you were my divine intervention today. Thank you."

Bishop exited the truck; Alex watched as he walked up to a small grassy knoll where his wife, Barbara, waited for him.

During the drive back to Wells Fargo, where Alex planned to reconnect with Agent Rodriguez and her entourage, his thoughts spiraled downward into darkness. Images of those who'd perished in the airport fire danced in his mind like puppets, their screams of pain drowning out all other sounds. He forced himself to replace the disturbing images with Caroline's angelic smile and Marcus with his intense, commanding green eyes. Nevertheless, endless questions continued to bombard his mind and left him with a pounding headache. Meanwhile, he had no doubt that he was being dragged deeper and deeper into the investigation by some undetermined force.

On Saturdays, the branch closed early, and the parking lot was empty. He arrived first, followed by the black surveillance van, which pulled up next to him. Before it came to a complete stop, Rodriguez jumped out.

Alex leaned back against the truck with his arms crossed; his dark scowl greeted her as she approached. Sensing his mood, she didn't speak.

A large billowing white cloud passed overhead and briefly blocked out the sun. Finally, he said, "I'm going home."

"Okay. We'll meet tomorrow and go over everything then."

"Not tomorrow," he snapped.

"Okay," she hesitantly said as concern furrowed her brow.

"I'll call you when I'm ready to talk." On that note, he climbed into the truck and drove off.

CHAPTER TWENTY-SEVEN

Lee County, North Carolina

THE BRAKES ON THE Silverado needed replacing, and Alex's neighbor volunteered to take care of it. Deciding to drop the truck off on his way home, he pulled into an open bay in the three-car garage behind Sam's house. A 1957 Corvette Stingray—which usually occupied the space—was at a car show in Charlotte.

He placed the key under the floor mat, closed the garage door, and crossed the backyard toward his place. Wendy, who stood at the kitchen window, smiled and waved at him.

It was a little past four in the afternoon; however, dark clouds from an approaching storm gave the impression it was dusk. The rolling thunder drew closer as Alex briskly walked along the path connecting the two properties. The front porch came into view as a loud crack resounded overhead and carried with it a flash of white light illuminating his surroundings. He reflexively ducked and threw up his arms. "Wow! That was close!"

Raindrops, the size of quarters, began pelting him, and he darted for the house.

He shook off the water at the front door and slipped out of his wet shoes and socks. Upon entering, he started for the master bedroom and stopped abruptly. Sensing a presence in the house, he held his breath and listened. Pounding rain on the roof masked all other noises.

From this angle, the living room was in full view. Nothing was out of place except for Sarah's picture, which now faced the door leading into the kitchen. *Somebody's in there.*

Retracing his steps, Alex stopped when he felt the front door at his back. Dark shadows cloaked the hallway, which led to the back bedroom. From his vantage point, he had a partial view of the master bedroom. *Could someone be in there as well?*

He sent a text message to Rodriguez. *I'm home—call 911. I have an unwelcome visitor hiding in the kitchen.*

While waiting for a response, he reached for one of the two baseball bats propped against the wall next to the door.

The phone vibrated with an incoming message: *Get out of there.*

Taking a firmer grip on the bat, he slid the phone into his pocket. "You there in the kitchen, put your hands in the air, and come out where I can see you. I'm armed." *I hope whoever it is doesn't come out shooting.*

The lightning and thunder had subsided, leaving the house shrouded in gloominess. Quiet, rhythmic rain danced across the roof as he restated his demands.

The back door opened, and heavy footsteps resounded as someone ran across the back deck. Not hesitating, Alex threw open the front door and sprinted across the porch. Reaching out with one hand, he vaulted over the railing and landed on bare feet. As if hunkered down at home plate, he raised the bat over his shoulder and waited. A second later, the home invader rounded the corner. He swung and connected with the intruder's gut. *Bam!* Crying out in pain, the man pitched forward as something flew out of his hand.

Sensing movement over his right shoulder, Alex raised his arm and deflected a blow from the other bat. It grazed the back of his head and connected with his right shoulder at the base of his neck. Stars danced before his eyes, and his knees buckled as darkness overtook him, but not before he heard someone yelling at the man lying on the ground next to him.

"Get up, you idiot! You can't do anything right. And grab those! The last thing we need is for you to leave them behind!"

"My ribs! He broke my ribs!"

CHAPTER TWENTY-EIGHT

"*C*APTAIN *DECKER, DO YOU hear me?*"

Alex's head and shoulder throbbed. He made a vain attempt to open his eyes without success as his mind sank back into itself.

"Captain, I'm Lieutenant Brian Wilcox with the Navy SEALs. We've got the others out, and now it's your turn. On your feet, flyboy."

Sand and dirt mixed with mucus and blood caked the insides of his nostrils and coated the skin around his mouth. Pain shot through his left side when he rolled onto his back and came to the conclusion he probably had a cracked rib or two. Rancid odors mixed with body sweat made him want to gag. After the beating, the insurgents urinated on him and left him passed out on the floor in the dark, dank room.

"Captain Decker! Can you hear me, sir?"

The voice wasn't the lieutenants.

He was jolted back into the present in a flash and remembered what transpired prior to blacking out. Going on the attack, he threw a wild punch in the direction of the voice.

"Hold on," the uniformed officer said while attempting to restrain Alex's flailing arms. "I'm on your side. I'm with the Lee County Sheriff's Department."

He stopped thrashing about and fell back onto the wet

ground. It had stopped raining; nevertheless, he was soaked to the bone and couldn't stop shivering.

"Are you able to stand?"

"Yes," Alex growled. However, his legs buckled beneath him when he tried. The officer helped him to his feet and onto the front porch, where he sank into one of the wooden rockers. Someone wrapped him in a thermal blanket—its warmth a welcome relief.

He placed a hand on the swollen shoulder muscle at the base of his neck and winced. Addressing the sheriff, he said, "I apologize for having to ask this, but could you please get me an ice pack from the freezer in the kitchen?"

The officer entered the house as his neighbor, Sam, climbed the stairs. "Are you all right? We heard the sirens. What happened?"

He glanced toward the road and counted three Lee County Sheriff vehicles parked haphazardly among the trees. "I think the same punks who were at the treehouse earlier broke into my place while I was in Raleigh."

Sam collapsed in the other rocker. "Really?"

"I surprised them, and one clobbered me when they made a run for it."

"Oh no. I left Wendy home alone," Sam said, his voice escalating in alarm. "I need to get back to her. Will you be all right? Maybe you should sleep at our place tonight?"

"No, I'm good. Tell Wendy not to worry. I'm sure the police will figure this out and apprehend those who are responsible."

The sheriff emerged from the house and handed the ice pack to Alex.

"Officer Davidson, could you have someone accompany my neighbor back to his place?"

The officer acknowledged the request and motioned for one of his men to come forward as Sam hurried down the steps.

An ambulance drove up at the same time an emergency EVAC helicopter landed on the rain-soaked grassy runway.

"I don't need an ambulance," Alex snapped. "And I don't need to be airlifted to a hospital. I'm fine!"

"The helicopter's not for you. It's for those guys," the officer said, pointing to the aircraft.

Three FBI agents Alex recognized exited the aircraft and sprinted toward him. At the same time, he registered a fourth agent in an FBI windbreaker jacket leaving the woods beyond the hangar. The man approached the officer escorting his neighbor back home, and the three of them entered the path leading to Sam's place.

Rodriguez covered the porch steps two at a time while Pete and Special Agent Dunn waited at the bottom. Her words came out in a rush. "You okay, cowboy?"

"Hey, guys. What took you so long? You almost missed the party."

She knelt in front of him. "What happened?"

To forestall any additional dialogue, he said. "Before we get started, Officer Davidson, I need to ask another favor. There are two plastic bags filled with discarded debris sitting on the floor in the pantry. Could you bring them out here, please?"

The officer's face registered his disdain at being sent on a fool's errand.

"Trust me, it's important."

Once the officer was out of earshot, Alex said, "There were two of them, one in the kitchen and one in my bedroom. He's the one I misread. The guy in the kitchen made a run for it out the back door. I caught up with him out here when he cleared the corner of the house and clobbered him in the gut with a bat. The other guy got me from behind with a second bat."

Officer Davidson came back empty-handed. "They weren't in the pantry," he said with a condescending tone. "Maybe you put them somewhere else."

"You're probably right," Alex said. "No worries. I'll get them after everyone is gone. Thanks."

Rodriguez showed her creds to the officer and introduced herself. "I need a private moment with Captain Decker if you don't mind."

Davidson glared down at Rodriguez from his bulky six-foot frame, apparently not happy having his territorial authority infringed on. "I'm curious. Why are you here?"

Giving him a disarming smile, she said, "I promise this won't take long. You'll be able to get Captain Decker's statement afterward."

He nodded toward the ambulance. "What about the paramedics?"

Alex waved them off. "Convey my appreciation for them coming out here, and let them know I'm okay. No blurred vision, nausea, or slurred speech. Ibuprofen should take care of the pain, which is bearable."

"You heard the man," Rodriguez said.

The officer scowled but refrained from saying anything as he set out in the direction of the paramedics.

Still holding the ice pack against his neck, he cautiously got to his feet. "The house needs to be dusted for prints. I want your guys to do it, not the locals."

"Since you're part of an ongoing FBI investigation, I'll enlighten them to the fact that this incident now falls under our jurisdiction. They won't be happy, but I'll deal with it."

"But first, I want to do a walkthrough and check if anything is missing. Let's go."

Pete and Agent Dunn remained outside while Rodriguez followed Alex into the house.

In the living room, he immediately noticed that Sarah's picture was back in its original location and visible from the front door. Smiling, he offered a quiet thank you to Marcus for the clue that informed him of the intruders earlier. He was coming to the realization that the two Bishop siblings were guiding him toward an unforeseen objective, and he needed to start trusting in that fact.

"The local cops are wasting their time searching the woods. Those two guys are long gone," Alex said. "On my way home, I noticed a late-model dark blue Ford truck parked a mile down the road at an abandoned farm. The bank owns the property, and I assumed it was a potential buyer. Now I'm convinced it was these guys."

Rodriguez followed him into the kitchen. It wasn't a surprise that he came up empty after checking the pantry for the discarded beer cans and cigarette butts from the treehouse.

Sensing his frustration, she asked, "What was in the trash bags?"

"I'll tell you later. Let me finish here first."

When they returned to the porch, Alex gave his statement to Officer Davidson. In the meantime, more FBI agents had arrived and begun a thorough search of the woods and outbuildings. The county sheriff, who wasn't thrilled about the Feds invading his turf, departed with the rest of the local authorities.

Pete remained behind at the house with the investigative team as Alex, Rodriguez, and Agent Dunn set off into the woods. The air smelled musky, and dark clouds threatened to deliver more rain by the end of the day. At the treehouse, he updated them on finding the beer cans and cigarette butts. "Someone's been camped out here, spying on me."

Leaning back against a tree, Alex crossed his arms in a subliminal sign of defiance. "I'm clueless as to how this break-in could have anything to do with your investigation. But since you've kept me in the dark about so many things, care to enlighten me?"

As if warding off a tension headache, she pinched the bridge of her nose with a thumb and forefinger. Finally, she said, "What you and I need to discuss will take some time. I'm going to be working here through the night with my team. In the meantime, I want you to go to a hotel and take Agent Dunn with you. We'll reconvene back here in the morning, and I'll go over everything with you then, including why I wanted you to meet with Jim Bishop today."

Alex stepped away from the tree. "I refuse to be put off any longer. I want the truth of what's going on and what Bishop has to do with it."

Putting up a hand in an attempt to defuse him, she said, "Calm down. You've had a horrific day, and you got clobbered with a bat. Get some rest. We'll talk in the morning first thing."

Throwing up his arms in frustration, he said, "Fine, although I have a better idea. I'm going to spend the night at the neighbors. Come on, Agent Dunn. I'll introduce you to some very nice people."

∞

As the two men disappeared into the woods, Rodriguez sat down on the bottom step of the ladder that led up to the treehouse. Intermittent droplets, leftover from the rain, pelted the ground around her, leaving divots in the dirt. A chipmunk darted through the underbrush as a squirrel scurried up a nearby tree, followed by its mate.

Enjoying the tranquility of her surroundings, Rodriguez understood why Captain Alex Decker chose this corner of the world to restart his life. It gave the impression it was insulated from the violence and wickedness found elsewhere in the world. Unfortunately, evil had invaded his sanctuary.

CHAPTER TWENTY-NINE

"No! I'm not buying it. It'll take solid evidence before you convince me of such a ridiculous accusation."

Rodriguez glanced at Pete, who sat next to her, operating the system's control panel in the surveillance van. The IT tech shrugged and said, "I said he wouldn't believe you."

Alex's nerves were already on edge following a sleepless night at his neighbor's house, and Rodriguez had just made a statement that sent him reeling. Luckily, the air-conditioning unit worked because the atmosphere in the van was heating up.

Rodriguez looked up at Alex, who towered over her. "Would you sit back down, please? You're giving me a kink in my neck."

With a disgruntled *harrumph,* he lowered himself onto a storage compartment that doubled as a bench.

"As I stated earlier, the FBI and CIA believe Jim Bishop is an arms dealer selling illegal weapons to numerous subversive factions around the world. And they don't have a clue as to how long it's been going on."

"And I already voiced my opinion," he snapped. "Though I've just met the Bishops, I'm not buying it. What's your proof?"

"Alex . . . just hear me out." Her words carried an edge of

frustration. "Bishop's been eluding the Feds for over a year. He came under suspicion when a customs inspector in Panama stepped in at the last minute because a coworker was in a car accident. During the inspection, they discovered military-grade weapons and ammunition concealed within the crates. The other inspector was on Bishop's payroll by all indications, although they never could prove it, for he died from his injuries.

"The CIA, in conjunction with the Panamanian officials, decided not to confiscate the guns. As an alternative, both parties agreed to track the contraband to its final destination. The shipment was delivered the following day to a drug lord in Colombia, which put it beyond Panama's jurisdiction. The CIA decided to sit on it for the time being. Their goal was to uncover the layers of Bishop's operation and identify his customers, but he's shrewd. They kept running into snags along the way. He's extensively connected around the globe, and they're certain he has inside informants that operate below their radar."

Rodriguez drank a sip of water and continued, "As you found out yesterday, Bishop's playing a key role in President Jabari's goal to rebuild the infrastructure of his country. Our president recommended Bishop for the position, unaware that he was under investigation. When the CIA and FBI found out about it, it was too late. The wheels were already set in motion."

Recalling Bishop's haggard appearance yesterday, Alex initially assumed it was due to Caroline's untimely death. Now he wondered if the man's illegal dealings were catching up with him.

Pete displayed a picture of the Côte d'Ivoire's president and a map of West Africa on split-screen. Rodriguez glanced at them and picked up where she left off. "In addition to being one of our allies, President Jabari is highly respected by the African Union. The country's natural resources are oil and diamonds, and it's the largest exporter of cocoa in the world."

Growing impatient, Alex fidgeted on the uncomfortable

bench. "In any given situation, there's always the downside. What's this one?"

"Côte d'Ivoire, also known as the Ivory Coast, has had its allotment of dictators, coups, and civil wars through the years. President Jabari assumed office in June of 2015. Nevertheless, militants with a strong affiliation to his predecessor, Francois Abioye, remain active in the north. Using his involvement with President Jabari's undertaking as a front, the CIA believes Bishop is shipping weapons concealed in his freight and selling them to rebels in the north."

"And again, where's the proof?"

"I'm getting to that. My team identified the mysterious passenger while we were in DC."

"What!"

"His name was Tony Domonkos Gulyas. As you recall, he traveled with false documents, and we couldn't find a match for his DNA. By backtracking through Barbara and Jim's affiliation with that of her father, we found Gulyas."

That got Alex's attention. His frustration dissipated, and his right foot bounced with nervous energy.

Rodriguez presented a grainy picture of a younger version of Gulyas on her iPad. "Tony, as he was known, had a longstanding working relationship with Barbara Bishop's father, Howard Ramsey. Now, do you get the connection we've drawn between Bishop and Tony, in that they both reported directly to Ramsey back in the day?"

Alex still wasn't convinced. He perceived there were too many gaps in what she had shared thus far. "Go on," he said with an impatient gesture.

"We recovered a handful of raw diamonds among the charred remains of the travel shoulder bag Tony had with him on the plane. Soil samples embedded in the stones identified them as blood diamonds from a specific northern region of Côte d'Ivoire."

"You've got to be kidding!" Alex sprang to his feet and struck the back of his head—still tender from the previous night's escapades—on an overhead storage compartment. "Ouch!"

"Cowboy, it might be healthier if you remained seated."

Rubbing the bruise, he lowered to the bench as she continued. "It's well-documented that during the nineties, the inhumane treatment of people who were forced to extract the blood diamonds in the same region gained international attention. All mining operations were shut down in 2005. Nevertheless, the problem still existed in isolated pockets. The conclusion we've come to is that Abioye supporters in the north are paying Bishop with diamonds in exchange for the weapons."

Skepticism showed on Alex's face. "You're saying the few diamonds this Tony fella had on him were payment for a shipment of weapons?"

"No. The stones he had were just a sampling. On Thursday, one of my team members came across uncut diamonds in the ashes of a military transport cage that contained a K-9 traveling on the same plane as Tony Gulyas. I had them tested, and they came from the same region. We believe the stones found in the cage were payment meant for Jim Bishop in exchange for weapons, and Tony was his frontman."

CHAPTER THIRTY

"STOP RIGHT THERE," ALEX interrupted. "It's been three weeks since the fire, and your guy just found the diamonds?"

Rodriguez rose and, using the Keurig, made a cup of coffee and added sugar. "The Army transport cage, which contained a German shepherd, was in the cargo bin of the airplane that caught fire. The animal was inbound from Europe via Atlanta. The dog's remains were tagged and put on hold at the morgue. However, it got our attention when no one from Fort Bragg inquired about the animal. In checking, we were told that the Army didn't have any record of a military canine in transit from Europe during that week or the next. On Thursday, one of my men picked up the burned cage while cataloging items from the wreckage, and it broke apart. The diamonds were discovered in a false bottom."

Alex released a slow whistle. "Now I can see how you've drawn a connection to Bishop and why you wanted me to get cozy with the man. Nevertheless, I have to take into consideration what he's doing to help President Jabari rebuild his country. Why would he sabotage that objective by selling guns to the opposition?"

"It's not the first time someone has buttered their bread from both sides of the table, nor will it be the last."

"Are you sure it's not the brother-in-law?" Alex said. "I got the impression Bishop doesn't care for him."

"The CIA and FBI are investigating Blake Sanders also, and thus far, he is clean, not even a speeding ticket."

"What's Sanders's bio?"

Taking her seat, she blew on the hot coffee, took a sip, and set the cup down. "Blake is in his late fifties and grew up in the mountains of West Virginia prior to enlisting in the Army after high school. He attended UNC in Chapel Hill on the heels of completing his tour of duty, which is where he met Bishop's sister. They married soon after graduation, and from there, his career took many directions until he hooked up with Bishop ten years ago.

"Any of Blake's offspring floating around?"

Rodriguez opened a file on her iPad and summarized the report on Sanders. "He has two sons and a daughter. Richard, the oldest son, is in his late thirties and works for his father. The daughter is married to a lawyer who specializes in international business law. And yes, the son-in-law works for Daddy Sanders too. The youngest son, Dwight Sanders, went on a summer trek down to South America in between his junior and senior years of college and went missing. Sanders tried to find him, but Dwight never showed back up. Blake has three young-adult grandchildren, who are also on the payroll."

"Tight little camp. Too tight, if you ask me."

Nodding in agreement, Rodriguez added, "As Bishop shared yesterday, Blake and his wife have a lovely home on the outskirts of Charleston. Correction. It's a mansion, and the daughter and her husband live in the heart of Charleston's historic district—four blocks from the Battery."

Taking care not to collide with the overhead compartment, Alex got to his feet. "I need a cup of real coffee and a shower. Am I allowed to go into my house yet?"

Pete scowled at Alex, who still wore the same clothes

from the previous day when he landed in the patch of murky water. "Where'd you sleep last night, hopefully not between clean sheets?"

"I spent the night on a chaise lounge in Sam's screened-in porch. Jeff had the couch in the living room but left before dawn."

"You may want to consider burning those," Pete added, scrunching his nose in disdain.

Giving the tech a thumbs-up, Alex said, "Come on, Special Agent Rodriguez. I'll get cleaned up while you brew a pot of coffee."

"Me?" she snapped.

He lifted an eyebrow. "You do know what a kitchen is used for, don't you?"

"Yes, of course. I use it to warm up leftovers in the microwave."

Opening the back door, he motioned with his arm. "Let's go. I'll teach you how to make a pot of coffee the old-fashioned way."

Rodriguez turned to Pete. "We okay?"

"Give me a second." The tech typed something on a keyboard and handed over two button-sized disks. "They're fully charged and good for the next twenty-four hours."

She dropped one of the small disks in her pants pocket and handed the second one to Alex.

Palming it, he said, "What's this—a listening device?"

"No. It's a voice scrambler. It creates white noise in case somebody is eavesdropping. It's not an issue if we're inside the van, but out in the open, someone might be listening."

CHAPTER THIRTY-ONE

ALEX GRABBED A SHOWER and a change of clothes. Feeling more human, he paused in front of the fireplace on his way to the kitchen. He traced the outline of his wife's cheek down to her neck in the picture with an index finger. "You were right, babe. Trouble inadvertently finds me no matter where I go."

In the kitchen, he poured a cup of coffee and popped a couple of Ibuprofen into his mouth prior to joining Rodriguez on the back deck. As he settled into the patio chair next to her, she asked, "How's the head and shoulder?"

He rotated his head in a circle and felt the vertebrae in the neck release. He gingerly repeated the move with his right shoulder. "Better, manageable. The hot shower helped."

She sipped coffee and placed the cup down. "You should've had the paramedics check you out last night."

"Would you've bothered?"

"Of course not. By the way, did the kitten get out while your guests were here? I didn't see him in the house."

"I called my neighbor, Sam, after I left the Newman's and asked if his grandsons might like to have it. He checked with his wife, Wendy, and said the boys would be thrilled. I picked up some kitty toys, food, and a litter box and dropped it off on my way home."

"That was a good idea." Looking at the hangar, she said, "So that's Amelia."

Earlier, on his way back from the neighbor's, he had opened the bay doors to air out the hangar after the rain. The front of the red plane glistened in the sunlight. "Yep, she's the current love in my life."

"And it's the same airplane you performed those crazy stunts in that you mentioned yesterday to Bishop?"

"Yes. I've rebuilt the engine half a dozen times. Amelia and I have been through a lot together over the years."

She gave him a quizzical glance. "Flying commercial jets must be monotonous when compared to a vintage biplane or the F/A-18 Hornet."

"I'm happy sitting in anything that flies, especially if I'm at the controls." Changing the subject, he said, "I hate to deviate from my favorite topic, but there is something you haven't addressed yet. If Tony was transporting the diamonds for Bishop, who were the thugs that tried to kidnap him?"

"Good question." Rodriguez shifted in the chair and turned to him. "We presume they work for the man we caught on video standing at the gate window. For now, it's only conjecture, but if Tony did play a significant role in Bishop's world, it's possible they were after the stones and decided to take him as a bonus, maybe to hold him for ransom."

"And you think the goons who broke into my house are working for our mystery man from the airport."

"Correct. Bishop doesn't have a clue as to your involvement in any of this, which puts him on the backburner for now. Adding to it, we discovered someone was tailing you while we were in DC."

"I knew it!" Alex did a fist-pump, then sobered. "How'd you find out?"

She picked up her coffee cup but didn't take a drink. "Agent Dunn spotted him on Tuesday after returning from Virginia.

He noticed the man tracking your whereabouts as you exited the building, and we downloaded his picture from the security cameras. He's a mercenary, ex-military."

Alex cut in. "You think the guy who tailed me in DC and the ones who broke into my house are connected. Maybe they believe I know something about the diamonds since I'm working with you on the investigation."

"It's a good assumption. You said you found evidence that someone was in the woods keeping an eye on you since you came back from DC. Then it shouldn't be a surprise that we located listening devices planted throughout the house and in the hangar when we ran a scan last night."

His blood pressure rose as his temper flared. "Who are these jerks? And what do they want with me?"

"You're definitely on someone's radar, and we need to find out who it is. We're installing motion-activated cameras and a security system in and around your house and the hangar. Pete will download an app onto your cell phone that will allow you to view them. We've replaced your laptop in the office with one of ours and moved you to a more secure internet provider."

"Wow, thanks for the toys," he said flatly. He wasn't happy to have his privacy infringed upon, especially by unspecified individuals.

Rodriguez's brow creased with concern. "There's something else we're taking into consideration. You collided with the third man as he made his escape during the fire. Given the right opportunity, he probably thinks you can identify him, which may be another reason they're keeping an eye on you."

He tentatively fingered the bruised muscle at the base of his neck. "They must've returned, realized I collected the beer cans and cigarette butts, and came for them. I was going to ask you to test them for fingerprints and DNA."

Alex paused, and in his mind's eye, focused on the two men he encountered during the break-in. "The guy in the kitchen wasn't ex-military, and the ones staked out at the treehouse were bumbling idiots. On the other hand, I think the man who clobbered me was in charge and shouldn't be taken lightly."

"Exactly. For that reason, I've assigned Agent Dunn to be with you 24/7 for now. You get to stay home and work on your airplanes, which should make you happy."

Alex shot up from the chair and confronted her. "I'm on lockdown with an FBI agent as my babysitter!"

"Calm down, cowboy. You get to play with your man toys."

"You want me to hang around here while you straighten out this mess. That's not my style, *Agent Rodriguez!*"

Erupting from the depth of his gut, he had no intention of reining it in this time. Pacing back and forth, he lectured Rodriguez on the current atrocities in the world. "While we've sat around these past few weeks digging through the ashes of the airplane and tinkering with speculations, some idiot shot down a Malaysia Airlines plane over northern Ukraine, killing two hundred and ninety-five civilians. Israel and the Gaza Strip are exchanging missiles again and killing civilians while Nigeria is imploding upon itself. Al-Shabaab and the Al-Qaida are terrorizing Somalia while ISIS and ISIL are doing their best to rip Iraq and Syria apart. That's after so many American soldiers died on their turf fighting to bring peace to a place where conflict has existed since Adam and Eve left the garden. By the way—" He paused to take a breath. "Isn't it a contradiction in words, fighting for peace?"

"Anything else?"

Alex didn't hear her. "And here in the States, students are gunning down their classmates with semiautomatic weapons. Meanwhile, the black and white population continues to be at odds with each other and, at times, escalating into mob violence. Now you tell me Bishop's selling arms to militant factions in Côte d'Ivoire for payoff in blood diamonds, which your man *just* discovered in a US Army canine cage.

"To top it off, last night, a couple of derelicts broke into my house. One creamed me with my favorite bat, then stole it! In the middle of all this, you want me to hang around here while you figure it all out. That's not going to happen." Alex stood facing her with his jaw set and hands-on-hips while waiting for a response.

Rodriguez sat with her elbows resting on the armrests with her fingers intertwined. A smile started at the corner of her mouth and reached her eyes.

"What's so funny?" he barked.

"Welcome back to the world of the living, Captain," she said with a twinkle in her eye.

"What?"

"I suggest we put the issues of the Middle East, Ukraine, Nigeria, and our own country on hold for the time being. First, we solve our problem, and then we take on the others. Deal?"

He exhaled slowly, his temper tantrum dissolving into thin air.

She motioned for him to take a seat as she lifted the cup of cold coffee to her lips.

"I don't need a babysitter," he said, refusing to budge.

Agent Dunn emerged from the corner of the house. "That's not what I hear. I leave you alone for a few days, and what happens? You get thrashed and burglarized."

CHAPTER THIRTY-TWO

THEY PUT OFF FURTHER discussion until Alex made breakfast. Agent Dunn declined the invitation to join them, saying he was helping Pete test the newly installed surveillance equipment.

The tantalizing aroma of bacon frying in the pan made Alex's stomach rumble. He was starving and in need of sustenance. The coffee helped clear his foggy brain, a byproduct of his limited sleep the previous night.

Snagging a cooked morsel, he chewed on it as he digested what Rodriguez had shared with him during the past hour. Caroline's face resurfaced as he closed his eyes. There was little doubt it was her voice that haunted his dreams, though her words remained distorted, not unlike a bad phone connection.

Once the food was ready, Rodriguez sat at the kitchen table, her plate laden with scrambled eggs, bacon, sliced tomatoes, toast, and a glass of orange juice. She speared a tomato slice with a fork and held it up. "Raw vegetables for breakfast! Where are the fried potatoes?"

"I believe tomatoes are considered to be a fruit," he said and tossed a piece into his mouth.

Rolling her eyes, she picked up the glass of juice. "Canned or frozen?"

He pointed at the juicer sitting next to the toaster on the counter.

"A man who knows his way around the kitchen. Good for you."

She sat the orange juice down and stared at its contents as her smile faded.

Studying her downcast eyes, he speculated on where her mind had gone. "Does your husband cook for you?"

She lifted her chin. "What? Oh, his culinary forte is anything cooked on the grill."

Alex pushed his empty plate aside. "A talent passed down through the ages since the first caveman discovered fire. Although, I would think bacon and eggs on the barbecue could be a challenge. How does he pull that one off?"

By mentioning her husband, he hoped she would open up about the kidnapping. Pete had confided in him, and he didn't want to break that trust. Unfortunately, she didn't take the bait and picked up where they left off earlier. "You ready to hear about Gulyas and Ramsey?"

He rose to clear the table. "Let's go for a walk while we talk."

Outside, they followed a deer trail, which led to a small fishing pond at the back of his property. Shafts of light filtered through the trees and danced on the ground as they walked.

"Okay, enough with the suspense," Alex said. "What intel have you discovered about the man with the leather shoulder bag?"

"Tony was originally from Hungary and immigrated to the States with his family when he was fifteen. At eighteen, he became a US citizen and enlisted in the Army. He was fluent in German, Italian, French, and Russian and the language of his heritage. Not long after his tour of duty was up, he went to work for Howard Ramsey, Barbara Bishop's father."

It was getting warmer, and Rodriguez paused to take off her FBI jacket and secure it around her waist. "Their relationship remained solid for thirty-six years until the old man died a year ago."

At the pond, Rodriguez sat down on a large boulder at the water's edge. "Ramsey started his international importing business early on and became well established by the time he was thirty. He specialized in acquiring and importing high-end art and custom-made furnishings from around the world. Through his family, who had money and social standing within Charleston's wealthy upper class, his client list grew."

Alex stood nearby in the shade of an oak tree. "You believe Gulyas teamed up with Bishop after the old man died. Why?"

"Even at his advanced age, Tony had unique skills that would benefit Bishop."

Grabbing his interest, he drew closer. "Unique skills? How so?"

"From what we've learned thus far, Tony specialized in problem-solving while staying in the shadows. He must've traveled in disguise and with forged documents because—as I mentioned earlier—he didn't show up on any of our face-recognition databases.

"Ramsey's family, including Barbara Bishop, were clueless to the fact that the old man didn't always operate on the up-and-up when dealing with a difficult vendor. He would solicit his friend's help, and Tony would intervene, at which point a seller would suddenly have a change of heart."

Alex brought up something he had been contemplating since learning about Tony. "Wouldn't Caroline have recognized Tony at some point during the flight?"

"Maybe, but remember, Mrs. Bishop had a falling out with her father years ago after she became engaged to her husband. We can assume he never met the Bishop children."

Inhaling slowly, he considered Rodriguez's words. "It's unfortunate they were on the same flight. What are the odds?"

She nodded in agreement and rose. "It's lovely here, but we need to get back."

The storm that came through the previous day had given spring a helping hand. Yellow dandelions and wildflowers peppered the ground along the path that led to the house. Rodriguez dodged a muddy wet patch as she spoke. "The only way we're going to get these bozos is if we draw them out into the open, whoever they are."

"If you want them to come for the diamonds, you could use me as bait since I've captured their interest," Alex smiled.

She stopped abruptly and dismissed the suggestion with her hand. "No."

"Why not? They've already made a house call. We could invite them to dinner!"

Alex sensed her apprehension and didn't give her the chance to negate his idea. "You believe the man in the window, the thugs at the airport, and the idiots that were here last night are in this together. I agree that the best way to catch them is to offer the diamonds as the main course and bring them out of hiding." Taking her arm, he propelled her forward toward the surveillance van. "Let's go. It's time we go on the offensive and put a plan together."

CHAPTER THIRTY-THREE

LEX BRUSHED ASIDE A hanging limb as they cleared the woods. "Who else knows that you have the diamonds?"

"Pete, the agent that found them, Agent Dunn, myself, and now you. One more thing," she added as the surveillance van came into view. "Someone's hacking into our systems and accessing files, reports, and emails about this investigation. Pete's trying to figure out who it is and is getting nowhere. Because of that, I'm not documenting anything in our system regarding the stones until we know who and what we're dealing with on this."

"And I assumed this was going to be easy."

Agent Dunn exited the van as they approached and handed Rodriguez and Alex each a bottle of water. Alex downed half the liquid, paused, and started to take another drink when the trailhead leading to his neighbors caught his attention. Speaking to Dunn, he said, "Turn around for me, please."

"Why?"

Circling with his index finger, he said, "Show me the back of your jacket."

The agent's brow furrowed in confusion, but he complied.

Alex examined the large yellow letters on the back of the agent's FBI windbreaker while directing his next question to

Rodriguez. "Are you aware of any FBI agents arriving here last night prior to the three of you showing up in the helicopter?"

"No, the only uniforms here were county and local police. My team was still at the warehouse in Greensboro when Pete, Jeff, and I snagged the ride on the helicopter here. Why?"

"I don't believe it." Exploding, Alex hit the side of the van with an open palm and winced. "Ouch."

Rodriguez and Dunn—surprised by this sudden outburst— spoke in unison. "What is it?"

Flexing his fingers and shaking it off, he said, "It's possible the man, who we spotted during the fire at the airport, was here last night passing himself off as an FBI agent."

Rodriguez's eyes widened in disbelief. "What are you saying?"

"A man in an FBI windbreaker came out of the woods just as the helicopter landed and accompanied my neighbor back home. He was probably doing reconnaissance to make sure his buddies didn't leave evidence behind. I only saw him from the back, but I figure it had to be him."

"That was a bold and stupid move on his part," Rodriguez said with excitement. "Now, we can get a good description of him from your neighbors."

Agent Dunn grabbed Alex's arm. "We got this, Rod. Come on, cowboy."

∞

Sitting around the kitchen table, Alex updated Sam and Wendy on the break-in, keeping it brief. He soon steered their conversation in a different direction. "Sam, did the FBI agent who escorted you home last night give you his name?"

Sam squinted his eyes as if searching through the archives of his mind. "Now that you mention it, I'm not sure he did, although he was here for quite a while talking to us."

"Describe the man to me," Dunn said. "I'll know who it is."

Focusing on Alex, Sam said, "He had dark hair, the same color as yours, and was shorter and thinner than you."

Wendy cocked her head and studied her neighbor's features as if seeing him for the first time. "As I recall, he had a cleft chin similar to yours. Matter-of-fact, the FBI agent could've passed as your brother, although his eyes were a lighter shade of blue, and he wore glasses, the frameless type."

Sitting forward in the chair, Sam said, "It just came to me that he mentioned he was from western Pennsylvania. The town was called Sharp Village, Sharp, something?"

Alex's voice was barely audible as he spoke, "Sharpsville."

"Yes, that's it," Wendy sang out. "Aren't you from around there?"

"Hermitage, the next town over." The words caught in his throat as if he had swallowed poison.

"The agent mentioned he still had a mother, brother, and sister living there," Wendy added.

Absently scratching his unshaven chin, Sam said, "It was at that point I asked him if he had a family of his own. He said his wife had passed away a few years ago."

To Alex's ears, his friend's words were distorted and echoed as if they were conversing in a tunnel. His skin became bathed in perspiration, and his hands and feet tingled from lack of oxygen.

"Oh, I just remembered," Wendy said as she reached for a business card sitting on the small table next to her. "He handed me this as he was leaving."

Alex read the name on the card and abruptly stood, nearly knocking his chair over. "Excuse me. I need to use your bathroom."

He hurried down the hallway and hastily closed the door behind him. He extracted the bottle of anti-anxiety pills prescribed by Dr. Fletcher from a pants pocket with a shaky hand. Leaning over the sink, he palmed water into his mouth and downed one of the tablets, then slid to the floor and leaned back against the tub. Once the pill began to take effect, he used a handkerchief to pick up the FBI business card, which had fallen to the floor, taking care not to contact it with his fingers. As he reread the FBI agent's name, he considered—not for the first time—the extreme measures his unknown adversaries were taking to bait him.

CHAPTER THIRTY-FOUR

U PON EXITING SAM AND Wendy's house, Dunn confronted Alex. "What's wrong?"

Carefully unfolding the handkerchief, he showed the agent the FBI business card. "The name and phone numbers on it belong to my brother. Everything the man shared with those two mirrors my life. I need to fill Rodriguez in on what we learned. You stay here; I don't want to leave them alone."

Dunn agreed. "Go."

As he sprinted along the path, he soon realized it was a mistake to run back. The physical exertion brought on another anxiety attack. Lightheaded, he stumbled inside the surveillance van and collapsed to the floor. For a second time in less than twenty-four hours, he was back in Afghanistan, and an avalanche of fears assaulted him.

Two specific outcomes were needed as Alex, Chris, and others sliced through the night sky in the mountainous region of Mir Samir. The first was to take out a cache of weapons and heavy artillery stashed within various caves in the area. The second was to create a diversion as SEAL Team Four slipped into a nearby village and extracted four Marines held by Taliban rebels.

The sky lit up as they dropped their payload on the hills west of the village. During their first pass, Alex detected two S-125 Neva missiles locked on his plane. He released decoy flares and executed a maneuver perfected during his early barnstorming days. The first missile passed beneath him; the next one detonated too close for him to react. Shrapnel ripped through the F-18 Hornet's engine and left-wing, and the shock wave from the explosion sent the plane spiraling out of control. Alex ejected before the plane erupted into a ball of flames.

They were on him as soon as he hit the ground. With his hands tied, they dragged him by the boots toward their compound in the heart of the village while intermittently punching and kicking him.

What if the op had failed, and the SEALs had never made it? If they did, would they know he was here and needed rescuing also? An onslaught of thoughts flooded his mind, none of them good.

Wait! He heard a woman's voice. *Where am I?*

"Pete! Hand me a paper bag. Here, breathe into this, cowboy. Your anxiety pills, do you have them with you?"

In a hoarse voice, he said, "Took . . . already. Not . . . helping."

Rodriguez leaned in, her breath grazing his cheek as she spoke. "I want you to visualize that Sarah's in front of you. Gaze into her eyes. Do you see her?"

He did, then Caroline Bishop's face replaced Sarah's as Rodriguez began reciting the twenty-third Psalm. It was Caroline's voice he heard, the one from his dreams, not Rodriguez's.

"Yea, though I walk through the valley of the shadow of death, I will fear no evil, for thou art with me; thy rod and thy staff they comfort me . . . ."

By the time the agent finished the familiar biblical scripture, the tunnel vision had dissipated along with his fears, and Caroline's image faded.

Settling on the floor next to him, she said, "So what got your knickers all in a wad, cowboy?"

"The man, masquerading as an FBI agent, has done his research. He disguised himself as my brother and went into great detail while talking to my neighbors about his personal life, which was a carbon copy of mine."

He handed Rodriguez the FBI agent's business card still wrapped in the handkerchief. "The name and phone numbers on it belong to my brother. Trust me, Danny's not a Fed. He's a vice president with one of the local banks in Pittsburgh."

Placing the card in a plastic evidence bag, she examined the front and back. "I have to give the man credit. It appears authentic, even down to the water markings. The real question is, who is this guy, and what are he and his buddies up to?"

Standing, she helped Alex to his feet and withdrew her phone. "I'm going to request the county sheriff's office loan us one of their men to keep an eye on your place and the neighbors' for the time being."

Alex reached out to stop her. "I don't think that's a good idea."

"Because?"

Still shaky, he lowered himself into one of the nearby chairs. "If Jim Bishop is as devious as you believe, he's probably infiltrated all levels of authority within the state. It'll get his attention if you solicit help from the sheriff's department. Until we ID these guys, wouldn't it be best to keep it in-house?"

She pocketed the phone. "You're right. I'll get the Charlotte office to loan us a field agent or two. Also, change of plans. You wanted in on this, and you've got your wish. But only for your input, not as the bait. Agreed?"

He was glad she had changed her mind and planned to navigate the landmines of her stubbornness later. "I agree." *For now, that is.*

"Pete, put one of our team members on surveillance here until they send us someone from Charlotte to keep an eye on things."

Turning back to Alex, she said, "Bishop's next shipment is due to arrive in Africa a week from today. We have confirmation that the crates contain weapons. It's a golden opportunity for us to catch him in the act. First, we need to figure out who we're dealing with here. You and Agent Dunn will stay with my team at the Airport Marriott for the time being. The two of you can go that way now; Pete and I'll be right behind you."

Glancing at the time, she said, "On your way, grab some lunch for us, and we'll reconvene at the warehouse, where we'll start putting a plan in place to draw these guys out into the open."

CHAPTER THIRTY-FIVE

I T WAS APPROACHING MIDNIGHT, and they were still at it. The day had been grueling, and to top it off, he was once again functioning with minimal sleep. The quiet background hum of white noise in the conference room was taking its toll on him. In addition, the bump on his head and bruised shoulder were throbbing.

They'd finally come up with a plan to draw the bad guys out into the open using the diamonds as an incentive. It played out on the whiteboard; however, from his point of view, there were too many variables overshadowing the potential for success, coupled with the fact that Rodriguez refused to solicit help from her team on this mission.

Agent Dunn and Rodriguez sat across from each other at the conference table, mapping out final details. Alex paced back and forth behind Pete, who sat in front of a laptop and a desktop computer. A half dozen flat-screen monitors rested on Ikea shelving behind the makeshift workstation, one of them showing a split-screen live feed of his property.

Alex approached an interior window, which gave a view of the warehouse below. Various sections of the twisted and blackened Galaxy airplane, tagged with inventory numbers, lay strewn about the floor. Due to the late hour, the building was quiet except for a skeleton crew of FAA and FBI investigative agents sifting through charred remains. The rest of the team had gone back to the hotel.

His facial features were drawn tight as he addressed the others in the conference room. "Guys, can you go grab a cup of coffee and give me a minute with Maria?"

Rodriguez stretched her arms over her head and yawned. "We're done here. Pete, you and Agent Dunn go on to the hotel. Alex will ride with me."

Once they were alone, she stood and tossed empty food containers into the trash. "You're miffed. What's up?"

"It's insane to do this without backup and not solicit help from your FBI buddies. At least bring the rest of your team in on this. If not, these guys will get the diamonds, and you'll end up dead."

"As I said before, someone's hacking into our systems and databases—the fewer people who are aware of the stones, the better. I reassigned the agent who discovered them and sent him back to DC, which leaves the four of us, and I'm keeping it that way. No further discussion is necessary."

He crossed the room in three strides and stood towering over her. "What is going on with you? Why don't you want to use your team, at least?"

"I don't need to explain myself to you."

She turned to leave. Alex grabbed her arm and spun her around to face him. It was futile to argue with her, and for that reason, he pushed it back on her. "You're keeping something from me. What is it?"

Jerking her arm free, she glared at him. "I'm not bringing anyone else in on this, and that's final. But, by all means," she spat out between clenched teeth, "if you have a *better* idea, do tell."

Exhaling slowly, he spoke, keeping his voice calm. "All I'm

asking is for you to take a step back and reconsider what you're up against here. We're totally in the dark as to who these guys are and what they're capable of doing."

"Okay, I'll sleep on it. Are you happy now?"

Alex tossed an empty water bottle into a recycle bin. "Anyone ever told you that you're as stubborn as a mule?"

Rodriguez grabbed her FBI jacket and laptop bag and switched off the conference room lights. "Yes, at least twenty times a day."

MONDAY, MAY 7
MARRIOTT AIRPORT HOTEL
GREENSBORO, NORTH CAROLINA
1:12 A.M.

Agent Dunn was snoring softly in the other bed as Alex slipped into the bathroom. The agent would discover what he was up to soon enough. For now, Alex decided to keep the man in the dark until he talked to General Pritchard.

Locking the door first, he turned on the shower for background noise and reached for the secure satellite phone. The general picked up on the first ring, sounding groggy from being awakened. Alex sat down on the lowered toilet seat lid. "I apologize, sir. It's the first chance I've had to call you all day."

The general cleared his throat. "Sorry, I don't have anything new regarding Professor Mitchell."

"This isn't about the kidnapping. I need help, sir."

The general came fully awake. "Okay, I'm listening."

Alex rose and began to pace in the small confines of the bathroom. "I previously mentioned that I'm helping Agent Rodriguez investigate the airplane fire, which has led us to something bigger. One of Rodriguez's agents discovered a stash of diamonds in the ashes of the airplane last week. Circumstantial evidence, which I don't have time to get into right now, connected them to a businessman named Jim Bishop. The FBI and CIA believe Bishop is an illegal arms dealer. He's presently under investigation for selling weapons to rebels in Africa, who were paying him with blood diamonds from a northern province of Côte d'Ivoire."

"No way," Pritchard uttered in disbelief. "At present, Jim Bishop's working with the president of Côte d'Ivoire as a consultant in a major undertaking. An arms dealer, what a ridiculous notion."

"You do know him?"

"Sure do. Jim's a good friend. Linda and I had dinner with the Bishops two months ago here in Washington."

Before the conversation got sidetracked by the general delving into Bishop's admirable qualities, Alex broke in. "There's more. Besides Bishop, there's another group interested in the diamonds. Someone broke into my house yesterday. Since I'm the odd man out and not a Fed, it's the consensus they're stalking me to get intel on the stones. In addition to the mayhem it has created, a hacker is poking around inside the FBI's database and mainframe. Agent Rodriguez's primary goal right now is to catch these guys first and focus on Bishop after they're in custody."

"What's the next step?"

"She wants to use the diamonds to draw them out into the open. I suggested she use me as the bait; however, she didn't go for it. She's come up with a cockamamie plan without using her team as reinforcement and putting herself in the cross-hairs. It's as if she doesn't trust anyone at this point except those of us who have knowledge of the stones."

"She's lost faith in the FBI due to the fact they haven't located her husband, and it's impairing her judgment," the general stated.

Alex had an idea. "Since she refuses to use her people, any chance you could solicit help from Lieutenant Wilcox and SEAL Team Four if they're available?"

"I'll look into it after we hang up." The general paused and sighed heavily. "She won't like it that you've gone behind her back; still, I'm glad you called me. Maria is an excellent agent. I wouldn't want her to jeopardize her career, her reputation, or her life at this point. I'll get back to you as soon as I have more info."

Alex typed a number on the phone and forwarded the text. "The cell number I just sent you belongs to Pete Creighton, the IT tech on Rodriguez's team. He's the one who confided in me about the kidnapping, and he's working with us on this investigation. If something urgent comes up, call him if you're unable to reach me. I'll give Pete a heads-up that we talked."

"Sounds good. Watch your back."

Alex's next call was to the chief pilot.

"What's up?" Robert said in a raspy voice and yawned.

"Something important has surfaced regarding the investigation I'm working on with Agent Rodriguez. I need to see you."

The tone in Alex's voice cut through Robert's brain fog. "Right now?"

"Five-thirty a.m. at the Airport Marriott."

"That's it! I'll never get back to sleep."

"I need some shut-eye first. I'm running on empty."

"Make some coffee. I'm on my way," Robert said and disconnected the call.

CHAPTER THIRTY-SIX

ALEX TRIED IN VAIN to catch some shut-eye; however, the cacophony of snoring made it impossible. Once Robert arrived, he enlightened the chief pilot and Agent Dunn on what was in the works, after which they attempted to get some sleep.

Robert, who was lying on the bed beside Alex, bolted upright when the call came in at 5:07 a.m.

Lowering his feet to the floor, Alex answered the secure cell phone on the first ring. "Yes, sir. Any news?"

The general's voice was charged with adrenaline. "You're in luck. Brian and his team were coming off R and R and not reassigned yet. They're on their way there right now and will be landing within the hour."

Alex breathed a deep sigh of relief. "You made my day, sir, and it hasn't even started yet. Inform the lieutenant and his second-in-command to meet me here at the Airport Marriott." Alex picked up a small folder sitting on the nightstand, which contained his room key. Smiling, he added, "I'm in room three-three-three." He had asked Dunn to get them the room, hoping it would bring them good luck.

"Anything else?"

"No, that's it for now." Alex stood and stretched. "I hope Agent Rodriguez doesn't shoot me when she learns what I've done."

"Good luck with that one."

Alex entered the conference room accompanied by the others. "Good morning, Agent Rodriguez, Agent Dunn, Pete. I want to introduce Lieutenant Brian Wilcox and his second-in-command, Master Chief Enrique Avelino, of the Navy SEALs. Of course, you've already met Captain Jacobson."

If eyes could shoot darts and hit the bullseye dead center, Rodriguez would be a champion on the pro-circuit. "What are they doing here?"

"Maria, we need to talk." He gestured toward the hallway.

Leaping to her feet, Rodriguez stomped out of the room.

"We'll be right back, guys," he said, following her out.

In the hallway, he instinctively recoiled when she abruptly spun on him.

"I understand why you're mad," he said, holding up both hands, palms out. "Let me explain. Lieutenant Wilcox and his SEALs team are here to help us. And Robert is one of the best strategic planners I know. I've briefed him already. You'll do yourself a favor by listening to what he has to say."

She opened her mouth to speak and closed it, her temper tantrum rendering her speechless.

The intent of his next words was meant to disarm her. "I want to get these guys as much as you do, but not by forcing them into a shootout, which could happen if we go with your plan, potentially getting you killed. The SEALs are pros at this and will cover our backs."

Rodriguez breezed past him on her way back to the conference room. "You're not off the hook by any means."

WEDNESDAY, MAY 9
GREENSBORO, NORTH CAROLINA
OFF-SITE WAREHOUSE
10:30 A.M.

They had spent the past two days mapping out every scenario possible until they came up with a plan that they agreed was rock-solid. Bolstered by a round of morning coffee that pumped caffeine into everyone's veins, Rodriguez began a final run-through. "My boss, Richman, confirmed he received the encrypted email I sent last night informing him that we'd recovered the raw diamonds from the ashes of the airplane wreckage. It also mentioned that Agent Dunn and I would take the last flight out tonight for DC, and we'll have the diamonds with us."

They were confident the unidentified hacker would snag the secure email and pass on the news. The drive to the airport would offer their potential assailants the opportunity to intercept Rodriguez and Dunn. Clothed in darkness, the Navy SEALs would track the two agents from above in a UH-60 Black Hawk helicopter. Alex planned to accompany them. They'd put together a couple of back-up plans in case the two agents were intercepted at the airport or after they arrived in DC. Rodriguez and Dunn would be armed, vested, and ready in case the situation escalated.

"Okay, the clock's counting down," Rodriguez said, tapping her knuckles on the conference table for luck. "Anything else?"

No one responded.

"Alex?"

"I'm good," he said as he continued to sift through Bishop's and Sanders's FBI files in front of him.

Rodriguez downed the last swallow of coffee and stood. "Then it's a go. We'll take a break; we'll all meet back here at six p.m. and leave for the airport as soon as it's dark."

Alex remained seated as the others filed out of the room, his attention on a specific report.

Drawing near, she leaned in and skimmed the document, which contained a detailed report on Jim Bishop. "Why are you bothering with that now? Bishop's not our objective at this point. Besides, you've read through the files a hundred times already."

"I keep thinking I'm missing something. By the way, it says here Blake's oldest son, Richard, had a wife, and she ran off with some guy a few years ago. They have a son, Rudolph. Who names their kid after a reindeer?"

"Give me a break, cowboy," Rodriguez said with annoyance. "The CIA have vetted Blake and his family; they're clean."

"I was just wondering what became of the wife. Besides, it'd be beneficial if we had updated pictures of Richard and his son. The ones we have on file are old."

"Right now? Oh, all right." She went to the door and called Pete's name, who was down the hall in the breakroom.

Alex walked over to the whiteboard laden with aerial shots of the route they were taking to the airport that evening and a multitude of Post-it notes. He added eight by ten black-and-white photographs of Jim Bishop and Blake Sanders to the collection. Stepping back, he studied the images of the two men and finally gave up. "Agent Dunn's waiting for me downstairs. I'm going home to pick up some clean clothes and get my mail. Since the cat is out of the bag, I'm sure these idiots have lost interest in me. I may take Jeff up for a spin around the block in Amelia."

"I'd rather you didn't. Remember, I sent the field agent, who was keeping an eye on your place and the neighbors', back to Charlotte after your friends, Wendy and Sam, departed for the cruise two days ago, which you persuaded me to send them on; I might add." She pointed at the active monitor screens mounted above the computer console table. "Pete's keeping an eye on the surveillance cameras throughout your property. All I'm asking is that you play it safe for now."

Giving her a thumbs-up, Alex grabbed his leather flight jacket and left. In the hallway, he ran into the technician. "Pete,

I need current pictures of Blake's son, Richard, and the grandson. The Intel on Richard is sketchy, and there's a gap in the filing of his income tax returns. He was in the Air Force early on, which puts him close to my age. Dig more into his history and send it to my cell phone. And get me whatever you can dig up regarding Richard's ex-wife while you're at it."

"Will do," Pete mumbled with a mouth full of a ham and cheese sandwich.

CHAPTER THIRTY-SEVEN

LEE COUNTY, NORTH CAROLINA

AGENT DUNN SAT ON the worn sofa, thumbing through an airplane magazine, when Alex emerged from the bedroom, dressed in worn jeans and an old football jersey. "Any time you want a flying lesson, I'm your guy."

"That's just what I need, an expensive hobby to add to the college tuition I'm funding for my two kids over the next six years."

Alex started for the kitchen carrying a tactical backpack slung over his left shoulder. "I need to get some things from the hangar. I'm also going to refuel Amelia while I'm at it. Want to help?"

∞

Inside the hangar, he opened a breaker box on the far wall and detached the false cover. After entering an access code on the hidden keypad, a section of the wood paneling slid back, exposing a secret compartment that contained a variety of handguns, automatic weapons, and a sniper rifle.

"Woo!" Dunn exclaimed. "You prepping for Armageddon?"

Alex handed Dunn the open backpack to hold, which contained a military-grade first-aid kit, the NVGs, and additional clothing. He added an assault vest; withdrawing a Sig P229, he placed it in a holster at his waist beneath his shirt. The Smith &Wesson M&P 9mm had remained strapped to his ankle since the break-in on Saturday night. He added two extra magazines for the Sig and one for the 9mm. "If you'll take the backpack to the house, I'll pull the plane out of the hangar."

∞

Inhaling the spring air, Alex sighed with relief. The day was perfect, warm, and sunny. Even though he believed he was no longer on anyone's radar since the email had been sent, he knew Rodriguez was taking measures to guarantee the safety of his friends and family, including himself, until the assailants were apprehended. Following the break-in and what they'd discovered afterward, FBI field agents in Pennsylvania were assigned to keep his family under 24/7 surveillance.

On Monday, his neighbors, Wendy and Sam, were taken to Charleston in a limousine driven by an FBI agent disguised as a chauffeur. The couple was surprised and delighted after receiving a telephone call Sunday informing them that the first-place winners of a five-day cruise to the Bahamas had to cancel at the last minute. They were the runners-up in a contest they didn't remember entering.

Along with Dr. Newman's family, Robert and his family were relocated to an undisclosed location on Tuesday until it was designated safe for them to return home. Due to commitments that he couldn't reschedule, Dr. Newman had delayed his departure and planned to join with his family by noon today.

Alex parked Amelia beside the aboveground fuel storage tank and relaxed, letting the tension of the past few weeks melt away. Since he promised Rodriguez he wouldn't take Amelia up for a spin, he made up his mind to wash the plane instead and, if time allowed, apply a coat of wax after refueling.

Two hours later, Alex heard Dunn humming to himself as they worked their way down opposite sides of the aircraft. As they finished up, Alex had a premonition someone was watching them. Checking the surveillance cameras from the app on his cell phone, he detected nothing out of the ordinary. Glancing under the belly of the airplane, he spotted Dunn's legs on the other side. "Agent Dunn, we may have company."

The agent bent down, and their eyes met. "Time to go, Captain."

Alex nodded in agreement and reached for the open bottle of liquid wax that sat next to his foot. It wasn't there, and he spotted it a few feet away. *Marcus?*

Walking over, he bent down to retrieve the bottle as rounds from a semiautomatic weapon pelted the ground where he previously stood.

Thap, thap, thap. "Sniper, take cover!" Alex dove to the right, rolled, and was back on his feet. Running a zigzag pattern as bullets sprayed the terrain around him, a bullet grazed his left arm as he dove into the underbrush. Keeping low, he crawled further into the thicket and took cover behind a fallen tree.

The instant the sniper redirected his aim, Alex popped his head up and witnessed the aboveground fuel-storage tank exploding into flames, taking Amelia out with it.

"No!" With adrenaline coursing through his veins and still holding the bottle of wax, he tossed it aside and withdrew the Sig from its holster.

As soon as the shooting stopped, Alex crawled to the edge of the woods and positioned himself behind a large oak. Using the tree as a shield, he surveyed the damage. The fire blazed out of control; at least, it was a safe distance from the hangar and the woods. It was unsettling that he couldn't see Agent Dunn from this location.

"Please, God, let him be okay," he said under his breath.

He checked the trees on the other side of the runway near the road where the sniper would be hiding. Nothing moved. He waited.

There he goes!

Leaving the safety of the oak tree, Alex sprinted down the driveway. He reached the road just as a truck pulled out onto the highway, sped north, and disappeared around a curve. Breathing hard, he hissed, "You and I aren't finished yet."

Sirens rang out in the distance as he raced back to the fire. Alex circled the blaze in search of his friend. Noticing a pair of legs on the ground protruding from the backside of the hangar, he rounded the corner of the building and discovered the agent lying motionless on the ground but still breathing.

Holstering the Sig at his waist, Alex reached down and gently shook him, taking care to avoid the growing bloodstain on his left shoulder. "Dunn, can you hear me?"

The agent appeared dazed as he glanced around, taking in his surroundings. A trickle of blood ran down the side of his face. "Did you get him?"

Alex kneeled next to the agent. "Take it easy there, buddy. A bullet got you in the shoulder."

The agent's eyes grew wide with horror. "He shot you too!"

Alex glanced down and started laughing. The front of his shirt was stained the color of blood. "It's airplane wax."

Dunn moaned as he attempted to get up and abruptly sat back on his heels, knees bent.

"Go slow. You might also have a concussion. Your head is bleeding."

Dunn grimaced as he placed a palm on the bullet wound to stop the bleeding. "What a lousy way to screw up a beautiful day. While going for cover, I got hit and collided with the corner of the building. Apparently, the impact knocked me out."

The sirens grew louder as Alex helped his friend to his feet. "We need to get out of here before the first responders arrive."

When they reached the back of the house, Alex said, "Wait here. I'll be right back."

In the kitchen, he grabbed the backpack and a bottle of

water. When he returned, the man's pallor was white. He withdrew a clean sock from the bag and pressed it to the agent's injured shoulder, and they set out for the woods. Reaching the entrance to the path leading to his neighbors' place, Alex paused and glanced back at the burning wreckage that was his plane, Amelia.

"I'm sorry, cowboy," Dunn said.

"So am I," Alex said, his voice cracking as he spoke.

They disappeared into the woods as a fire truck, and two county police cars pulled into the driveway.

CHAPTER THIRTY-EIGHT

"Rod! We got a hit; email's been hacked!" Pete's fingers flew on the keyboard as he bounced up and down, his enthusiasm barely contained.

Crossing the room in three strides, Rodriguez reached him and studied what was on the flat screen. "I was beginning to worry that we didn't give him enough time."

"I'm tracing it now, and our buddies at Langley are also helping."

"Good. Maybe we'll finally get 'im."

Pete frantically entered a variety of codes into the computer. "This is going to take a while. Would you grab me a power drink from the breakroom?"

She hesitated, not wanting to miss this opportunity. "Okay, but call out if you get a hit."

His eyes were riveted to the monitor as he waved her off.

On the way to the breakroom, Rodriguez's secure satellite phone rang. Glancing at it, she noted the caller ID was blocked. "Hello."

"I've been anticipating this conversation for weeks. I know so much about you; it's as if we're old friends."

"Who is this?" she snapped, coming to an abrupt stop in the hallway.

"Why, this is the call you've been waiting for, Agent Rodriguez."

In a choked voice, she said, "Carl?"

"Oh, of course, you want to talk to your husband," the stranger said, his tone taunting her. "Professor, tell your wife how much you miss her."

"Maria?"

She choked out the next words. "Are you okay?"

"I'm good," he responded in a sleepy voice. "I miss you. Promise you'll take care and stay out of harm's way. Love you."

Carl's response was the same one he gave whenever she was out of town, which was disturbing, considering the severity of the situation.

The caller was back online. "Enough with the romantic chit-chat. It's time to get down to business."

A short time later, Rodriguez re-entered the conference room, and Pete handed her a copy of a flight reservation. "Blake Sanders is on the move. He's booked on the red-eye flight out of Atlanta tonight to the Canary Islands via Madrid, where he'll link up with his wife, who is finishing a shopping spree in Europe." The excitement in Pete's voice was palpable. "And get this, after the Canary Islands, Mr. and Mrs. Sanders are catching a Viking River Cruise, which will depart out of Amsterdam."

Their eyes met, and Pete verbalized what was on both their minds. "The Canary Islands are only a spit away from Côte d'Ivoire. Bishop's latest shipment is due in a week. I lay odds that Sanders is going to collect the payment in person, after which, he'll take the diamonds to Amsterdam to sell on the black market."

Rodriguez, mentally juggling the phone call with her husband

and his kidnapper, and the situation unfolding at hand, nodded in agreement. "Where's Bishop?"

"Still at home, where he has been for the past four weeks. He canceled all travel plans indefinitely."

She paced as her brow deepened into a frown. "We were wrong; Bishop and the brother-in-law are in this together."

Pete's SAT phone rang. "Hello." He paused and listened. "When? No! Okay, I'll tell her." He disconnected and spun around in his chair. "Dr. Newman is missing. The receptionist at his office said a county sheriff picked him up prior to our guys arriving. They checked the security cameras in front of the building. The license plate on the patrol car had been reported stolen some time ago. Plus, in the video, the officer kept his hat low on the brow, casting a shadow across his face so they couldn't ID him."

She threw up her hands in frustration. "This can't be happening. Get ahold of Alex and Dunn and tell them to get back here ASAP. And inform them about the doctor's abduction."

Pete punched in the captain's number; it went to voicemail. He tried Dunn's line with no response and redialed both numbers with no success. Disconnecting, he glanced around. Rodriguez wasn't in the room. He ran out into the hallway and called her name. Someone on the floor of the warehouse below yelled back that she had just left the building.

Pete spun around, his eyes focused on the table in the conference room. The briefcase containing the diamonds was gone.

On the far side of the room, his workstation exploded, sending surges of electricity through the air. Pete dove to the floor in the hallway and peered inside. The force of the power surge sent the bank of monitors sailing through the air. The overhead lights exploded as his computer melted into a black glob, and toxic smoke rolled in waves across the ceiling. The sprinkler system failed to activate as flames licked their way up the wall behind the workstation. The same electrical surge tore through the warehouse. Screams could be heard from below as everyone ran from the building.

An agent on all fours appeared next to Pete. "We need to get out of here."

"I'll be right back."

"Don't go in there—" The man's words broke off into a coughing spasm.

Pete yanked off his Linkin Park T-shirt and tied it around his head, covering his nose and mouth, then he crawled into the smoke-filled room on his hands and knees. His vision blurred with tears each time he coughed. Not giving up, he continued inching forward. The travel bag containing his backup laptop sat on the floor beneath the conference table. No longer able to see, he reached out and came up empty.

CHAPTER THIRTY-NINE

LEE COUNTY, NORTH CAROLINA

ALEX EASED AGENT DUNN down onto the back steps at Sam and Wendy's house. After passing his cell phone to the agent, he dug out the first-aid kit from the backpack. "Call Rodriguez and fill her in as to what's happened."

Following two failed attempts, Dunn frowned and stared at the screen. "It went to voicemail."

Alex exchanged a pill and a bottle of water for the cell phone. "Take this; it'll help with the pain." He tried Pete and connected with him on the first ring.

"I called you guys numerous times and didn't get an answer," the younger man exclaimed, followed by a coughing fit.

"A sniper tried to take us out. We're at my neighbors' place now." Scanning the woods from where they came, he continued, "Are the SEALs with the helicopter?"

Pete paused as if digesting this latest news. "Yes, they're standing by, ready to go."

Alex studied the smoke trailing across the sky from his place. "They can track my location via my phone. Tell them to pick us up in the clearing behind the garage and put a rush on it. They'll need to approach from the south because the county sheriff and a fire truck are at my place. Also, Agent Dunn took a bullet in the shoulder and may have a concussion. He's mobile, but their medic will need to check him out." He disconnected.

The agent winced as Alex replaced the bloody sock with a sterile dressing. He inspected the knot on his friend's forehead and checked the man's eyes for clarity. "Hang in there, buddy. Cavalry's on its way."

Pete called back, informing them the SEALs were airborne and would be there soon.

Alex, keeping a watchful eye on the trailhead leading to his house, added in reply, "I need to talk to Rodriguez."

"She left with the diamonds," Pete said, his voice hoarse. "That's not all. Dr. Newman's missing. Someone posing as a county sheriff picked him up prior to our guys arriving, and the cruiser they left in had stolen plates."

"No!"

"There's more." Pete broke into another coughing fit before he could continue. "Someone tried to kill me!"

"How's that even possible? You're inside the secure warehouse complex."

"A major electrical power surge bypassed the circuit breakers, creating various fires throughout the building. To top it off, the sprinkler system and fire alarm were disabled. If I hadn't stepped out of the conference room to find Rod, I would've been cooked to a crisp," Pete said with a shaky voice. "The warehouse is ablaze. The fire department is here also."

Walking back and forth in front of Agent Dunn, Alex verbalized what he was thinking. "She must've gotten a call just before the fire started. There's no doubt she was told they have the professor and want to exchange him for the stones. If they do have him, you and I both know that's not going to happen. They'll end up dead."

"Man, I hope not. I never mentioned that Professor Mitchell was my instructor at Georgetown University. At his recommendation, Rod brought me in as an intern, and I never left."

"I'm glad. I need you there to help me figure out what's going on. What else can you give me?"

"I was able to rescue my backup laptop from the fire, though it nearly did me in, and I've got her on-screen. The tracking device hidden in the lining of the briefcase with the diamonds is providing a strong signal. As an extra safety measure, I dropped another one in the left pocket of her jacket earlier today, although I doubt she's aware of it. You'll have the same onscreen images I do from both devices in the helicopter."

Alex noticed the chopper approaching in the distance. "Anything else?"

"Regarding your earlier request, I couldn't dig up any current records of Richard Sanders's wife and the mechanic she allegedly left town with: no work histories, tax returns, or driver's licenses. They may be in Mexico. Want me to check?"

"Don't bother. I doubt the two of them made it out of the county. Doesn't Richard Sanders live somewhere around here?"

"Yes. Richard and his son, Rudy, have a place that backs up to the Uwharrie National Forest."

"Wait a minute." Alex stopped in his tracks. "The grandson's name in Sanders's file wasn't Rudy. It said something different."

"Hold on a sec; I'll verify. Got it; the grandson's given name is Rudolph. Rudy's a nickname."

Alex recalled Rodriguez's altercation with a young punk named Rudy at Bubba's café weeks ago. In his mind, the arrogant redneck, the diamonds, and the mercenaries at the airport were an improbable mix at this point.

Helping Agent Dunn to his feet, they made their way to the open field as the helicopter drew closer. Holding the phone to his ear, he said, "Were you able to ascertain who hacked the email yet?"

"Unfortunately, no, I'm still working on it. Man, I hope the professor's still alive," Pete said with a melancholy edge to his voice. "And, I hope you get to Rodriguez in time."

The wind kicked up around Alex as the helicopter's skids settled on a patch of sunbaked red dirt. "SEALs are here. Don't lose hope, Pete. We'll find them both and Dr. Newman, I promise."

CHAPTER FORTY

RODRIGUEZ DROVE AROUND TO the back of Copal's Grill and parked next to the dumpster. A man, backlit by the sun, appeared out of nowhere. Tapping on the driver's side window with the nozzle of a Sig Sauer, he motioned for her to get out. As she exited, he jabbed the gun into her ribs.

With lightning speed, she batted the gun away with her left hand and drew back the right to deliver a hard knuckle jab to the man's throat. Before delivering the punch, a gun pressed at the base of her neck stopped her.

"Hello, sweet thing," the assailant at her back said, his words drawn out in a thick southern accent. "You remember my cousin, Dave."

The cousin—who stood next to the open door—shoved his gun into his waistband and proceeded to bind her hands behind her back with flex-cuffs as the other man stepped forward. "I've been lookin' forward to this, Agent Rodriguez. You're just as pretty as I remember."

The intent of his words was unmistakable, and his foul body odor combined with the smell of cigarettes and alcohol nearly made her gag. She recognized him immediately. "You're still up to no good, Rudy."

"We were offered a lovely bonus if we delivered you alive, so don't do anything fancy. Got it?" he said, waving the gun in front of Rodriquez as if it were a toy.

A silver SUV rounded the corner of the building and pulled up next to them. The other cousin climbed out from the driver's side, and Rudy shoved Rodriquez toward him. "Hold her while I check for weapons, and shoot her in the knee if she tries any of that tae kwon do stuff."

Rudy confiscated her FBI badge and satellite phone. Next, he ran his hands up and down her body, all the while smiling. Extracting the gun hidden beneath a pant leg at her ankle and a second one from the shoulder holster, he said, "Good. You're not wearing a wire."

"You're an idiot," she spat out. "The restaurant security cameras are catching all of this."

"Tough luck, babe. I used them for target practice while waiting for you to show up."

Rudy retrieved the case containing the diamonds from her car and transferred the stones into a small, tattered gym bag. He tossed the briefcase, along with her FBI badge and phone, into the dumpster. "Time to take a little ride, pretty thing," Rudy said as he shoved her into the backseat of the SUV and climbed in next to her. "I would blindfold you, but in this case—" He smirked. "It won't be necessary. You ain't coming back here."

Uwharrie National Forest, North Carolina

Alex sat next to Lieutenant Wilcox on the helicopter floor while the medic worked on Agent Dunn's shoulder. The rest of SEAL Team Four—dressed in camouflage fatigues and face paint—were squeezed in around them. Each SEAL hugged a Colt M4A1 rifle to their chest, except for the one who carried a Knight's Armament Mk 11 SWS 7.62 sniper rifle.

His cell phone vibrated; it was an email from Pete, which

contained three attachments: the first photograph was a younger version of Blake Sanders. The second photo was of a younger version of his son, Richard, in an Air Force uniform. The third one was an updated picture of Rudy. Alex immediately recognized the punk from the diner. He flipped back to Blake, and Richard's photographs as vague memories surfaced, and the rhythmic *wuppa wuppa* vibration of the helicopter receded to the background.

It was during his first tour in the Mediterranean. He and his wingman, Chris, had just landed at the US Izmir Air Base in Turkey. They had brought their jets in for major overhaul and repairs. Alex was on his way to the mess hall to meet up with Chris and happened upon an argument at full throttle.

"You're such an idiot. Everything's going to blow up in your face if you don't stop scrounging around for an easy buck."

Not wanting to intrude, Alex remained out of sight in the shadow of a building in the hope that the two men would move on, but Chris caught up with him before they did. "Why are you standing here? Come on, I'm starving," his friend said as he hurriedly bypassed him.

When they cleared the corner, Alex was surprised to discover the man handing out the reprimand to a second lieutenant was a civilian. In a feeble attempt to conceal the fact he had overheard them, he addressed the lieutenant. "Excuse me. We just flew in, and we're trying to find the mess hall."

"It's that way," the tall, middle-aged American answered, his tone heated.

Once again aware of his current surroundings, Alex's eyes flew open. The men he had come across nearly two decades ago were Blake Sanders and his son, Richard.

Brian, the SEAL team leader, nudged Alex's shoe with his boot to get his attention. "Are you sure you want to go in first?" he asked for the third time. "They may shoot you as soon as they spot you."

"I want to get them talking and extract info from them before you come barging in."

"Or we could persuade them to surrender and confess to their sins with a little underhanded coaxing."

"Not a good idea," Alex said, shaking his head. "I want to determine if Bishop or Sanders have anything to do with this. There's someone smarter than these goons pulling strings."

Brian acquiesced. "All right. Do me a favor, though, be careful. From what I gather, you chased the sniper through the woods with the Sig in one hand and the 9mm in the other."

Alex eyed Agent Dunn, who winked back at him.

They weren't able to proceed under cover of darkness as initially planned. However, the Nighthawk helicopter, equipped with stealth technology, approached the LZ undetected, the same way it did earlier when they picked up Alex and Agent Dunn.

Addressing his men, Brian said, "We're half a klick out. Once we're on the ground, spread out and stay sharp. Agent Dunn stays here. The medic and Alex are with me."

They released the fast ropes out each side of the chopper and were through the doors in an instant. On the ground, they scattered, moving cautiously through the underbrush until the cabin came into view. Alex, the only man not in fatigues, crouched down next to Brian behind a granite outcropping. The lieutenant quietly spoke into his tactical throat mic. "Smitty, Sit Rep."

Alex heard the SEAL's response in his earpiece. "Two pickup trucks parked in the driveway. A silver SUV just drove up. Three men and one woman are getting out. The woman's being taken inside by one of the tangos at gunpoint. The other two are entering the woods, which gives us a total of five tangos outside guarding the house. Two pit bulls in the kennel outback. Will tranquilize them on your signal."

The next person to arrive was Richard Sanders in a pickup truck, which Alex recognized as the same truck he saw leaving his place after the exchange of gunfire.

Richard climbed out and nodded to one of the guards, who lingered next to a large River Birch tree and stepped into the cabin.

Not long after, a silver Cadillac XTS sedan pulled up next to the SUV. "Bingo," Alex whispered in response as soon as he saw Blake Sanders climb out of the vehicle.

Blake scanned the woods then joined the others in the cabin.

The SEAL's commander signaled to Alex that it was time to go, and he shook his head no in response. They needed one more car to arrive with Dr. Newman. Five minutes later, they heard a vehicle coming up the gravel driveway. Alex was filled with apprehension as he started second-guessing his gut instincts. What if he was wrong and its occupant wasn't Dr. Newman in his abductor company but Jim Bishop? What if Rodriguez and the Feds were on the right track from the beginning, and Bishop was the mastermind behind all of this?

CHAPTER FORTY-ONE

LATE AFTERNOON SUNLIGHT SPILLED in through a dirty window spotlighting dancing dust particles in the musty air, which reeked of male body odor. Rodriguez sat at the far end of a rustic table and methodically scanned the one-room kitchen-dining-living area. Mentally cataloging every detail, she added the skinning knives, which hung in a bracket next to the sink, and the fireplace poker on the floor near the hearth as plausible weapons. Though her hands remained tied behind her back, her feet were unbound, which would help once she made a move to take control of the situation.

She could disable an adversary with one kick to the solar plexus, windpipe, or the groin and would enjoy doing the latter to Rudy, who had licked his lips and just blew her a kiss. For now, her number-one priority was to learn what they knew about her husband's whereabouts.

Blake interrupted her musings. "Agent Rodriguez, I want to thank you for being so cooperative."

"Where's my husband?" she asked for the third time to no avail. Her steely eyes remained fixed on his.

Across the room, Richard leaned against the sink. His hand rested on her gun, which lay on the counter while keeping his weapon pointed at her. "I think it's ironic an FBI agent can't keep tabs on her ol' man."

"Shut up," Blake snapped, then dismissively addressed Rodriguez. "I would like to help you find him. Unfortunately, I have a plane to catch."

"You don't have a clue where he is, do you?" Her words were laced with malice as she continued. "You only used him as a ploy to get me here."

Blake reached for the gym bag resting in the center of the table. "Don't be discouraged. The professor may show back up someday. Sad to say, you'll be dead."

They didn't have a clue as to Carl's whereabouts. Rodriguez mentally berated herself for not immediately recognizing the deception and acting upon it. Instead, she thoughtlessly abandoned years of experience and played right into their hands.

The front door opened, and the party grew in number. A Lee County sheriff walked in with Dr. Newman.

The doctor's eyes surveyed the room. "Where are my wife and children?" He grabbed the sheriff's forearm. "You said they'd be here waiting."

Rodriguez's heart raced as her temper flared. The man in uniform was Officer Davidson, the same person who'd responded to the break-in at Alex's house.

Roughly grabbing the doctor's arm, Blake propelled Newman toward Rudy. "Tie him up."

Dr. Newman spun around and nearly collided with Blake. "What's going on? I don't understand."

Rudy shoved the doctor into a chair across from Rodriguez and secured his hands behind his back. The man's face paled as his eyes darted back and forth, taking in his surroundings. "Where's my family?"

"Put a lid on it, doc," Blake snapped as he handed an envelope to the sheriff. "As usual, your assistance is greatly appreciated, Officer Davidson."

While Sanders concluded his business with the officer, Rodriguez quietly ran through her options. Blake wasn't the type to stick around when it was time to dispose of her and the doctor, leaving only Richard and Rudy. She would make her move then and deal with the guards outside after getting hold of Richard's cell phone and calling Pete.

Catching Dr. Newman's attention, she asked him why he hadn't waited for her men.

"The sheriff came in the office right before your agents were scheduled to arrive. He said you sent him." His shoulders slumped. "I should've called you."

"That's okay. Everything's going to be fine," Rodriguez said in a futile attempt to alleviate the doctor's anxiety.

"What about my family?" Apprehension resonated in the doctor's voice as he asked, "Are they okay?"

Rodriguez forced a reassuring smile. "They're in a secure location. Don't worry about them."

Once the sheriff departed, Blake focused on his guests. "Agent Rodriguez, Dr. Newman, it's been a pleasure."

At the door, he paused. "Rudy, stay alert. I'm counting on you to make sure your father doesn't screw this up like he did at the airport."

Richard stepped forward and got in his father's face. "What happened then wasn't my fault," he said between gritted teeth. "You got your diamonds, and I took care of the captain. We're both winners here."

Rodriguez was on her feet. "What are you saying?" Rudy shoved her back down onto the chair. Shaking off his hand, she said, "What happened to Alex?"

Ignoring her outburst and that of his son's, Blake said, "Get rid of the bodies and clear out of here as soon as you're done. And make sure the two of you have a good alibi for today. That also goes for your two cousins, Rudy." And he was gone.

CHAPTER FORTY-TWO

SIGNALING WITH THE RUGER, Richard motioned for Rodriguez and Dr. Newman to stand. "Okay, folks, time to take a little walk in the woods."

Grabbing Rodriguez by the arm, Rudy jerked her to her feet. Her gun still lay on the kitchen counter. Acting as if she was off-balance, she stepped in that direction. As a further distraction, she asked why they'd kidnapped the doctor as she inched closer to the gun.

Richard's mouth twisted into a menacing grin. "An alcoholic tells his sponsor everything, right, doc? So what did Captain Decker say about me? Never mind. You and the captain can reminisce after you two meet up in hell."

"Are you talking about me?"

All heads turned.

Alex stood at the front door, the youngest cousin holding him at gunpoint. "Look what I caught trying to break up your party, Uncle Richard."

They couldn't fail to notice the dark red stain on the front of Alex's shirt.

"You're shot!" Rodriguez cried out.

"I saw you go down with my own eyes!" Richard exclaimed as he stared at his nemesis in disbelief. "You should be dead."

"Sorry to disappoint you," Alex said with a shrug.

Pointing his gun at Alex's chest, Richard shouted, "Then what's on your shirt if it's not blood?"

"Airplane wax. Oops, you missed."

Richard's cheeks were beet red, and he rounded on the cousin. "What happened? Where'd you find him?"

Surprised by the outburst, the young man stepped back in reflex. "I . . . he came at me from behind and put a chokehold on my neck with his arm. I nailed him with an elbow to the ribs and a head butt. He stumbled backward, and I got my gun on him, so's he couldn't do anything else."

"Any weapons?"

The cousin handed over the Sig Sauer and 9mm. "He had these on him."

Richard shook his head. "I don't like this. Go tell the others what's happened and double-check to make sure he's alone."

As the cousin departed, he confronted Alex. "How'd you find us?"

Holding his hand up high so as not to alarm Richard, he approached Rodriguez, excused himself, and slowly reached into one of the pockets on her jacket. He withdrew a small disk, placed it on the table, and held up his cell phone. "Tracked it with an app on my iPhone."

"Rudy, grab that thing and his phone. Smash them both."

Richard shoved Alex into a chair and motioned for Rodriguez and the doctor to sit back down. "We're not going anywhere until I'm sure it's safe."

Alex spoke to his friends. "You guys okay?"

"They're fine . . . for now," Richard said, moving to the kitchen window and peering out. Anxiously fingering his unshaven chin, he turned and addressed Alex. "Where's that agent you were with earlier at your place?"

Alex shrugged. "He caught one of your bullets in the shoulder. I left him behind when I heard the sirens approaching. I knew he would be in good hands, and I needed to get out of there if I was going to track down the diamonds and Agent Rodriguez. Pete called me and informed me they both had vanished. Oops, it looks like you missed your mark on that one also."

"What are you talking about?"

"The fire at the warehouse. Pete got out unscathed."

"What fire?" Rodriguez asked.

Richard shook his head in confusion. "I have no idea what you're talking about, and there's no way you came here alone. Rudy, check the windows in both back bedrooms."

Rejoining the small group, he said, "I didn't catch sight of anything, Pop. Besides, our guys outside would signal us if something was wrong."

"Get over here and help me keep an eye on them." Richard picked up Rodriguez's gun and handed it to Rudy, who held them at gunpoint.

Stepping away from the window, Richard glared at Alex. "You're akin to my worst nightmare that just won't quit. Ever since I spotted you at the airport, you've been sticking your nose into my business just like last time. I wanted to take you out last Saturday when you and Bishop were coming in for a landing. It's too bad that we still need him, so I had to pass on the moment."

Alex had been waiting for the perfect opening and grabbed it. "I guess it wouldn't go over well if you took down the boss of your little operation."

Richard scoffed at the idea. "Mr. Good Samaritan was never part of this. He's our scapegoat in case something goes wrong."

Relief washed over Alex; simultaneously, he experienced the firm grip of his invisible friend on his right shoulder. He knew that he wasn't the only one in the room liberated from the burden of uncertainty regarding Jim Bishop, although for different reasons.

"I still don't get it," he said, his brow knitting together in confusion. "Why do you have it in for me?"

"You've got to be joking! You and your buddy, Chris, couldn't let it go. I had a sweet thing going until you overheard my father and me talking."

Spittle flew through the air as he continued. "I spent eight lousy years in Leavenworth on account of you two. At least your friend got his when his plane took a nosedive on that aircraft carrier. I more or less forgot about you until I saw you at the airport three weeks ago. Then, of all things, I discovered you live half an hour from here. I couldn't believe it."

Confused at first, a heartbeat later, something registered in Alex's brain. "I remember reading in the *Stars and Stripes* that the MPs busted a smuggling ring at Izmir. That was you? Trust me, Chris and I had nothing to do with it!"

"Liar," Richard bellowed, the muscles in his neck taut with rage. "It's time I take you out back and bury you next to my . . ."

Richard didn't finish, and Alex took advantage of the void. "Out of curiosity, does your wife's ghost ever haunt your dreams?"

His presence forgotten at this point, Rudy stepped in front of his father. "What's he talking about, Daddy?"

In one swift movement, Richard side-stepped his son. Pointing his gun at Alex's chest, he said, "I've had my fill of you!"

Unyielding, Rudy poked his father with the nozzle of Rodriguez's gun to get the man's attention. "Why'd he say that about Mom?"

"Don't worry," Alex said, nodding toward the front door. "Your daddy can tell you and the SEALs all about it."

Richard glanced over his shoulder, where three Navy SEALs stood just inside the door with Colt M4 semiautomatic weapons trained on him. Consumed by madness, Richard squeezed the trigger.

The bullet slammed into Alex's chest and propelled him backward. The last thing he recalled was Rodriguez and Dr. Newman yelling, "No!"

CHAPTER FORTY-THREE

B RIAN REPLACED THE TWO rounds he had fired earlier and set his weapon aside. "Well, Captain, you got what you wanted, though you nearly got killed in the process."

Alex held an ice pack against the dark bruise on his chest beneath the shirt. "It was worth it. We now have proof it was Blake, not Bishop, dealing in weapons on the black market. Plus, everything Richard said earlier was in front of witnesses and recorded by your guys."

"While the medic was checking you out, I had Rudy call his grandfather and inform him that everything went according to plan. Blake won't discover the truth until we've got him under lock and key."

Crime scene tape encircled the house and blocked the driveway at street level. *First, the airport, then at my place, and now here.* Alex surmised if they kept this up, the whole state would soon be wrapped in the yellow police tape.

Floodlights illuminated the grounds around them. The two men, talking and taking in the scene, sat on the edge of the front porch. The invasion of FBI field agents and the canine team had silenced the cicadas, crickets, and bullfrogs.

Brian hopped down to the ground and stretched. "My guys had Richard in the crosshairs through the kitchen window, but you wanted him taken alive. You played it close, my friend. It was a good thing you had the Kevlar vest on under that ridiculous shirt. Did you say the stain is from airplane wax?"

Glancing down, Alex smiled. "Yeah. Richard believed he shot me in the heart back at my place. Since he missed the first time, I guess he had to give it another go. I'm grateful there was a futon behind my chair to break the fall, or else I'd also have a concussion."

Brian handed over Alex's satellite phone. "Considering what the jerk tried to do to you, I admit I enjoyed popping him in the elbow and knee. Once the wounds heal, he'll remember this day every time it rains."

Alex slid down off the porch landing next to the SEAL team leader. "Richard and the others are your prisoners. This operation now falls under NCIS jurisdiction."

"Yep, that's what I've been told." Brian gathered up his gear and signaled his men that it was time to leave. "I wonder how those boys are going to like Hotel Guantanamo."

"Rodriguez believes after Blake's son-in-law learns about their location, he'll start calling in favors. No worries, we'll have nabbed Blake by then," Alex said with confidence.

Brian signaled to Enrique to give him another minute and turned back to Alex. "From what I understand, our next stop is Africa, and you're coming along for the ride. What I don't get is why? Your friend Bishop's off the hook."

"I need to follow this through to the end. I owe it to the Bishops' two children."

Brian shrugged. "Okay, by me. I'll catch up with you and Agent Rodriguez on Sunday in Côte d'Ivoire."

AIRPORT MARRIOTT HOTEL
GREENSBORO, NORTH CAROLINA
11:39 P.M.

The late-night Marriott guest-services rep at the front desk greeted Rodriguez and Alex as they made their way to the elevators.

"Come on, Rod. Let me buy you a drink to cheer you up. Nothing's open, but there's a vending machine next to the indoor swimming pool."

Rodriguez had sulked during the hour drive from Richard's place. Alex made every effort to engage her in conversation; she was unresponsive, her jaw set with eyes glued to the road as she drove.

Pressing the elevator button, she said, "There's no need for you to stay here tonight. Take my car and go home."

"Can't. Didn't Pete tell you? They have an all-points bulletin out with my name on it. Richard left a parting gift of two kilos of cocaine stashed under the back seat of my truck, and someone placed an anonymous call informing the local authorities. They're also looking for me in connection with the fire at my place."

Rodriguez regarded him, her voice mournful as she spoke. "I forgot about Amelia. I'm so sorry, Alex."

"Thanks," he choked out as a lump formed in his throat. Unable to meet the agent's eyes, he said, "Everything should be straightened out by morning. In the meantime, I think it's best to stay here with you and your team versus spending the night in jail."

She turned and headed down the hallway. "Come on. Let's have that drink. I'll buy."

Pete came across them a little while later, sitting beside the indoor pool. High on adrenaline and rambling, he said, "What a night! It's amazing how everything worked out okay. The fire at the warehouse was something else. That was a brilliant idea,

Captain, letting Sanders go so we could catch him with the goods in Africa." Pete downed a sip from the Red Bull can he held. "I still haven't nailed down who's hacking into our databases. Whoever it is, they're a genius. Although since someone tried to kill me, I must be getting close to nailing him." He took a breath and noticed Rodriguez and Alex weren't listening to him. They sat rigid across from each other, staring off in different directions. "Did I interrupt something? It's been a rough night."

Rodriguez glared at Pete.

Alex intervened, preventing her from saying something she would regret later. "I told your boss how I initially heard about the professor's kidnapping."

"Oh," Pete responded, choosing not to comment further.

"The truth of the matter is, if you hadn't confided in me beforehand, I wouldn't have guessed what was going on or why she ran off."

"Don't you think I know that?" Fuming, Rodriguez exited the lounge chair and walked to the far end of the pool and back, all the while mumbling to herself.

Pete hesitantly asked, "Why are you so mad, Rod? You're safe, and so is Dr. Newman. Plus, you got a confirmation that Blake is the arms dealer, not Bishop."

Stopping abruptly, her eyes filled with tears of self-loathing. "I should've recognized it was a recording of Carl on the phone from one of our earlier conversations. I don't have a clue as to how they got it. Just the same, I was an idiot for not realizing it was a ruse." Directing her words at Pete, she said, "Alex's been trying to convince me otherwise. That said, I could've gotten everyone killed. And I still don't know what's happened to my husband." Deflated, she collapsed into a nearby chair.

Alex rose and went to her. Kneeling, he lifted her chin and met her eyes. "Maria, I promise we'll find your husband. You've got to believe that."

For a time, the only sound came from the swimming pool's

filtering system. Finally, she gave him a weak smile. "Okay, but one more thing," she said in a hushed tone. "By bringing in the Navy SEALs, you saved my job and my credibility. It's beyond my understanding as to how you pulled it off, but I appreciate what you did, all of it."

He squeezed her hand in silent response.

To help ease the tension, Pete asked, "What's next?"

Alex got to his feet. "Rodriguez and I are going to visit the Bishops in the morning. Unfortunately, we need to tell them about Blake and his band of mercenaries."

CHAPTER FORTY-FOUR

Jim Bishop led Alex and Rodriguez into the living room, where Barbara greeted them warmly. Their hostess wore a spring-colored cotton dress with just a hint of stylish jewelry at her neck and matching earrings. Alex speculated she wouldn't receive her guests in any other fashion.

In contrast, Bishop was dressed for comfort in a golf shirt and dark khaki pants. He motioned toward the sitting area in front of the white marble fireplace. Rodriguez and Alex made themselves comfortable in the two upholstered winged-backed chairs as the Bishops settled in across from them on the couch. Barbara was the first to speak. "Jim hasn't stopped talking about his ride in your airplane, Captain. He had such a marvelous time."

Alex smiled at Bishop in agreement. "It was a perfect day." As they continued with pleasantries, he studied the faces and body language of his host and hostess. The changes he had previously noticed in Jim were visible in his wife as well. She had lost weight, and the grief was more noticeable on her. There were dark circles under her eyes, causing him to regret what information he and Rodriguez were about to impart upon them.

Addressing the agent, Barbara asked, "And what brings you here today?"

Rodriguez sat forward in the chair, closing the distance between them. "As Captain Decker mentioned to you on the phone, I'm in charge of the FBI's investigation of the Galaxy airplane explosion at the airport."

"I see," Barbara said with a hint of wariness in her voice.

"The Captain also shared with you that he's working with us on behalf of the airline. During our ongoing investigation, we became aware of a separate set of circumstances. We're here today to inform you of our findings, as well as what has transpired within the past twenty-four hours. Mr. Bishop—"

Bishop interrupted her before she could continue. "Please call me Jim."

She took a breath and started again. "Very well, Jim. Unfortunately, what I have to share with you isn't pleasant. You two have suffered so much heartache and loss already, and for that reason, I deeply regret the purpose of our visit."

Reaching for his wife's hand, Jim stiffened. "Is this about Caroline and the fire?"

"No. As I mentioned, this is a separate matter." She hesitated then continued. "The FBI and CIA are involved in another investigation focusing on the criminal activities of your brother-in-law, Blake, his son, and three grandsons. At first, both agencies believed you were the one trafficking arms on the black market. Now we have proof that you weren't involved in your brother-in-law's illegal operation."

"Oh dear," Barbara gasped as Bishop sat back, his eyes wide in shock.

"We now have proof that Blake is selling guns to drug lords, terrorists, and warlords in various third-world countries. We also confirmed he exploited his business relationship with you in order to transport the weapons hidden within the freight containers."

Visibly shaken, Bishop paled from the impact of the news. However, it was Barbara who caught Alex's attention. She remained stoic, with no reaction, except for a slight tick at the corner of her mouth. He speculated she knew something about it, or at the very least, had her suspicions.

Finding his voice, Bishop asked, "Are you sure?"

"I won't go into great detail at this time, but as of last night, your nephew, Richard, and great-nephews are in the custody of the US Navy SEALs. They're being detained at Guantanamo Bay for questioning."

Bishop shot forward on the couch, his chest heaving. "Why there?"

"The FBI and CIA confirmed a number of the weapons were stolen from US military bases, and they need to identify who among the ranks are working for your brother-in-law."

"What about Blake? Where is he?" Barbara said flatly.

"On a plane bound for the Canary Islands. From there, he's chartered a plane to take him to Côte d'Ivoire. We believe he plans to be on-site when the next shipment arrives Monday night. We've verified the inbound freight has weapons and heavy artillery concealed amongst the building supplies and farming equipment."

Bishop collapsed back against the cushions of the couch, his mouth agape, his breathing erratic.

Alex rose and laid a hand on the man's shoulder. "Jim? Are you all right?"

A few tense moments passed before Bishop's eyes cleared. Lifting his head, their eyes met, and he let out a long, slow sigh. "I had no idea. It's just a lot to take in."

He sat back down as Rodriguez continued. "We're mindful of the fact that you're working with President Jabari to rebuild the infrastructure of his country, and we don't want that relationship jeopardized because of Blake's transgressions. To fix this, we're going to need your help."

In a raspy voice, he said, "What do you need me to do?"

"Timing on this is crucial. The captain and I want to be there before the shipment arrives. We're booked on a flight for Abidjan, Côte d'Ivoire, via New York and Brussels tomorrow morning. I would like you to go with us."

Shifting his position on the couch, Bishop squeezed his wife's hand and met her eyes. Though no words were exchanged, they appeared to have come to an agreement.

Bishop addressed Rodriguez. "If you give me the flight number and departure time, I'll meet you at the airport."

Acknowledging the request with a nod, she continued, "One more thing. Before leaving for Africa, I need you to call President Jabari and request a private meeting with him on Sunday morning. We want to inform him about the shipment of weapons in person and the measures we're taking to apprehend Blake and those involved. Captain Decker and I will accompany you."

No one spoke as silence filled the room, and Alex continued watching Barbara. Unlike her husband, she gave no indication that she was surprised or taken aback by the news. Sensing his eyes upon her, she looked in his direction.

Now that he had her attention, he verbalized what was on his mind. "Barbara, do you remember a man named Tony Domonkos Gulyas?"

Her gaze didn't waver, though the color drained from her face.

Bishop answered for his wife. "Yes, we knew him back in the day. He worked for her father."

Out of the corner of his eye, Alex noticed Rodriguez's perplexed expression as he proceeded. "Barbara, what can you tell me about Tony?"

Puzzled, Bishop glanced at his wife, then at his guest. "How is that relevant to what we're discussing here?"

Ignoring Jim, Alex continued, his tone encouraging as he restated the question.

Meeting his eyes, she said, "Tony was my father's closest and only friend. He worked for my father for many years. However, now that Daddy's gone, I've no idea what became of him."

"Did you ask Mr. Gulyas to do a favor for you lately, maybe to check into Blake's business dealings?"

"Why do you ask?" she said in a weak voice, her lower lip quivering.

"Barbara, what's wrong?" Bishop said, his apprehension palpable.

Pushing her husband's hand away, she rose from the couch and approached the fireplace. Gripping the mantel for support, she said, "Has something happened to Tony?"

CHAPTER FORTY-FIVE

BISHOP ROSE, CLOSING THE distance between them. Gently laying a hand on her arm, he said, "What is it, darling? Tell me."

She met his eyes. "I'm so sorry. You were aware that I'd had my suspicions about Blake for some time. You have such a forgiving and compassionate heart; you refused to believe he was trouble."

With tears spilling forth, she continued. "I mentioned something to Marcus, and he told me he would check into it. He was shot and killed five weeks later."

He took her in his arms, and she sobbed against his shoulder; her remaining words muffled.

Finally, with red, swollen eyes, she addressed Rodriguez. "I never believed Andrea shot our son. Marcus was the boy's mentor." Sighing heavily, she added, "They were very close."

"All the evidence pointed to the boy," Bishop said. "During the hearing, two policemen testified they'd witnessed Marcus and Andrea arguing in the parking lot of the community center during a routine drive-by. They were the first to arrive after the shooting and caught the boy fleeing the scene. It was an open-and-shut case, even though Andrea repeatedly stated he didn't own a gun and was in the middle of apologizing to Marcus when he got shot. We believed him then and still do today."

Barbara straightened and wiped tears from her cheek with the back of her hand. Facing Alex, she said, "As I previously told you, my father disowned me once we became engaged and didn't attend our wedding. He also ordered my mother and brothers not to have anything to do with us. Since both my brothers worked for my father, they had no choice. We hadn't seen or heard from any of them since. However, to our surprise, Daddy showed up at Marcus's funeral. He expressed his condolences and his regrets for the lost years between us.

"He wasn't sorry. Not really," Barbara added, the words mixed with bitterness. "He was dying and wanted to make restitution for his sins. A few weeks after Marcus's funeral, he had his own memorial service; we didn't attend."

She reached for a tissue from a box sitting on a nearby table and dried her eyes. "That's when Tony called me. He said no one should ever turn their back on family and gave me his personal cell phone number. As far as I know, my father was the only other person to have it. Tony said if I ever needed anything to call him." She paused. "I need to sit down."

As they settled in, Rodriguez remained standing. "May I get you some water, Barbara?"

"No. Thank you, dear." Barbara motioned for the agent to take a seat as she resumed her story. "I visited Andrea at the jail following his arrest."

Squeezing her husband's hand, she said, "Jim wasn't aware of it at the time; I told him afterward. I needed Andrea to tell me in person that he shot my son. Instead, he wept and said, 'Marcus was the only person who believed in me. Why would I shoot him?' I was convinced at that moment the boy didn't do it."

Offering some back-story, Jim said, "Andrea was eleven years old when our son arrested him for stealing. He received a one-year probation and community service as a first-time offender. From that moment on, Marcus took the boy under his wing and got him involved with a church basketball team that he coached.

Andrea came from a broken home and grew up in the foster-care system. Barbara shared with me what had transpired during the visit with Andrea, and I agreed with her. There's no doubt in our minds that he's innocent."

Barbara laid a hand on her husband's arm. "I believe I'll have that drink of water. Do you mind, dear? And please bring some for our guests also," she added as he stood and went to the kitchen.

When Bishop came back with the drinks, she continued, "We hired one of the best defense lawyers in the state. Regrettably, he couldn't discredit the testimony of the two police officers. Andrea was tried as an adult at seventeen and sentenced to life in prison for voluntary manslaughter."

"Our lawyer has submitted an appeal; it's going to take time," Bishop said, further clarifying what they were facing. "We make a point to visit Andrea every week and take books for him to read. We also gave him Marcus's Bible, which he treasures."

Barbara filled them in on the rest. "After they sentenced Andrea to prison, I called Tony. I told him that I'd spoken with Marcus about my suspicions regarding Blake and wondered if that conversation was connected in any way to our son's untimely death. Tony promised to look into it and get back to me later."

Jim bolted upright, exhibiting surprise mixed with apprehension.

Unaware of her husband's reaction, Barbara asked, "I haven't heard from him. Has something happened to Tony?"

The agent chose her words carefully prior to responding. "I regret to inform you that your friend is dead."

Tears filled her eyes, and she began to cry, her chest heaving in between the sobs. "Tell me that's not true."

"It was an accident. It happened quickly, and I promise your friend didn't suffer."

In a choked voice, Barbara asked, "Is this connected to Blake in any way?"

Rodriguez paused, then said, "Matter of fact, that's one of the reasons we're here. Tony had a shoulder bag with him, which contained a sample of uncut diamonds, which came from others meant for Blake, which he never received. We have the stones and have ascertained they were payment in exchange for weapons your brother-in-law sold to guerrilla militants in the northern region of Côte d'Ivoire. We believe Tony was bringing the diamonds to you, along with other evidence regarding Blake's illegal operation."

This last tidbit got an immediate reaction from Bishop. "Are you serious?"

Nodding in response, Rodriquez continued. "I realize it won't ease the pain of loss regarding your son and your friend, but please understand that Tony's involvement led us to Blake's unlawful dealings and who's most assuredly responsible for Marcus' death."

She shook her head as if wishing it to all go away and collapsed into her husband's arms and quietly wept.

Allowing the Bishops some time alone, Alex and Rodriguez rose and made their way out to the backyard. He led the way to a gazebo, which stood in the center of a rose garden where they reclined in overstuffed lawn chairs.

Rodriguez massaged her temples. "We should go and give them some privacy. Before we do, though, I need to make sure Bishop calls President Jabari. He probably won't come with us now, and I wouldn't blame him."

Settling back on the comfortable cushions, Alex said, "He may surprise you."

She eyed him keenly. "What compelled you to ask Barbara about Tony?"

He shrugged. "Not sure. It was just a hunch."

"The two cops who testified against Andrea were obviously on Blake's payroll."

"I agree," Alex said.

"I'll do what I can to get the boy released as soon as we're back from Africa."

"I guess we better come back then."

"I'm counting on it."

A heartbeat or two later, he said, "I'm proud of you, Rod."

"Why?"

He smiled. "Because you made up your mind to go to Africa without me having to convince you."

"I still hate flying."

"I haven't forgotten," Alex said, then added, "Why didn't you tell Barbara that Tony died in the same airplane fire as Caroline?"

Rodriguez rotated her head to dispel unwanted tension in her neck as she spoke. "There's no need. Considering the circumstances, I doubt the Bishops watched the news after the fire. Even if they did, we intentionally blurred the faces of Tony and the others on the film released to the public since it was an ongoing investigation. After we get back, I'll have his body released to the Bishops in a sealed coffin and make up something for the death certificate. That way, they'll never learn what truly happened to him."

They quietly sat, enjoying the peace and serenity of the Bishops' backyard. Alex heard a familiar sound and opened his eyes. Glancing toward the western sky, he blinked twice to make sure it wasn't a mirage. "Hey, look at that!"

"What?" she said, following his gaze.

A red vintage Stearman WWII biplane drew closer and lazily dipped its wings back and forth as it passed overhead.

CHAPTER FORTY-SIX

B ISHOP PLACED A CALL to Barbara while they waited at the Newark Airport for their connection to Brussels. Afterward, he informed Rodriguez and Alex that his wife said she would be okay during his absence. Now that they were in the air, Bishop didn't seem convinced. Sitting across the aisle from Alex, he stared at the inactive entertainment screen embedded in the seatback in front of him, and his posture gave the impression that life was seeping from his soul.

In the seat next to Alex, Rodriguez was quite the opposite of their traveling companion. She was in constant motion, fidgeting like a two-year-old until the plane banked right over the water immediately after takeoff. White knuckles showed through her golden-brown skin as she gripped the armrest and pinched her eyes closed, thus shutting out the world around her.

Alex leaned in and spoke into her ear. "Breathe, Maria."

Opening one eye, she squinted at him before turning toward the window. With a fleeting glance at the dark slate-blue bay below, she slammed the window shade closed and resumed her earlier position, white knuckles and all.

As soon as the flight attendant completed the familiar in-flight announcements, Rodriguez spoke, her voice barely audible. "Do you remember when TWA Flight Eight Hundred exploded twelve-and-a-half minutes after takeoff from JFK on July 17, 1996? Faulty wiring transmitted a spark into the central fuel tank. There were no survivors."

He placed a hand on her arm and squeezed it. "Maria, nothing's going to happen to us. Not now, or in Africa. It's going to be okay."

The tension in her jaw muscles remained as she confronted him. "I usually end up with a coach seat in the last row next to the bathroom. How'd you get us in first class? Who do you know?"

"I called in an IOU from a friend who thinks a lot of you."

"Really? Who is it?"

He flashed a mischievous grin. "Sorry, if I told you, I'd have to kill you."

"Aren't you the funny one?"

The flight attendant was taking drink orders and their dinner selections. Noticing that Bishop declined both the drink and the meal, Alex reached across the aisle and got his attention. "It's a long trip, and you'll need your strength. Please eat something." Bishop yielded to the request and gave the flight attendant his order.

That problem solved, Alex set out to overcome the other one. "I'll make you a deal, Maria."

She stared at the blank screen in front of her as if she didn't hear him.

He considered it a newly acquired habit she must've learned from Bishop. "I'll give you the name of your secret admirer after you fill me in on everything you've learned about your husband's kidnapping."

The attractive flight attendant interrupted them just then. "Excuse me, would you care for a drink before we serve dinner?"

"A glass of white wine," Rodriguez briskly stated. "Make that two glasses."

"Of course, one for you and one for the gentleman."

"No, two for me," she said with a forced smile.

The attendant blinked. "Oh." She glanced at Bishop and back at Alex. "Is he with you too?" she asked in a low voice.

"Yes. It's been a rough week, and flying makes my friend nervous," Alex said, giving a small nod in Rodriguez's direction.

"I'll get those drinks for you right away, ma'am. What would you like, Mr. Decker?"

"Just water, please."

After the drinks arrived, Alex picked up the conversation from where they left off. "Okay, walk me through it from the beginning. I'm all ears."

She absently fingered the linen napkin sitting next to a small cup of warm mixed nuts as she gave an overview of Carl's abduction.

Her face flushed with anger, she said, "There are no leads, and my CIA and FBI comrades aren't capable of locating him. Plus, the kidnappers haven't contacted me regarding a ransom. The only call I've gotten was initiated by Blake to get the diamonds."

By the time the appetizers were served, she had regained some of her composure. "When I got the call, I honestly believed it was Carl."

"I would've responded the same way if someone kidnapped my wife."

She acknowledged his honesty with a nod. "Blake would've won if you hadn't brought in the SEAL team, and we'd all be dead . . . you, Pete, Dr. Newman, and me."

"He's not going to come out the winner on this one. We're not going to let him."

After dinner, he noticed her eyelids growing heavy. "Get some sleep. You're going to need it. We've got a lot to do after we get to Africa."

Compressing a button, she lowered the first-class seat into a makeshift bed and laid back. "Cowboy?"

Reaching over, he drew the blanket up over her shoulders. "I'm here."

"You didn't tell me who my secret admirer is yet."

"It'll keep until tomorrow."

∞

To Alex's relief, Bishop ate most of his dinner. However, once the meal service was served and the cabin lights dimmed, he continued to stare into space with a worried frown creasing his brow.

"Enough of this," Alex mumbled to himself. He got up and approached the front galley, where the first-class flight attendants were eating their meals. The blonde, who'd served him earlier, stepped forward. "Is there something you need, Mr. Decker?"

He presented his Galaxy Airlines and Homeland Security creds to the young woman. "My friend, Mr. Bishop, is going through a rough time. I'd like to speak to him in private, if possible. Could we use the galley area after you're finished eating? It won't take long, and I believe it'll make him feel better."

She glanced at her coworkers and considered his request. "I'll need to remain in the area. That being said, I believe I can arrange it. Give us a couple of minutes."

A short time later, Alex beckoned Bishop to follow him to the first-class galley. Without going into great detail, Alex spoke of Marcus's sudden appearance in the cockpit of his airplane prior to the one Caroline was on catching fire.

"He insisted I change gates, which I did. Your son saved my life and those of the passengers and crew members on the plane."

Bishop became unsteady and reached for the galley countertop for support. "What're you saying?"

"I promise you I'm not making any of this up. The whole experience is still a mystery to me. There're two other times Marcus has saved my life within the past few days." Alex gave an overview of the house break-in and the positioning of Sarah's framed photograph, warning him that someone was hiding in the kitchen. He explained how the repositioning of the bottle of airplane wax had caused him to move out of harm's way as Richard sprayed the area with bullets.

Spellbound, Bishop was wide-eyed, and the realization of what Alex was saying took hold.

"There's something else," Alex said as he continued. "I saw Caroline's face in the rearview mirror of my truck when you and I got in it last Saturday at Starbucks. Up until that moment, I've never experienced the depth of grace and unconditional love I felt radiating from her. She turned to you, and I sensed her love pouring forth to you. I also got the impression she was worried about you."

Still gripping the counter, Bishop swallowed hard.

"Since the fire, I've sensed both their presences, especially in my dreams."

Pondering Alex's words, Bishop grew pensive. "I've sensed them at times, but I've never mentioned it to Barbara for fear she would think I was nuts."

"My words fail to fully express the love I've sensed your son and daughter have for you and your wife. Nevertheless, I hope I've done them justice by what I've shared with you now."

Reaching out, Bishop embraced Alex. "Thank you, Captain."

They separated, and Bishop brushed the tears away with the back of his hand. "If you don't mind, I would like you to share this with Barbara when we get back home."

"It would be my pleasure. One more thing, I wanted to let you know Agent Rodriguez has made arrangements to reopen Andrea's case. She intends to have the boy released into your custody as soon as possible until it's resolved."

Bishop bowed his head and, in a quiet voice, said, "Thank you, God, for answering our prayers and bringing these servants of yours into our lives."

Once he had finished praying, Alex suggested he call his wife on the satellite phone and share the good news about Andrea.

Returning to his seat, Alex leaned across Rodriguez and opened the window shade. The night sky was clear and sprinkled with twinkling stars.

Hello, Kitten. I hope you had a good day.

Alex reclined the first-class seatback into the makeshift bed. After spreading the coverlet over his legs, he fluffed the pillow and got comfortable. He closed his eyes, and an image of Sarah slowly materialized in his mind; she was smiling.

I know I need to learn to let you go, but not yet.

CHAPTER FORTY-SEVEN

S WITCHING SEATS WITH RODRIGUEZ, Alex sat next to the window during the final leg of their trip as they flew south across France, Spain, and western Africa. From his vantage point, he watched as the pilot skillfully maneuvered the plane around mile-high storm clouds on their final approach to Abidjan's international airport. Gazing down, he noticed intermittent tributaries and inlets woven among the lush green landscape comparable to the coastal area of southern Florida. The one major exception was the pristine beaches, which weren't populated with internationally prominent first-class resorts as of yet.

Abidjan's city center, with its modern high-rise buildings, appeared in the distance as the aircraft touched down on the runway. After clearing customs, Alex, Bishop, and Agent Rodriguez hailed a cab, which drove them to the Novotel Hotel in the center of town.

Exhausted from the twenty-five-hour trip, they enjoyed a quiet dinner in their three-bedroom presidential suite prior to calling it a night. Nevertheless, sleep eluded Alex, and he was rummaging around in the small kitchen in an attempt to make coffee when his SAT phone rang. "Isn't it past your bedtime, General?"

"Can't sleep with all that's going on," the general's husky voice boomed. "You?"

"No." He poured coffee into a cup, quickly added sugar and cream, and took a sip.

"Are you free to talk?"

"Hold on." With coffee cup in hand, he returned to the bedroom and closed the door. "I'm good now."

"How's Bishop doing?"

Alex walked over to the large window with its majestic view of the sleeping city. "I imagine he'll feel better after we meet with President Jabari. Bishop gave the president the impression Rodriguez and I are subcontractors working with him. I hope he doesn't toss us in a dungeon once he learns the truth of why we're here."

"You're such an optimist."

Glancing around the bedroom, he said, "Before I forget, I want to thank you for the nice digs and the first-class seats on our flights here. Maria's curious as to who's picking up the check for our upgraded travel arrangements."

"Inform her that Uncle Sam is paying the tab. For what you and your friends are about to undertake, it's the least we could do. Regarding a different matter, how miffed is she that the Navy SEALs are now lead in this mission?"

"The truth is I think she's relieved. She asked who I called to put those wheels in motion; I didn't tell her yet. I wasn't sure you wanted her to know about your involvement."

"If it comes up again, you can tell her. But for now, you two need to stay focused on what lies in front of you. Call me after you meet with the president, and watch your back."

"Will do."

SUNDAY, MAY 13
ABIDJAN, CÔTE D'IVOIRE, AFRICA
10:30 A.M.

Bishop and Rodriguez occupied the back seat of the outdated taxi during the short trip to the palace. Alex sat in the front next to the driver and mentally cataloged his surroundings.

They passed newly constructed high-rise buildings among intermittent older ones; their crumbling facades punctuated with bullet holes and broken glass belied the country's not-too-distant turbulent past and subsequent rebirth under their new leader. The FBI files Alex read through prior to embarking on this trip described in great detail President Jabari's passion and love for Côte d'Ivoire and its people.

As the taxi meandered through the maze of streets and congestion, Alex observed the women, both young and old, who wore ankle-length cotton dresses with vibrantly colored designs and matching headwraps. The men were in colorful T-shirts and jeans or cutoffs, and uniformed policemen and soldiers carrying semiautomatic weapons walked the streets in pairs. The temperature registered in the mid-eighties and each person's dark brown skin glistened with moisture due to the high humidity.

The taxi pulled up to the palace's main gate, and Bishop handed their passports to one of the guards. Another soldier circled the car with a bomb-detecting canine, while a third one trailed behind with an under-vehicle search mirror, checking for explosives. Once given the go-ahead, the driver followed the red-brick road leading to the Presidential Palace. An expansive rectangular building came into view, and Alex thought it resembled a modern-day concert hall or federal building, more so than a palace.

The taxi pulled to a stop at the main entrance, and Bishop guided them inside, where they encountered two soldiers with AK-47 assault rifles. A third soldier confiscated their mobile phones with the promise the items would be returned at the end of their visit.

After stepping through the full-body scanner, Phillippe, the president's assistant, greeted them and escorted them to a conference room on the mezzanine level.

"Please make yourselves comfortable. President Jabari will be with you shortly," Philippe said and withdrew, closing the door behind him.

As they each grabbed a seat at the sizeable wood-inlaid conference table, Alex surveyed his surroundings. Two large landscape paintings occupied the space above an elaborately carved credenza at one end, and elegant drapes framed large windows at the other. Marble flooring, the color of amber, added to the tasteful decor.

At precisely eleven o'clock, President Jabari entered the room and greeted Bishop with a welcoming handshake. After introductions were made, the president walked to the table's far side and took a seat. Addressing Bishop, he said, "I'm very pleased with the progress of the housing development. My advisors inform me that most of the homes will be ready for occupancy by the time the new production plant is in operation. That's a remarkable accomplishment, considering the obstacles you and the contractors have encountered along the way. Thank you for your commitment to keeping everything on track, Jim."

Bishop shifted uncomfortably in his chair. "You're welcome, sir."

"You requested this meeting," the president said, his English laced with strong French inflections. "Is there something important you wish to discuss?"

"Yes. Unfortunately, I must share some disturbing news with you."

CHAPTER FORTY-EIGHT

PRESIDENT JABARI GAVE NO reaction to Bishop's statement but for a slight tic of his jaw muscles. "Go on. I'm listening."

Clearing his throat, Bishop continued. "On Thursday, I found out my brother-in-law, Blake Sanders, has been selling arms to militant rebels within your country. We have confirmation that the latest shipment of weapons is due to arrive here tomorrow night. I've allowed Blake to combine his freight with mine as an opportunity presented itself to give him a discounted rate on shipping costs, which I now realize was a major mistake. He led me to believe his cargo contained farm equipment and building supplies." As Bishop continued with his story, the president's eyes narrowed while processing the additional information. "I should've been more diligent regarding my brother-in-law's affairs, and I take full responsibility for my negligence."

During the uncomfortable silence that followed, Alex studied the man sitting across the table from him. The president looked decades younger than his sixty-plus years and moved with the agility of a man half his age when he had entered the room earlier. The lines around his eyes framed the inherent wisdom he had gained through the years.

President Jabari rose from his chair without saying a word and walked over to the telephone sitting on the credenza. Pressing a number which connected him directly to his assistant, he said, "Philippe, contact the San Pedro harbor master, General Francoise, and Colonel Nguessan, and inform them I need to see them immediately. Clear my schedule for the rest of the day, and let my wife know I won't be able to go to the dinner party with her tonight."

Disconnecting the call, the president approached his three guests as they simultaneously rose. Addressing Alex first, he said, "Mr. Decker."

"Yes, sir?"

The president's dark brown-black eyes scanned Alex's tall, fit stature prior to making eye contact. "Mercenary or military?"

Alex pulled out his credentials and passed them to the president. "Ex-US Navy pilot, sir. At present, I'm a captain with a commercial airline in the States."

Handing back the TSA/Homeland Security and Galaxy Airline's ID badges, the president asked, "So why are you here?"

"To assist Jim Bishop in apprehending his brother-in-law. I'm also here to help you identify and arrest the militants who are buying the weapons."

"You're a friend of Jim's?"

"Yes, sir. However, it's more complicated than that, but to save time, I won't go into it."

Considering Alex's response, the president massaged his chin with his thumb and forefinger. Satisfied with his answers, he continued. "And why are you here, Ms. Rodriguez?"

The man towered over her, and she had to lift her head to meet his eyes. "I catch bad guys."

"CIA?'

Shaking her head in response, she presented her FBI badge.

"A little off your turf, aren't you, Agent Rodriguez?"

"I'm here in conjunction with the US Navy SEALs who are handling this mission."

Politely gesturing with his hand to get the president's

attention, Alex said, "Excuse me, sir, I think I should mention our President and the chairman of the Joint Chiefs of Staff know we're here and authorized the SEALs involvement."

Rodriguez's head spun around so fast, Alex was surprised it didn't fly off her shoulders, and her scowl told him they would revisit this bit of information at another time.

Addressing Rodriguez, the president said, "How did you, Captain Decker, and the SEALs become involved with this situation?"

Regaining her composure, she said, "Five weeks ago, an airplane caught fire and exploded at an airport in the States. The plane belonged to Galaxy Airlines, the same airline that employs Captain Decker. Regrettably, Mr. Bishop's daughter, who was a flight attendant with that airline, was one of those killed in the fire."

The president broke off and leveled his eyes on Bishop. "I had no idea." Moving closer, he said, "Didn't you lose your son last year?"

"Yes, we did," Bishop said, his voice subdued.

President Jabari motioned with his hand for Rodriguez to continue. "Captain Decker was assisting me with the investigation when one of my men discovered diamonds in the ashes of the plane. They were payment for weapons Bishop's brother-in-law sold to militant rebels here in your country. The Navy SEALs stepped in after Sanders's grandson kidnapped me while I had the stones in my possession and apprehended Sanders's son and three grandsons when they rescued me.

"We allowed Blake Sanders to leave the country with the diamonds so we could track his whereabouts, plus verify his next objective. We've confirmed that he's on his way here. As Captain Decker mentioned, we're here to catch Blake Sanders during the next handoff and to help you identify the rebels who are buying the weapons."

President Jabari grew pensive as if trying to sift through what was the truth and what wasn't. His brow creased in a sympathetic frown as he faced Bishop. "Please accept my sincerest condolences for your loss. And thank you for being forthright with this information." He paused, possibly weighing his options, then added, "We'll figure this mess out first. I'll address your part in it afterward, Jim."

"Fair enough, sir," Bishop solemnly responded.

Addressing the three of them, he said, "Considering the magnitude of this situation, I imagine none of you have eaten for a while."

They slowly nodded their heads in unison.

He approached the credenza and rang his assistant for the second time. "Philippe, arrange to have lunch made for us. We'll also need good strong coffee. Were you able to reach General Francoise and Colonel Nguessan? Good. Tell the cook to make enough food for five. Also, I want this room scanned for listening devices while we wait for the general and colonel to arrive."

After hanging up, he said, "I imagine your Navy SEALs have a plan in place. If you don't mind, I prefer to wait until the others get here to discuss it. Please make yourselves comfortable while we wait."

CHAPTER FORTY-NINE

I
N THE BLINK OF an eye, the predawn sky changed from dark purple to vibrant peach as lights in the buildings outside the window flickered to life. Breathing deeply, Alex rotated his head in a circle in an attempt to alleviate the tension in his neck and shoulders while trying to remember the last time he had enjoyed a full night's sleep, one not steeped in apprehension, nightmares, and visiting spirits. His stomach was tied in knots, and he imagined the others in the room were experiencing the same sense of uneasiness.

Sitting on the edge of the couch, Bishop held a cup of cold coffee as Rodriguez paced back and forth with a hand tucked under each armpit as if trying to still them. Pete, who was positioned at a desk in the far corner, rhythmically tapped on his laptop. A cable ran from the computer to a television mounted on the wall a few feet away, offering them a clear view of the customs area inside the San Pedro shipyard. The freighter containing Bishop's and Sanders's shipment had arrived the previous night, at which point dock workers unloaded the containers and placed them in a warehouse, where they waited to be cleared by a customs inspector this morning.

Blake Sanders and his two mercenary bodyguards had arrived the previous day and occupied a suite in the Sofitel Hotel located a few blocks from the Novotel. It frustrated Alex that the man was so close, yet they had to wait for him to make the next move.

General Francoise had given the SEALs access to the customs area during the night. They had installed high-tech hidden cameras, which currently streamed a live feed to the large flat-screen via Pete's laptop. The SEAL team had also placed tracking devices inside the crates that belonged to Blake.

Colonel Nguessan— director-general of the National Police and superior commander of the National Gendarmerie—arrived with President Jabari. Alex withdrew from the sliding glass windows and greeted their guests with a handshake. "No activity yet, Mr. President. Please help yourselves to the breakfast buffet."

An assortment of covered serving dishes laden with hot food, fruit, and pastries sat on the dining table. To anyone outside the small gathering in the room, it appeared as if the president was having breakfast with Bishop and his two associates. It wasn't a surprise that the elaborate banquet went untouched.

"Here we go," Pete said.

Rising to his feet, Bishop joined the others as all eyes became transfixed on what was taking place on the television screen. In the background, uniformed soldiers, armed with semiautomatic weapons, patrolled the warehouse with trained detection dogs as they searched for hidden explosives and drugs. The customs inspector, who was in his mid-thirties and wearing a tan uniform with gold braids on the lapels, stepped through a door on the left.

Sanders and his bodyguards were visible in the lower corner of the screen, eating breakfast delivered by room service. The SEALs also had installed cameras and listening devices through-out Blake's hotel suite prior to their arrival.

The room grew silent as Alex, along with the others, watched the inspector methodically work his way up and down each aisle with a clipboard in hand. Everyone had a copy of the customs manifest highlighting the pieces belonging to Bishop and Sanders, plus their location.

Time dragged on until Rodriguez said, "Did you catch that? Is it my imagination, or did he bypass a crate belonging to Blake?"

Glancing at his copy of the manifest, the inspector stepped in front of a large container, which they knew belonged to Bishop. He signaled it to be opened, verified that it contained machinery parts for the new factory, and had it resealed.

Time passed at a turtle's pace before Pete pointed to his laptop. "There! He did it again."

When the inspector concluded examining the rest of the freight, they had visual and recorded confirmation that he bypassed each of the containers that belonged to Sanders.

Speaking to their two guests, Rodriguez said, "Mr. President, now we can understand how Blake's shipments are bypassing customs."

Colonel Nguessan's eyes narrowed as he intensely stared at the screen. "That's my idiot nephew," he said heatedly. "I recommended him for the job."

Bishop turned to address the colonel-major. "Sir, we can't control the choices others make, even if they're family. It's not an easy lesson to learn. I'm walking that path myself right now, and I understand that it's a hard pill to swallow."

"My men will take it from here," President Jabari said. "Agent Rodriguez, I want to thank you for loaning us your IT technician. He's agreed to assist my security team in monitoring the movement of the freight until it reaches its final destination."

"Pete's one of the best. However, don't forget I need him back."

Acknowledging her comment with a nod, he added, "Are you sure you don't want our help in dealing with Sanders? I've got men I trust."

"Thank you, sir, but the SEALs have got this one covered. And thank you for agreeing to let us extradite Sanders to the States once we have him in custody. From what we've been able to ascertain thus far, he's been at this for some time. It's imperative that we learn the extent of his network and global customer base, and he's the only one with all the answers."

President Jabari approached Bishop. "Jim, once you are back in the States, I've no doubt the FBI and CIA are going to need your help to sort through your brother-in-law's affairs. In any event, I trust you'll still be able to finish the work you started here in Côte d'Ivoire?"

Relief mixed with gratitude washed over Bishop. "Mr. President, I promise I will do all I can in support of your efforts, and thank you for allowing me to continue."

Félix Houphouët-Boigny International Airport
Abidjan, Côte d'Ivoire, Africa
Six Hours Later

Brian's secure phone rang, and the SEAL team leader put it on speaker so the others could hear the update. Master Chief Enrique Avelino and Smitty, an IT technician, both with the Navy SEALs, were huddled together with two military police from the president's secret service in a hotel room directly below Blake's suite. They were monitoring his activities via the hidden cameras.

"Party's over," Enrique said. "Sanders received payment, and we've recorded the transaction. The SEAL's tone carried little emotion despite the gravity of their forthcoming undertaking. "The client left immediately following the handoff. We have confirmation he was picked up a few blocks from here by Colonel Nguessan's men. Sanders and his two bodyguards just exited the hotel and are coming your way."

"Roger that," Brian said and disconnected the call. "Look

alive, everybody. They're thirty minutes out. Remember, we need to take Blake Sanders alive."

Rodriguez, Alex, and Bishop, along with Brian and the rest of the SEAL team, were staked out inside a maintenance hangar at the airport. The airplane, which Sanders chartered for his flight back to the Canary Islands, sat on the tarmac out front. Unbeknownst to the cockpit crew, the SEALs had installed audio-and-visual equipment inside the aircraft, giving them a clear interior view.

Twenty-five minutes later, Johnson, an African-American Navy SEAL, dressed in a ground-service uniform, bounded up the stairs, and entered the cockpit. "Captain, here are your papers. The plane's fueled, catered, and ready to go. Remind your passengers they'll need to check in with the customs officer in the hangar. And as a special treat, the caterer made coffee for you from our own Côte d'Ivoire beans." He handed the captain and first officer each a cup. "Enjoy."

Before long, a black sedan pulled up next to the Citation CJ3 airplane. Sanders climbed out and ascended the stairs to the aircraft, two at a time. His two bodyguards paused to scan the surrounding area, then retrieved their luggage from the car's trunk and joined their boss.

Sanders leaned in through the open cockpit door. "We're all here, Captain. We can leave now."

The pilot pivoted in his seat. "Sir, you and your two friends are required to check-in with the customs officer and show your passports and visas before we're permitted to leave. He's waiting for you in the hangar. It shouldn't take long."

"No need, we already took care of it." Sanders presented the documents, which were stamped by the same customs officer who had inspected the cargo earlier in the day.

The captain scanned each one and handed them back. "Okay, it looks like we're good to go. If you'll please be seated, we should be on our way shortly."

Sanders closed the cockpit door and joined his men in the cabin. He relaxed in one of the plush leather seats and got ready for the six-hour flight back to the Canary Islands. However, the plane wasn't moving, and the front door remained open. Losing patience, he instructed one of his men to investigate the cause of the delay.

Inside the cockpit, the bodyguard found the two pilots asleep and swore under his breath when he spotted several men in military uniform with assault rifles closing in on the aircraft.

"What's holding us up?" Blake yelled. Before he got an answer, movement outside the passenger window caught his attention. At first, he believed his eyes were playing tricks. Captain Decker, Agent Rodriguez, and his brother-in-law stood below on the tarmac. US Navy SEALs and Côte d'Ivoire militia formed a semicircle behind them with guns drawn. "You've got to be joking! This isn't happening."

∞

Agent Rodriguez raised the megaphone to her lips. "Sanders, you and your men are going to do as I say. One by one, you'll move to the open door, place your weapons on the floor, and descend the stairs; hands up where we can see them. We've got cameras streaming live footage from inside the airplane and can hear everything you say. Now move it, you first."

Sanders rose and proceeded to the front door. Pausing at the top of the stairs, he shook his head in disbelief. "I don't have any weapons on me." Raising his hands, he descended the stairs. One of the Navy SEALs frisked him once he reached the bottom step and pulled him aside.

The first bodyguard did as instructed and descended the stairs. He was checked for weapons and ushered out of the way as the second bodyguard followed suit. When he reached the bottom, he didn't wait to be searched but immediately stepped over next to his boss. Sanders slipped behind the mercenary and—using him as a shield—grabbed a Beretta 9mm holstered beneath the man's jacket and pointed it at Jim Bishop.

"No, don't." Holding her hands up, Rodriguez jumped in front of Bishop.

Smiling, Sanders placed the gun beneath his chin. They heard a loud pop, and he collapsed to the asphalt.

Two SEALs body-slammed the mercenaries to the ground as Alex, Rodriguez, and Brian ran to Sanders. Alex knelt beside him; it was no use, for a significant portion of the man's head was missing.

In frustration, Rodriguez repeatedly punched the air with her fist. "No. No. No!"

As he stood, Alex noticed Bishop stood frozen in place. Approaching his friend, he quietly spoke his name.

Hearing Alex's voice, Bishop tore his gaze away from his brother-in-law's body. "Is he dead?"

"Yes, I am afraid so. I'm sorry."

"I need to call my wife." Bishop withdrew his cell phone and walked away.

Meanwhile, Rodriguez stopped her ranting long enough to phone President Jabari as Alex distanced himself from the others and called General Pritchard.

His friend picked up on the first ring. "Did everything go as planned?"

"Unfortunately, no, sir." Alex filled him in on the details of the past twenty-four hours since the cargo ship had docked in the harbor, up to and including when Blake Sanders took his own life. "It's going to be a challenge for Bishop and Rodriguez to sort through Sanders's illegal affairs now that he's dead."

"I have some news which is going to help the situation," the general said. "And I hope you're sitting down because you're not going to believe what I'm about to tell you. Pete found out Blake Sanders's younger son—the one who was presumed dead—is very much alive. With s help from Navy Intelligence, your IT buddy is having fun hacking into Dwight's hard drive as we speak. We've discovered that Dwight is the mastermind behind this whole mess. The bonus is that Pete remembered this guy from his university days."

"You're serious?"

"Yes. Pete and his friends at Langley identified Dwight as the one hacking into the FBI and CIA security systems. That's not all; Dwight deleted his school records, social security number, and birth certificate. Plus, we haven't dug up any pictures of him. It's as if he never existed; thanks to Pete, we have proof that he does. You finish up on your end, and we'll circle back afterward. For now, I think it's best if you didn't mention anything to Bishop, but Rodriguez should be informed."

CHAPTER FIFTY

MID-MORNING SUNLIGHT STREAMED IN through the sliding glass doors, which offered a view of the spacious wraparound balcony. In contrast, Alex thought the dark menacing clouds that painted the sky in the west corresponded with the mood of the other occupant in the room.

He poured a cup of coffee and sat down in an overstuffed chair across from Rodriguez, who had squatter's rights on the couch. She wore jeans and a baggy T-shirt, and he couldn't help noticing the dark circles that framed her chocolate brown eyes and puffy face. *She looks as tired as I feel.*

Ignoring his presence, Rodriguez sipped orange juice while thumbing through a tourist magazine that emphasized must-see attractions in the area. An aura of calm replaced the tension in the room from the previous day. Nevertheless, the energy radiating off the agent was anything but serene as she dramatically flipped a page, nearly tearing it in half.

Without looking up, she said, "Bishop's packing. He's catching a flight this afternoon to the Canary Islands, where he'll join his sister. From there, they'll fly home together. General

Francoise is making the necessary arrangements to have Sanders's body shipped back to the States. As far as Sanders's wife knows, Blake was allegedly killed by a street gang while overseeing the delivery of the shipment to his customer. The truth will come out soon enough, and it will give her time to deal with his death."

She glanced his way, not making eye contact, then continued unloading her frustrations on the defenseless magazine. "We have reservations on a flight out this evening. I guess your days of working with the FBI have come to an end."

Alex moved to the couch after she grudgingly forfeited space for him to sit. Hoping to cut through her darkened mood, he smiled and said, "You'll not get rid of me that easily."

Her head popped up, and her eyes narrowed with suspicion. "Oh, really."

"I wanted to wait until we were alone to share some surprising news. Bishop has enough on his plate right now, and I didn't want to burden him with this."

"For crying out loud, just spit it out!"

Alex glanced over his shoulder to make sure the door to Bishop's bedroom was closed and reached for the remote control on the table in front of them. He pressed a button, and contemporary French music came through on speakers affixed to the wall across from them. Moving closer, he said, "Blake's youngest son, Dwight, is still alive."

She launched herself off the couch. With hands-on-hips, she glared at Alex. "How'd you acquire that intel? Been chatting with your buddies in the White House *again?*"

Tilting his head toward Bishop's bedroom, he signaled for her to lower her voice. "Maria, please sit down."

Seething, her nostrils flared like a crazed dog ready to pounce. "You have anybody else in your back pocket meddling in this investigation that I've been kept in the dark about?"

"No one. Besides, given the opportunity, I would've told you about General Pritchard's involvement eventually. That's how I got the SEALs to help us. "

"Are you referring to the IOU that came signed, sealed, and delivered by none other than our President and the Chairman of the Joint Chief of Staff?" she heatedly replied. "Thanks for keeping me abreast on that one, flyboy." Pivoting on her heels, she stomped off toward her bedroom and slammed the door closed.

He needed to let her know what he had found out, but it wasn't going to happen now. *That woman's got some serious anger-management issues. Or maybe she needs her husband to come home.*

President Jabari called Rodriguez in the afternoon with an update. She rejoined Alex in the living room, apparently coming to terms with his cardinal sins, and put the call on speaker. "I thought the two of you would be interested to learn there are warrants out for Sanders's two bodyguards in Argentina, Ecuador, China, and Israel; however, they'll be serving time in our prison first, along with the customs inspector."

His voice was clear and concise as he continued. "Colonel Nguessan informed me that Liberian rebels rendezvoused with the two trucks containing the weapons on an isolated road at our border to the west. I'm pleased to learn it wasn't any of our people."

He thanked Rodriguez for handing over the diamonds, both those located in a safe at Sanders's hotel in the Canary Islands and the ones used as payment for the latest shipment. "We still need to investigate how the Liberian rebels acquired the diamonds in the first place. However, we were able to track down the illegal mining operation's location in the north using the report you gave us from the samples tested. I appreciate what you, Captain Decker, and the Navy SEALs have done for my people and my country. I trust your next visit will be under more favorable conditions."

∞

Alex was in the middle of packing when his satellite phone rang. "I hope you have some good news because Rodriguez is royally miffed."

"I can only imagine," General Pritchard said, sounding sympathetic. "I believe what I'm about to tell you will help the situation. They located her husband."

"He's alive?" Alex said with a gasp. Flooded with relief, he dropped down onto the edge of the bed.

"That's right. Your travel arrangements are going to change once we've verified the intel. Call me once you get to the airport. I should have confirmation on the professor's location by then, and I'll give you the updated itinerary. Meanwhile, don't say anything to Maria until we've substantiated Carl's whereabouts."

FÉLIX HOUPHOUËT-BOIGNY INTERNATIONAL AIRPORT
ABIDJAN, CÔTE D'IVOIRE, AFRICA
9:30 P.M.

"I don't get it," Rodriguez said, her voice rising with each syllable. "Why are we being rerouted to Miami via Lisbon? The plane to Brussels is still showing on time."

"You can go on to DC if you wish," Alex said, not hiding his grin as they headed to their gate. "I'm going to Miami to help plan the rescue of your husband. I just thought you might want to come along."

She grabbed his arm, forcing him to stop in his tracks. "What are you saying?"

Alex noticed two businessmen within hearing distance and ushered her toward an alcove in the concourse where they could talk privately. "Maria, if you calm down, I'll tell you what I've learned about Carl and where we go from here."

Her brow knitted together in a scowl as she crossed her arms. "I'm waiting."

Shaking his head, he continued. "Okay. While you were in the restroom, I got a phone call from General Pritchard. They've located your husband. He's in Belize."

"He's alive!" Pressing her hand to her lips, she fought back the tears.

"Yes, he is."

Her knees gave way, and she collapsed in a nearby chair, staring up at him in bewilderment.

"You and I are flying to Miami, where we'll meet with the FBI team in charge of the kidnapping investigation."

Her ingrained sense of determination and single-mindedness was back. "That would be Agent Fillmore and his incompetent band of agents. Who has Carl, and where is he?" she asked with an edge to her voice.

He held up a hand. "Let me finish."

She paused briefly before restating the question. "Alex, who kidnapped my husband?"

Alex lowered himself into a chair next to her. "Blake's son, Dwight Sanders."

Her eyes wide with surprise, she said, "No!"

"I wanted to tell you about Dwight this morning. You didn't give me a chance. Pete and the guys at Langley identified Dwight as the one hacking into the FBI and CIA security systems. He's the one managing the family business, not Blake. After orchestrating his disappearance, he hacked into multiple systems and deleted all records of his existence. That's about the time he got involved with selling arms on the black market. Thus far, Intel shows that Blake was probably the only one who knew his son was still alive. I think it ironic that Richard was working for his younger brother and didn't have a clue."

Pausing to gather her thoughts, she finally asked, "How were they able to find Dwight and Carl?"

"Pete remembered the younger Sanders from his days

at the university. They were both in your husband's classes at Georgetown."

"Unbelievable!"

"Pete said something clicked in his brain and connected Dwight Sanders's name with a student who went missing prior to their senior year. He recalled that Dwight was a gifted genius in the areas of computer science and mathematics. Your husband tried to mentor him, but—to quote Pete—*the guy had a larger-than-life ego and was narcissistic. He gave your husband a hard time and considered himself above reproach.*"

"So it must've been Dwight who called me. If so, then it *was* Carl I spoke to on the phone and not a recording."

"I would agree. And I bet it was Dwight who showed up at my house posing as an FBI agent the night of the break-in. At first, I suspected Richard; but later, I realized he couldn't have pulled it off."

"Since we have no idea what he looks like, he could be standing a few feet away, and we wouldn't have a clue," Rodriguez said, the absurdity evident in her voice.

Alex peered over his shoulder to verify no one was eavesdropping on them and said, "Let's hope not."

"Anything else?"

He leaned in closer. "From what I gather, your guys in Miami are convinced Dwight's primary reason for the kidnapping of your husband was not to use him to get to the diamonds. They've confirmed Dwight is developing military-grade anti-drone software and plans to sell it on the black market from the latest intel. With your husband's knowledge in that field, he would be worth his weight in gold to a person such as Dwight, who would exploit him."

Her eyes narrowed, and between taut lips, she voiced an unyielding opinion on the subject. "Carl would never compromise his values or his integrity. And he definitely wouldn't acquiesce to the demands of Dwight Sanders."

Reaching into his small travel bag, he withdrew two bottles of water, which he had purchased at the kiosk. Handing one to Rodriguez, he said, "We'll learn more after we reach Miami. By the way, we're traveling with false documents. Since Dwight is probably tracking our whereabouts, we don't want him to discover what we're up to right now. Two undercover agents are on their way to DC using our tickets. They gave me our new passports and tickets while you were freshening up in the ladies' room. Unfortunately, we're in coach this time."

She studied the passport he handed her. It looked valid. "You are aware that I could arrest you after we land in Miami for entering the United States with false creds?"

Dismissing the possibility, he took her arm in his. "They're about to call our flight, Ms. Sanchez. What say we go get your husband?"

CHAPTER FIFTY-ONE

THE SECURE SATELLITE PHONE rang for the umpteenth time. Dwight checked the screen and chose to answer it to alleviate another voicemail containing his brother-in-law's rantings. "What do you want now?" It baffled him how the man ever made it through law school. Paul had no spine, nor could he think for himself.

"I told you earlier," Paul said, speaking with a nasal twang. "Your mother keeps calling me in a panic. And now the Feds have frozen my assets and your father's. They showed up two hours ago at your parents' home in Charleston and presented your mother with a search warrant. They've also been to their places in West Palm Beach and Palm Springs. It's complete chaos here, and she's driving me crazy. You need to do something."

As he listened to Paul whine, Dwight keyed in the password to Blake's investment accounts and wasn't surprised at being denied access. "I told you over and over, not to worry. My mother's in the dark as to what her husband was involved in. Without my father to substantiate anything, the Feds have nothing to go on. They're just fishing. Besides, I told Blake not to flaunt his money, and we both know how my mother loves her shopping sprees. Now she's calling you to bail her out. Not my problem."

"What about me?" Paul pleaded. "I'm surprised they aren't at my door yet. What should I do when they show up?"

"Haven't you been listening? Keep your mouth shut and let them have whatever they want. If you've done as I've instructed through the years, they won't connect you to my father's illegal transactions or mine." Unbeknownst to his brother-in-law, Dwight checked Paul's underhanded dealings regularly and was confident the Feds wouldn't uncover anything.

"You can't blow me off like that," Paul screamed into the phone. "This is your doing, all of it. And I'm caught right in the middle."

"You screw up, Paul, and I'll have one of my guys cut out your tongue and feed it, along with you, to the sharks. Am I clear on this?" Dwight's voice was calm as he spoke; nevertheless, the threat was unmistakable.

He heard erratic breathing on the line and presumed the wimp was crying. Not expecting a response, he continued, "As soon as we hang up, smash the SIM card and burner phone we're talking on and dispose of it before the Feds get there."

Paul wasn't ready to let it go. "Don't you care what happens to your brother and nephews? What's to become of my two sons? The Feds aren't telling me where they're located."

"They're at Guantanamo Naval Base. And for all I care, they can rot there." Dwight disconnected the call, hacked into his father's offshore accounts, and transferred the funds to his banks in the Cayman Islands and Switzerland. "Mom may be working at Walmart once this is over."

Satisfied the funds were secure, he keyed in the flight reservation info for Agent Rodriguez and Captain Decker, confirming they were back in the States. Hacking into one of the military satellites, Dwight soon had a video feed of Rodriguez entering her condo in Alexandria, Virginia, and the captain at home in North Carolina.

"Good, now I can focus on more important matters." He couldn't believe less than forty-eight hours ago his father was killed by a small band of guerrillas while delivering the latest shipment in Africa, and two of his top operatives, who were traveling with Blake, had ended up in jail. The fallout from it was giving him a migraine.

Another bone of contention was the fact that he had just learned his uncle, Captain Decker, and Rodriguez were in Abidjan when the shipment arrived on Monday night. Intel regarding their unexpected visit was sketchy. Nevertheless, with Richard in custody, he had little doubt their visit was in some way related to his father's demise. More importantly, Dwight wanted to find out what had happened to the shipment of guns and the diamonds.

Adding to the pandemonium—after the debacle at Richard's cabin—his brother and nephews were arrested for kidnapping Rodriguez and Dr. Newman and the attempted murder of Captain Decker, not once but twice. "What idiots!"

It wasn't the first time he had questioned his parental lineage. He bore no resemblance in appearance, intelligence, or personality to his redneck brother, Richard, or his wannabe-princess sister, who was married to Paul, the floundering lawyer. And there was little doubt his nephews came from the same gene pool as his older brother.

Smiling, Dwight recalled when he had attended Marcus Bishop's funeral portraying himself as one of Marcus's high-school buddies. The deception and disguise worked for his aunt and uncle, who were oblivious to the fact that the man in their midst was their nephew and the one responsible for their son's death.

The one person Dwight trusted, to a limited degree, was his lieutenant, Ryan Borella. The man had zero interest in technology.

He was a hard-wired, old-school soldier to the core. Give him a weapon and something to shoot at, and he was happy.

Ryan Borella, his father, and the professor were the only ones aware of what Dwight looked like these days. Ever since childhood, he had had an infatuation with disguising himself and going about unnoticed. These days, he entertained himself by occasionally masquerading as the gardener or maintenance man and eavesdropping on Ryan or his men while pruning a rose bush or repairing a broken light.

At the family gathering following Caroline's memorial service, he had used the acne-scarred, chubby young man disguise, which was one of his favorites. It was the first time Dwight had laid eyes on the captain in person.

Back in the day, Dwight had found a picture of the Navy pilot on the internet during the time that Richard blamed Captain Decker for his downfall. He knew it was his brother's stupidity, not the captain, that landed Richard in Leavenworth. Nevertheless, he couldn't resist exploiting his brother's neurotic obsession regarding the captain and his father's wrath over the situation. During Richard's incarceration, Dwight shared updates regarding Captain Decker's continued military successes with his father and could only imagine the heated conversations it fueled between the two men.

Over the years, Dwight lost interest in the family drama. That's why it surprised him when Captain Decker resurfaced at Caroline's memorial service and began working with Agent Rodriguez.

Dwight couldn't trust his father, brother, or nephews to retrieve the diamonds without mishap, so he sent Ryan to DC to keep an eye on the captain and the agent. Meanwhile, he had kidnapped Professor Mitchell and planned to use him to get the stones if Richard failed. But the truth was, he had an ulterior motive for getting his hands on the professor that was worth more to him than the diamonds.

After he had Professor Mitchell stashed away on the island, Dwight chartered a private jet to Greensboro just in time to witness another mess his brother had created. Ryan called him at the hotel and reported about the botched break-in at Captain Decker's house. Dwight disguised himself as an FBI agent and roamed the property freely while searching for potential evidence connecting him to Richard and his nephews.

Given the opportunity, he couldn't resist masquerading himself as Captain Decker's brother in Pennsylvania. He wished he could've seen the captain's face the moment his neighbor handed him the embossed FBI business card with the brother's name on it.

Even after all that's happened, Captain Decker continues to come out unscathed. How is it possible? Choosing not to dwell on it, he focused instead on his latest enterprise and how to get the professor to assist him. If all else failed, Dwight would use Ryan to get what he wanted.

CHAPTER FIFTY-TWO

FBI SPECIAL AGENT LEONARD Fillmore rose to greet Rodriguez and Alex as they walked into the conference room. "Good. You made it. Come on in."

Alex shook hands with the seasoned field agent. Having heard stories about the man from Rodriguez based on her frustrations, he was determined to postpone judgment until he had a sense of how things progressed. "Thank you for letting me tag along."

A man, who was a foot shorter than Fillmore, stepped forward. Special Agent Hiroshi Oshiro from NCIS introduced himself. "To be honest, we received a call from the White House insisting we include you in this rescue mission, so welcome to our side of the fence, Captain."

Fillmore introduced them to the rest of the core-strategist team. "This is FBI Special Agent Ben Carter, Specialist Nancy Higgins with Navy Intelligence, Bob Hybarger, an anti-terrorist specialist with Homeland Security, NCIS intelligence analyst Tim Bakker, and my assistant Liz Cartwright."

Once the agents and Alex were seated, Fillmore began. "Liz is passing out a folder that contains everything we've learned about Professor Mitchell's kidnapping and Dwight Sanders. To save time, I'll summarize and address your questions after I finish.

"We've identified Dwight Sanders as our person of interest who abducted Professor Mitchell three weeks ago and is holding him on a small island off the coast of Belize. Within the past few days, we've discovered that Dwight is developing military-grade anti-drone software and plans to sell it on the black market. We believe he intends to utilize Professor Mitchell's knowledge and expertise in the field to achieve that goal."

Reflexively, Alex gripped Rodriguez's arm and—with a slight shake of his head—signaled her not to respond. Biting her lower lip, she shook off his hand while glaring at Agent Fillmore.

Unfazed, the agent continued. "Last Saturday, FBI Agent Pete Creighton from Agent Rodriguez's team contacted me as the lead on this investigation. He informed me that he had attended George-town University with a student named Dwight Sanders, and they were both in Professor Mitchell's IT classes. More importantly, Pete had a hunch that Dwight was still alive. Prior to catching his flight to Africa Sunday morning, Pete phoned back to tell me he and his buddies at Langley had located Dwight's compound.

"Once Pete arrived in Africa, he continued in his efforts to track down Dwight Sanders while assisting Rodriguez and the Navy SEALs with their mission to apprehend Dwight's father, Blake Sanders."

Fillmore glanced around the room to make sure he had their full attention until his eyes settled on Rodriguez, who sat across from him. "Pete called late Monday night to say he had verified Dwight was the person hacking into our systems. With that breakthrough and the help of Navy Intelligence, we had a game-changer. The IT techs hacked into Dwight Sanders's email and mainframe without detection. Since then, we've uncovered a wealth of information regarding Dwight's illegal operations."

Rodriguez interrupted him, her tone acrid. "I realize that I've been out of the country this week, so could someone tell me how Pete got involved and why I wasn't privy to any of it until now?"

This meeting just hit its first landmine, Alex thought.

Seemingly impervious to her outburst, Fillmore quickly said, "Let me defer your questions to Agent Carter."

The FBI agent sitting next to Fillmore nodded and smiled at Rodriguez. "There's not one simple answer to your question. If I may, I'd like to go over some background relative to Dwight Sanders's various enterprises first."

Rodriguez motioned with a condescending gesture for him to continue.

Carter selected a key on his laptop, and a list popped up on the whiteboard at the front of the room. "Completely separate from being an arms dealer, Dwight Sanders designs video games targeting teens and preteens. He used a variety of alias names for the copyrights and created a corporation to promote them. He positioned his lawyer as president and CEO. The profit margin is significant. The company is legitimate; finances are in line, taxes paid, dividends distributed to investors, etc."

"Excuse me for interrupting," Alex said, holding up his hand. "Who's the lawyer?"

"Dwight's brother-in-law, Paul Dyer."

Rodriguez's right leg bounced up and down, and Alex could sense she was losing patience with the drawn-out explanation. Nevertheless, Dyer's name got her attention.

"The FBI became interested in the video games after they discovered a pattern in connection with school shootings." Pointing to the list on the whiteboard, Agent Carter continued, "We discovered that each shooter favored those particular games. Further examinations of the interface design revealed a subliminal code that stimulates aggressive psychological behavior in the user. Agent Hybarger and his people with Homeland Security got involved then. Breaking it down, we found the games advocate violence, especially in support of white supremacy."

Acidic coffee rose to Alex's throat as Rodriguez shot forward in her seat. "Are you serious?"

In tandem, Carter and Hybarger confirmed the results by nodding. Carter added, "Dwight used the profit from the sale of the games via money laundering to pay off local officials, custom inspectors, and fund those who are stealing weapons from our military bases amongst other things. In the last twenty-four hours, we've tapped into two of his off-shore accounts and are tracking down the transfer of funds."

Alex read through the names listed on the whiteboard. Though he considered sitting in front of a computer playing video games a waste of time, he recognized a number of them.

Keeping his eyes on Rodriguez, Carter said, "Saturday evening, while you and Captain Decker were en route to Africa, Agent Pete Creighton spoke with General Pritchard regarding Dwight Sanders."

"General Pritchard?" Rodriguez turned to Alex and impaled him with invisible arrows.

Oh boy, there goes another landmine. Alex shrugged and gave her a half-hearted smile.

Agent Carter, oblivious to the growing hostility within the room, continued. "That's right. As per General Pritchard's directive, Pete telephoned Agent Fillmore. Agent Fillmore informed Pete about our investigation of the video games marketed by Sanders's son-in-law during the call. It verified in Pete's mind that Dwight was still alive, at which point he elected to search for a thumbprint buried in the designs' coding. After coming across a signature link, he broadened the search, and a synonym for the hidden code popped up in Belize. It's the name of the island where Dwight constructed his fortress, Isla de Quimera. Pete called back Sunday morning to inform Agent Fillmore of the island and that *Quimera* was the name of the game Dwight had designed and patented as a term project in their junior year at Georgetown."

Agent Fillmore reached for a button on his laptop, and a three-dimensional holographic image of an island came into view in the middle of the conference table. "Since you were in the middle of apprehending Dwight's father, we didn't want you distracted and instructed your agent not to mention anything at the time."

Alex glanced at Rodriguez. Her jaw muscles grew taut as she bit down, and he knew she was about to explode.

"Since the Navy SEALs were already involved with tracking Blake Sanders's activities and potential arrest, we contacted Specialist Higgins with Navy Intelligence for assistance. She allowed us to utilize the Navy's database and systems, eliminating the threat of Dwight discovering we were on to him. This image was downloaded on Sunday from one of the military satellites. The island is owned by a corporation within Dwight's umbrella and—as far as the Belize government is concerned—designated as an offshore software development lab."

Agent Oshiro spoke up for the first time since the start of the briefing. "Using the internet and other questionable world-wide networks, Dwight can manage the sales of arms to militant leaders and drug lords, plus work both sides of the fence in any conflicts without leaving the island. He has local police and customs inspectors around the world on his payroll, as you witnessed firsthand in Côte d'Ivoire. Once we have him in custody and gain full access to his computers, we'll be able to retrieve further information about his offshore accounts, which could add up to billions."

Rodriguez slammed her fist down on the table. "I don't care how wealthy Dwight is or how connected globally. What about my husband? Has anybody caught sight of him on this island?"

The room grew silent except for the white noise coming from the air-conditioning vents.

Agent Fillmore toggled some keys on his laptop, and Rodriguez sucked in an audible breath as a second holographic image of the island compound replaced the first one. Her husband stood sandwiched in between two bodyguards. The three-dimensional picture was shadowed in darkness and grainy as if taken at night. However, there was no mistake; it was Carl who stood on a berm, staring out at the water.

From Alex's vantage point, it appeared as if the professor was staring right at Rodriguez.

Not taking her eyes off the image, she spoke through clenched teeth. "When did you get this?"

In a calm, dogmatic tone, Fillmore said, "Navy Intelligence delivered this image to us Monday night. From what we've been able to ascertain, he's in good health."

Rodriguez flew out of her chair, knocking it over. Speaking in a terse, hostile voice, she said, "You received a satellite image of my husband on *Monday night* and didn't call me?"

Fillmore was on his feet; placing his hands on the table, he leaned in, and his posture was far from congenial. "You've harassed me continuously since your husband's kidnapping. May I remind you that you chose to remain in the field following Carl's abduction? You said you could stay focused on your investigations and wouldn't be distracted by this one. I preferred not to say anything when this came in so you could concentrate on *your investigation*, which was to apprehend Sanders and his band of thieves. There's no doubt in my mind Richman made a mistake in letting you stay active. You not only allowed yourself to be kidnapped by Sanders's grandson last week, but Blake Sanders killed himself while *you* were supervising his arrest Tuesday night. I can't imagine what else would've happened if you'd known all this was going on at the same time."

Rodriguez stormed out of the conference room. Alex was right behind her, but paused at the door, and addressed Agent Fillmore. "I get where you're coming from; nevertheless, you're wrong about her. She's one of the best, and you're selling her short." He couldn't help noticing that the others avoided eye contact as he looked around the table before walking out.

CHAPTER FIFTY-THREE

RODRIGUEZ REACHED FOR THE door handle on the driver's side of their rental, which set off the car's alarm. In her heated frenzy, she ignored the obnoxious noise and kept yanking on it.

As he approached, Alex pressed the key fob to silence the alarm and unlock the doors. "I'll drive," he said, pushing past her and climbing in behind the wheel.

Stomping around to the passenger side, she got in and closed the door hard enough to potentially knock the car out of alignment.

Alex keyed in "community park" on the GPS and merged into the early-morning traffic on 163rd Street. He turned into Biscayne Gardens Park a few minutes later and switched off the engine. Rodriguez jumped out and jogged over to a footpath that circled the gardens. He quickly caught up to her and allowed her to set the pace as they ran.

The park was not that big, and she picked up the cadence as they started the second lap. He speculated on how long she could keep it up in flats as his own feet began to burn due to the

$150 dress shoes he wore. Be that as it may, he was confident she currently felt only anger fueled by frustration and uncertainty.

Typical of Miami this time of year, the temperature was already in the eighties, with the humidity on the rise. Perspiration coated their exposed skin as they walked out the final lap. Taking a seat on a bench beneath the shade of a tree, he waited for her internal storm to pass.

Finally, she spoke. "How do you manage it?"

"What's that?"

"Life without Sarah."

"You've experienced firsthand how poorly I've handled it. Why do you ask?"

"Because," her voice cracked as she fought the tears pooling in her eyes. "I can't even imagine what you go through day after day. In DC, I hate going home because Carl isn't there. The rooms feel three times their size, and the silence is unbearable. I miss him greeting me as I walk through the door and saying my name with his silly gringo pronunciation of the Spanish *r*. I miss him telling me about his favorite students, the ones who are challenged yet determined. I miss him at breakfast and the warmth of him beside me in bed. I miss—I miss." Pressing a balled fist to her mouth, she rocked back and forth.

Placing an arm around her shoulders, he drew her close as she wept, his shirt soaking up the tears. Without saying a word, he took her hand in his and waited.

In time, she straightened and brushed away the tears with the back of her hand. "Thanks," she mumbled, not meeting Alex's eyes.

He retrieved a handkerchief from his back pocket and handed it to her. "You're welcome, but it's little payback for the times you coached me through the anxiety attacks."

"You and Sarah never had any children?"

"No, we wanted to wait until I got out of the service. Sarah was younger than me, and we felt we had time." He focused on the dancing shadows on the ground in front of them. "Then, she got sick."

"Sometimes, life doesn't go the way we imagined or hoped it would. Carl and I tried at first, but we were told we couldn't have children after running a gamut of tests. As time passed, we let our careers fill the void." She straightened and took a deep, cleansing breath. "It's obvious Dwight was the one who tried to kill Pete last week with that power surge. Thank goodness he failed."

Alex shifted his position so he could observe her reaction to his next words. "I agree, and I apologize for not telling you earlier that I hooked Pete up with General Pritchard. Everything was happening so fast, and I considered Pete a good backup if the general couldn't reach me. I had no clue as to what transpired afterward, and what Fillmore said was as much a surprise to me as it was for you."

She fixed her gaze on him while weighing in on an idea. "Should I go back to DC?"

"No. You're right where you belong; although, you do understand that you'll have to suck-up to Agent Fillmore before he allows us back in the meeting."

Rodriguez *harrumphed* and sat back, crossing her arms.

A hush fell over them, each lost in thought until Alex finally spoke. "Sarah and I celebrated our fifth anniversary on Ambergris Caye in Belize."

Rodriguez straightened. "Really?"

"From what I remember, the people of Belize were very hospitable and friendly. It probably helped us that English is their primary language since they were part of the British Commonwealth until they got their independence in September of 1981."

He had piqued her interest, and she said, "What else do you remember?"

"The turquoise blue waters are so clear it's possible to see fifty feet down. There's a coral reef, which runs the country's full length, teeming with a variety of brightly colored fish. Sarah and

I booked an all-day snorkeling expedition out to the Blue Hole, a large submarine sinkhole roughly nine hundred feet across and four hundred feet deep if memory serves. It was surreal, holding her hand and floating over the abyss. You've probably seen pictures of it on the internet or in *National Geographic*."

In sharing the story, he was aware that it hadn't sent him into a tailspin of sadness or depression as it had in the past. Memories of the trip flooded his mind, and he detected the hint of a smile reaching the corners of his mouth.

A heartbeat or two later, he said, "Ready to go back?"

She nodded.

On the way to the car, he asked, "Who's been taking out the trash in Carl's absence?"

"That's an easy answer," she said with a mischievous wink. "No one."

CHAPTER FIFTY-FOUR

D WIGHT'S WORLD HAD BEEN spinning out of control since the debacle in Africa. He wasn't surprised to find out that a gang of hoodlums hadn't killed his family's patriarch. Instead, Blake had taken his own life after being caught in the act of selling guns to Liberian rebels.

Hating disorganization with a passion and having zero tolerance for situations that didn't go as planned, Dwight was at his wit's end. Adding to his frustration, the prototype military drone he had stolen from Creech Air Force Base in Nevada sat in Belize City, concealed in a large shipping container. He had the schematics for it—which were also pilfered—but needed the drone itself for final testing of the beta software he had designed.

The season's first tropical storm had stalled eighty miles offshore. The gale winds of fifty-plus miles per hour made it impossible to maneuver through the turbulent water by boat to Belize City, typically a three-hour journey, to collect his prize. Regrettably, not all things could be downloaded from the internet. With its extensive global service, he doubted FedEx would deliver a stolen military drone to his little island off the coast of Central America.

The rain was relentless, and Dwight loathed Belize during its hot, rainy season. The humidity was equivalent to a sauna outside the comfort of the lab. Unfortunately, he had a problem with the military-grade drone-detection system he had created, and until it was solved, he was stuck here.

He intended to utilize Professor Mitchell's expertise and knowledge to resolve the issue once the storm passed, and he had the drone in his possession. Until now, he had kept the professor unscathed in case he needed to use him for leverage to get the diamonds. However, it no longer mattered since his informants said the Feds had given the stones to President Jabari.

The storm wasn't the only thing getting on Dwight's nerves. Since his abduction and arrival, Professor Mitchell had acted as if he were on vacation. It was a bizarre mindset since the man's every move was limited and well-guarded.

At first, he treated the professor as a guest. During a tour of the compound, Dwight described his global customer base and successful business ventures, the majority of which he had achieved through questionable means. Aside from that, he was confident the professor would agree to work with him once the man fully understood what Dwight had created and the magnitude of his intellect and successes.

Instead, Professor Mitchell shook his head in disgust. "What a waste of your innate gifts and talent," the professor said as if reprimanding one of his students. "You could use them to make this world a better place. Instead, you choose to help others destroy it. How pathetic."

Dwight was shocked by the response and enraged. If he hadn't needed the professor to help solve the drone's software problem, he would've ordered Ryan to put a bullet to the man's head. In place of it, he locked the professor in a windowless room that contained only a cot, sink, and toilet.

Dwight relocated the professor to a guest suite after calming down and allowed him to roam the compound at night under a heavy guard. He met with the man each day in the hopes something would come of their meetings. Despite his efforts, the professor never wavered from his Boy Scout mindset.

The vault-like door to the lab opened, and Ryan entered, interrupting Dwight's agitated musings. "What now?"

"I told you two days ago we needed to replace the men we lost in North Carolina and Africa. You never got back with me if it was a go. So?"

Pivoting in the chair, Dwight glared at the man. "I don't have time for this! Do I have to do your job too? They'll be under your command. Show some backbone and do what I hired you to do."

Pushing back, Ryan said, "I've worked with some of the recruits in the past, and I'm aware of the others by reputation. Since you like to micromanage, *your lordship*, I *assumed* you'd want to check them out on the internet before I bring them in."

"Clearly, you didn't hear me the first time since you're still here." Dwight turned back to the computer.

Ryan stormed out of the room, slamming the steel-reinforced door closed behind him, which was hard to do, considering it weighed two hundred pounds.

Dwight smiled for the first time in days; he delighted in getting under Ryan's skin. Unlike the professor, the tall, well-built mercenary detested being talked down to by anyone. What did the psychologist call it? Authority complex, or something comparable to it. Dwight was well aware that Ryan put a sergeant major in the hospital back in the day and got booted out of the Marines for it. Whenever Dwight hit a nerve, he made sure Ryan's hand wasn't on the 9mm holstered at his hip.

He checked the security monitors lining the wall above his workstation. Though it was early afternoon, it gave the impression it was dusk outside with the encroaching storm. He noticed Ryan's security detail huddled beneath the various buildings' eaves in an attempt to stay dry. "What wimps."

The island's isolated location and the extensive security

system were causing the guards to be lackadaisical in their duties at the moment, which he planned to reprimand Ryan for the next time they spoke.

The current weather conditions were of little consequence in the lab. The dehumidifiers and AC system hummed within the spacious lab's confines, thus maintaining a climate-controlled environment that was necessary for the highly sophisticated IT equipment Dwight required for his work.

Dissimilar to the ten-thousand-square-foot mega-mansions located throughout the Caribbean, Dwight's compound was more of a fortress and built to sustain a Category Five hurricane with its thick cinderblock and rebar-enforced walls. A maze of rooms that housed Ryan's men and a limited house staff encircled the main structure. The men had access to a gym, an Olympic-sized swimming pool, Jacuzzi, sauna, and game room, which contained billiard tables, multiple TV monitors displaying the various sports channels, and PCs loaded with Dwight's video games. Everything ran on solar-power energy with gas generators as backup.

Dwight's lab occupied one-third of the compound. He rarely slept in the master suite with its king-size bed and wraparound balcony. Though the view of the turquoise blue water was breathtaking from its floor-to-ceiling windows, he preferred to crash on the overstuffed couch in the lab. He was nocturnal by nature, and within the windowless confines, there were times he hadn't a clue if it were day or night.

He procured the very latest in electronics, and when time allowed, refurbished used laptops and PCs prior to selling them on eBay. It held no real financial benefits, but the work calmed his manic brain. Piles of discarded pieces of equipment, motherboards, and gutted PCs and laptops covered the floor and numerous tables.

The lab was a geek's vision of paradise. However, the five-hundred-square-foot dressing room—concealed behind a wall of mirrors in the bathroom—held the greater personal value. It contained Dwight's precious collection of disguises.

Ryan had free rein of the compound except for the lab. Though the mercenary had observed his boss in a variety of disguises through the years, the man didn't have a clue the secret room existed, and Dwight planned to keep it that way.

Raking his hands through his hair, Dwight let out an exasperated sigh. He was still picking up the pieces from his father's house of cards and didn't have time to babysit all the wannabe dictators and drug dealers in the world. Besides the drone-detection software, he was on the brink of developing a new high-tech program that would take drone warfare to a new level for decades to come. North Korea, Iran, and Pakistan had already expressed an interest, and Dwight didn't want to pass up this lucrative opportunity.

A *ping* announcing an incoming coded message caught his attention. "Now what?"

He groaned as he read the encrypted email. Due to his father's untimely death, one of his top three customers—a drug lord in South America—wanted to meet with him in person to discuss business going forward.

"No more middleman," Carlos Alvarez had written. "Now, I deal only with you."

One thing he had learned over the years, never make a valued customer an enemy. He would consent to the man's request and, wearing one of his disguises, meet with him. Ryan would accompany him, and if everything went well, Ryan could deal with the customer going forward.

CHAPTER FIFTY-FIVE

Eleven Hours Later

Inside the lab, the howling winds and pounding rain were inaudible as the storm bore down on them. Ryan barged in, drenched to the bone, and leaving a trail of sopping wet footprints.

Dwight went ballistic. "You're dripping water everywhere!" Ignoring Ryan's current state, he hurried to the bathroom and came back with a stack of towels. While scattering them on the tile floor, his tirade continued.

"We have a problem," Ryan said, ignoring his boss's rantings.

Circling Ryan, Dwight dropped towels at his feet and finally tossed one in the mercenary's direction. "What?"

"We've been monitoring a distress call from a yacht less than a mile to the south of here. The headcount includes eight passengers and the captain. They tried to make it to Belize City ahead of the storm. However, they developed engine trouble and have been adrift ever since."

"And this is my problem because?" Dwight's words seethed with indignation as he pushed the man toward the door, which wasn't an easy feat due to Ryan's size and bulk.

"The yacht began to list and take on water due to the storm. The occupants were able to escape into a life raft before it sank. The captain was the last to leave after signing off on the mayday call."

"So . . . not my problem," Dwight said, reaching for the door.

Ryan swatted his boss's hand away while using the towel to wipe water from his eyes. "I differ regarding that opinion."

"Why?"

"Because the current is bringing them to your little island, and they're using the compound lights as a beacon."

∞

Following the meeting at the Miami FBI field office, and per Agent Fillmore's directive, Alex and Rodriguez used their fake IDs to fly to Raleigh, where they joined Special Agent Belmont with the FBI and Pete, who had flown in from DC for a pre-arranged meeting with the Bishops. Barbara provided an old Christmas card, which she had dug out of the attic, containing a picture of Blake Sanders and his family. It was the only photograph the Bishops had of Dwight; he was about eight years old and dressed in a Grinch costume.

Pete offered what he recalled of his classmate, as did Jim and Barbara Bishop. Agent Belmont used their input to create various sketches depicting Dwight's features as they might be today. Everyone involved with this mission, including Brian and the SEALs team, committed the drawings and the compound schematics to memory before being airlifted to the USS *Fort McHenry* anchored off the coast of Belize. From there, they waited for the approaching storm to make landfall.

∞

It was a little past midnight as Alex, Rodriguez, and the SEALs sped toward the island of Quimera in one of the Navy's midsized amphibious boats. The landing party also included Special Agent Hiroshi Oshiro from NCIS and IT Specialist Nancy Higgins with Navy Intelligence.

The ocean swells were between eight and ten feet high, and waves incessantly broke over the bow. It was a rough ride, but the Mark V SOC was built to handle these types of conditions. Rocking back and forth in sync with the vessel's movement, Alex stood peering over the navigator's shoulder, who was tracking the tropical storm on a monitor via satellite. If the gale hadn't made its timely debut and danced across the Atlantic, moving toward southern Mexico and Belize, they would have had to go to Plan B. Currently, there wasn't a Plan B.

As they drew closer, the running lights were doused, and they used sonar and radar to make their way in the darkness. At the four-mile marker, the boat slowed, and the SEALs—outfitted in assault underwater gear—slid off the slanted aft deck and vanished into the black water. The Mark V proceeded to an uninhabited island a few miles away, where Alex and the others would wait for the all-clear signal.

Glancing at Rodriguez for the umpteenth time, Alex noted her stoic expression as she bounced about strapped in a seat designed for shock-mitigation in rough seas. He trusted the SEALs would locate her husband and prayed nothing happened to him during their assault of the island. Staring off in the distance, he saw the occasional flicker of lights from Dwight's island through the heavy rain.

They'd named the mission *locura pandimoniam*—a suggestion made by Rodriguez—for they intended to create a chaotic distraction. Meanwhile, the SEALs would infiltrate Dwight Sanders's compound, capture him, and rescue Professor Mitchell.

In preparation for the assault, they collected every graphic map and blueprint they could dig up for the island and its compound. Dwight was obsessive, compulsive, and paranoid. He had used multiple contractors from around the globe during the construction of the main house and attached buildings, creating a hodgepodge of plans, thus eliminating the possibility of anyone getting their hands on the exact layout. He went through five different crews alone while constructing the IT lab located in the heart of the compound. That was their prime target, for they knew Dwight would most likely be closeted within it during the storm.

First, the SEALs team had to infiltrate the island's highly sophisticated security system without detection then neutralize ten trained mercenaries patrolling the island.

Due to the compound's thick walls and solid construction, they weren't able to get voice recognition or infrared body heat readings to verify the professor's location inside the buildings. However, they had confirmation he was on the island. Before the storm hit, Professor Mitchell's image was picked up via satellite in the company of two guards while walking on the beach.

∞

Dwight had no idea his secluded island was under siege, not only on one front but two. The nine castaways, who were adrift in the life raft, paddled feverishly to reach the boat dock. The winds weren't as fierce on this side of the island, and soon one of the security guards was able to tie the floundering raft to a cleat on the dock. Waves bombarded its occupants as they clambered over the side and up the ladder, holding on for dear life.

The island had motion detection and landscaping lighting throughout the grounds. In contrast, floodlights illuminated the dock area where the security team scrambled in the torrential downpour to round up their uninvited guests.

Meanwhile, Pete, stationed on the *McHenry* and a team of IT specialists from Navy Intelligence, continued to track the SEALs' underwater progress. Earlier satellite images detected drones patrolling the skies day and night in a three-mile radius. The storm had eliminated that problem. With lightning speed, Pete hammered away on the keyboard in an attempt to spoof Dwight's server. Breaking into a wide grin, he transferred everything to a contingency server that he now controlled.

∞

With the IT techs' help back on the *McHenry*, the underwater and land security sensors and motion detectors were disabled. The SEAL twelve-man assault team rose from the black water and breached the island's north side without discovery. Thick tropical vegetation and scrub trees provided cover as they replaced their fins and goggles with weapons and night optics retrieved from the waterproof pouches attached to their H-harnesses. Splitting up into two-man teams, they spread out and worked their way toward the compound. One security guard—hunkered down out of the rain beneath an outcropping of foliage—was compromised, gagged, and bound, and his radio and weapons confiscated.

The security guard stationed inside the surveillance command center remained fixated on the scene to the south—lit up like New York City—and hadn't noticed the Navy SEAL enter until it was too late. He quickly overpowered the guard, shoved him bound and gagged into a closet, and verified that Pete's security tapes of the compound's north end were running in place of the system's real-time feed. If Dwight were keeping an eye on his island from inside the lab, he wouldn't have a clue as to what was taking place.

As they neared the boat dock, Enrique, the SEALs Chief, and Cooper spotted Ryan, who stood cloaked in darkness beneath a covered porch with an assault rifle slung over his shoulder. He watched the mayhem unfold before him as pounding rain and wind masked any sounds.

A strategically placed blow caught Ryan in the back of his neck, and a leg swipe dropped him to the ground, thus knocking the breath out of him. They flipped the mercenary onto his stomach, and Cooper gagged and bound him with flex cuffs. Enrique pressed a gun against Ryan's temple as Cooper confiscated the man's weapons and two-way radio. They dragged him deeper into the shadows, where the SEALs waited for further instructions from their team leader.

Inside the main compound building, a two-man assault team, each with a Sig P226, cautiously advanced along the eastern corridor, clearing each room one by one. At the far end, they reached what they knew to be the private guest quarters. With stealth-mode precision, they disabled the electronic security lock for the door and entered. Spreading out with one going to the left and the other to the right, they reconnected in the living room, where they happened upon the professor sitting in a comfortable chair, reading. One of the SEALs held a finger to his mouth, signaling the professor to remain quiet as they searched the remaining rooms. Discovering the quarters otherwise unoccupied, the lead SEAL spoke with a hushed voice into his throat mic and informed the team leader that they'd located the professor. Turning to the room's only occupant, he said, "Professor Mitchell; we're with the Navy SEALs. Please come with us."

Putting the book aside, the professor stood, reached for the rain slicker on the hook by the door, and quietly left with his rescuers.

In a different section of the building, Lieutenant Wilcox and two other team members reached the door to the lab. Brian activated his throat mic. "Enrique, Cooper, bring Ryan."

Soon the two SEALs arrived, dragging the uncooperative mercenary along with them as he squirmed and shoved, trying to break free from their grip. A background check revealed that Ryan had a black belt in tae kwon do; thus, his hands remained bound behind his back with flex cuffs and his feet with hammock straps.

When the threesome joined the team leader, Brian pressed a gun to Ryan's temple, and the mercenary went still. Enrique wrapped a second hammock strap around Ryan's upper body, securing his arms to his sides. Removing the flex cuffs, Brian placed the mercenary's right palm on the security-access panel. Cooper simultaneously held the man's forehead against the retinal scanner at eye level. They heard a click, and Brian pushed on the door as Enrique and Cooper dragged Ryan into a nearby alcove.

The plan was to apprehend Dwight first and secure the lab second. However, he was nowhere to be found. The lights and equipment were still on, including the surveillance monitors mounted on one wall. Brian quietly signaled for his men to spread out after noticing the half-eaten sandwich, an open bag of potato chips, and a soda can sitting next to a laptop and PC, both of which were in sleep mode. They took care not to set off any tripwires or hidden explosives as they searched the lab's perimeter and bathroom for another exit. It seemed the only way in or out was the door they came through, which didn't make sense. If there were a fire, Dwight would need an alternate exit. The SEAL team leader ordered Enrique and Cooper to bring Ryan. Once the mercenary was within arm's length, Brian removed the duct tape from Ryan's mouth. "Dwight was in here earlier. Where did he go?"

Glancing around the lab, Ryan responded flatly, "I haven't a clue. I'm not his keeper."

Brian grabbed the man by the shirt collar. Mere inches separated them as he demanded Ryan to tell him where Dwight was hiding.

The mercenary laughed with a thick, sinister sound that came from the gut. "Without Dwight," Ryan said with a sneer, "you have nothing."

"Get him out of here," Brian said sharply. "The rest of you clear this room of any detonation devices. Meanwhile, keep an eye out for a hidden safe room. Dwight has to be somewhere."

The SEAL team leader glanced at his watch, then up at the security monitors.

∞

As planned and right on schedule, the last of the survivors— a pretty blonde dressed in tight cutoffs, a tank top, and a life vest— reached for the security guard's hand while making her way onto the dock. Locking eyes with the stocky man dressed in fatigues, she gave him a bright smile and jabbed a small telescoping-baton into his solar plexus. In reflex, he bent over, gasping for air. She came down hard on the soft spot between his neck and shoulder with her elbow, and his eyes rolled back into their sockets. He pitched forward, landing on the rain-soaked boards with a *thump*.

The remaining FBI agents masquerading as the stricken passengers took their cue from the blonde and disarmed the rest of the guards. The mercenaries were rounded up and relocated to the game room, where three FBI agents kept an eye on them. Meanwhile, the others teamed up with the SEALs in conducting a thorough search of the main compound and various outbuildings in a determined effort to find Dwight.

CHAPTER FIFTY-SIX

THE LARGE RECREATION ROOM, which had been utilized by Dwight's security guards, became the temporary detention center. Rodriguez was the first one through the door with Alex, Agent Oshiro, and IT Specialist Nancy Higgins on her heels. She came to a stop in the middle of the room and turned in a circle looking for her husband as rainwater poured off her FBI rain slicker, creating a puddle at her feet.

Beyond the billiard tables, seven guards, including Ryan, were on their knees with their hands bound behind their backs. Three of Fillmore's agents, each holding a semiautomatic weapon confiscated during the takedown, kept a vigilant eye on their prisoners.

At one end of the room, Rodriguez noticed the groundskeeper, Miguel, who sat huddled together with his family on the U-shaped sectional couch in front of a large wall-mounted TV screen. She recalled from staffing reports that Miguel's brother, Luis, was in charge of maintaining the property. Their two wives prepared meals for the mercenaries, plus took care of the laundry and housekeeping duties.

The two Belizean women cowered farther into the corner of the couch as three SEALs, laden with full-assault gear, entered the room through a door that led to the mercenary's quarters.

Brian and his men made a beeline for Ryan; simultaneously, the mercenary was yanked to his feet by one of the FBI agents.

"Enough of your games," Brian said, spittle landing on Ryan's face as he spoke. "Tell me where Dwight is hiding."

Upon noticing the SEAL team leader, Rodriguez proceeded in that direction with Alex and the others trailing behind. A dozen small TVs, plus the large one at the far end of the room, displayed a variety of sports channels. The cacophony of noise was nerve-racking. As they approached, Brian yelled, "Would somebody turn those stupid things off before I use them for target practice?"

Raising her voice to be heard, Rodriguez shouted, "Brian, where's my husband? And where's Dwight?"

The team leader pointed over his shoulder with a thumb. "Professor Mitchell's sitting over there, but we haven't located Dwight yet."

The TVs went silent at the same time Rodriguez shrieked, "You've got to be joking!"

In the corner of the room, the professor sat playing video games on one of the PCs. Hearing her voice, he pushed back and rose from the chair. "Maria!"

When she didn't immediately respond, he began weaving his way through the FBI agents and mercenaries in her direction. "Maria, I'm over here!"

Rodriguez watched her husband stride toward her with arms outstretched, ready to embrace her. She marched right up to him and, rearing back, planted a right cross to his jaw. Those located in the vicinity, including Alex, gasped as the man's glasses flew through the air. Dazed, the professor cupped the bruised jaw with his hand.

"That's for nearly getting Pete, Dr. Newman, and Captain Decker killed," she spat out.

Alex and Brian stepped closer just as she kneed the man in the groin. His legs buckled, and two SEALs each grabbed an arm to keep him from falling. "And that's for kidnapping my husband, you worthless piece of cow manure."

Alex gripped her forearm. "What are you doing? Have you gone insane?"

Shrugging off his hand, she impaled him with eyes filled with venomous rage. Addressing the man they assumed was Professor Mitchell, she reached out and snatched a wig from his head. White hair fell to his shoulders. Next, she yanked off the fake mustache and nose putty, which revealed skin lacking in pigmentation. Blood coated his teeth, and a trickle of it ran from his nose. Having lost a blue contact lens during the altercation, it didn't go unnoticed that one of his eyes had a pink iris.

Grabbing a full fist of stringy hair, she pulled Dwight's face close to hers. "Where's my husband?" she hissed between clenched teeth.

The FBI agent standing next to Ryan was distracted by the confrontation between Rodriguez and Dwight Sanders. Ryan dropped to his knees and finished cutting through the bindings at his wrist and ankles with the tactical knife he had retrieved earlier from the heel of his boot. Before the agent could react, Ryan jumped up and seized the FBI agent's Berretta 9mm. He drove a fist into the man's gut, and in five quick strides, approached Dwight from behind.

Sensing movement, Rodriguez let go of Dwight's hair. Before they realized what was happening, Ryan had snaked an arm around his boss's neck in a chokehold and pressed the 9mm against his ear. Jerking Dwight away from the two SEALs who still held onto him, Ryan said, "Nobody move, or he's a dead man."

Brian raised his hands, palms out. "Take it easy. No need to be rash. I'm sure we can work something out."

Dwight clawed at the mercenary's arm with both hands, and in a raspy voice, said, "You're choking me. Let me go."

"Shut up," Ryan hissed in his boss's ear. "You're my ticket

out of here. What'd she call you? Oh yeah. You worthless piece of cow manure."

Releasing his grip on Ryan's arm, Dwight reached for a gun hidden inside the left pocket of his rain slicker and pointed it behind him, level with Ryan's heart.

The next thing they heard was the unmistakable *pop* from a gun. Ryan let go of Dwight and stumbled backward. Wide-eyed with shock, he looked down at the red stain on the chest of his fatigues. Reaching out, he took a step towards Dwight when his knees gave way, and he collapsed to the floor, face down.

Rodriguez moved to overtake Dwight; nevertheless, he anticipated it. Catching her midstride, he jammed his gun into her gut. "Back off, everyone just back off." Raising her hands, she complied, as did the others.

He spat out a combination of bloody mucus, including pieces of a broken tooth, onto the floor. He glared at Rodriguez while wiping his chin off with the back of his hand. "Woman, I've had enough of you meddling in my life."

Alex and Brian exchanged a look as Dwight raised the gun and pointed it at Rodriguez. Alex dove for her. At the same time, Brian ducked and ran full speed toward Dwight. The Navy SEAL tackled him to the floor, but not before Dwight fired off two rounds. Brian slammed an uppercut to the chin with his elbow. Dwight's head struck the floor with a loud thump, and he went limp.

Alex collided with Rodriguez, and they fell to the floor. He moaned as she tried to extricate herself from beneath him. He finally rolled off her onto his back, and she spotted a small hole and blood on the right shoulder of his FBI rain slicker. Blood was also dripping onto the floor from the crown of his head, where a bullet had grazed him. She was relieved the shot hadn't caught him between the eyes; even so, his breathing was labored.

"Brian, Alex's hit! Medic! I need a medic over here!" She knelt beside her motionless friend and checked his pupils, which were dilated. "Alex, can you hear me? Come on; stay with me."

∞

Alex was aware of people scurrying around him, barking orders. Through the fog of semi-consciousness, he recognized Rodriguez's and Brian's voices; who were the others? Should he know them?

He felt the jab of a needle going into his arm and was grateful when the pain in his shoulder subsided. He just wished someone would give him aspirin for the throbbing headache. He surrendered to sleep to escape it.

CHAPTER FIFTY-SEVEN

THEY AIRLIFTED ALEX TO the USS *Fort McHenry*. After stabilizing him, they transferred him to a hospital in Miami, where a medical team of highly qualified doctors and nurses performed surgery to relieve pressure on Alex's brain. Nevertheless, he remained in a coma, and the weeks turned into a month.

In his dreams, he could hear them discussing a patient who'd sustained a subdural hematoma caused by a glancing blow to the head from a bullet. They said there was a chance the man could lose full use of his motor skills. However, they wouldn't understand the extent of the damage until he awoke. *Are they talking about me?*

∞

He stirred, tried to swallow, and found his mouth was bone-dry. The room was in semidarkness, and the hospital was quiet due to the late hour. The only noise came from the machines monitoring his vitals. Sensing someone in the room with him, Alex tried to open his eyes, but it took too much effort. *Who's there?* Did he think it, or did he say it?

"Hello, Alex. God's a little busy right now, so he sent me." The man's tone was comforting as he placed a hand on Alex's injured shoulder. Intense heat radiated across his chest and down his arms and legs as the stranger began to pray. Upon finishing, he placed a hand on each side of Alex's head, and the ever-present headache dissipated.

"Everything is going to be okay, Alex. Give it time and rest for now."

No argument there, he groggily thought as he drifted off.

∞

Dragging a spoon through the mush that was his evening meal, Alex screwed up his mouth in disgust. For the past three days, since he had awoken, his culinary choices had consisted of chicken broth, tapioca pudding, apple sauce, and Jell-O. *If I weren't so weak, I'd escape this madness.*

For a moment, he imagined he smelled a mixture of garlic and savory pasta wafting in from the hallway, which made his stomach growl so loud he was sure the patient in the next room must've heard it. *I wish someone would please bring me a decent meal to eat!*

As if hearing his brooding mental request, Agent Rodriguez and Professor Mitchell entered the hospital room. They were laden with bags of food from Il Gabbiano restaurant. The overpowering aromas made his head spin, and his stomach growled again. "How'd you get all that past the Gestapo nurse, Von Uber-something?"

The professor closed the door as Rodriguez crossed the room and sat her bags down on the bed. "I can be charming when the occasion calls for it. Plus, we brought enough for the whole nursing staff, which we left in the breakroom prior to coming to find you."

She picked up his meal tray with the spoon stuck like an arrow in the center of the brown-and-green goop. "Yuck. It seems we got here just in the nick of time." Handing the tray to her husband, she said, "Darling, please go flush whatever this is down the toilet."

Professor Mitchell deposited his bags on the bed next to the others before heading to the bathroom to dispose of the tray with its mystery-meal. In the meantime, Rodriguez extracted a variety of fancy takeout dishes from her parcels and placed them on the bedside table.

"I wanted to keep it simple for your first real meal. I'm afraid I went a bit overboard, so take it slow, cowboy. The nurses can always warm something up for you later."

His mouth watered as she opened each container. There was cheese-stuffed tortellini in a white wine cream sauce with bacon; breasts of chicken filled with ham, fontina cheese, and asparagus; risotto with scallops, shrimp, mussels, and lobster bits; and his favorite, veal sautéed in lemon butter, capers, and white wine with steamed asparagus. She unwrapped freshly baked garlic bread with melted cheese on top, and he moaned with pleasure at the sight of it.

"Rod, feed that boy something," her husband said as he rejoined them. "You're torturing him, and that goes for me too. I've endured smelling the food ever since we left the restaurant."

Laughing, she fixed a small plate for Alex with a sample from each container and a larger one for the professor as he arranged two chairs for them to sit on. After preparing a plate for herself, she sat down next to her husband and dug in.

Closing his eyes, Alex let the first bite of real food fill his senses. Methodically chewing each morsel that followed, his palate awakened to the taste of butter, cheese, wine, garlic, and pasta. The next sampling contained bits of bacon, or was it prosciutto? It didn't matter; it all tasted fantastic. He devoured the last tidbit and announced, "This is the best meal ever! Thank you."

Rodriguez finished hers at the same time. "It's the least I can do since you took a bullet for me."

His brow furrowed as he tried to recall the events that had landed him here.

Setting her plate down, she rose and approached the bed. "Do you remember what happened?"

"Only bits and pieces. Brian was here earlier and filled me in on some of it." Meeting the professor's eyes, he said, "From what I gather, at first they presumed Dwight figured out what was happening and disguised himself as you in an attempt to escape. They found out differently afterward."

Carl handed his empty plate to his wife and stood. "That's true. There's a hidden passageway connecting the safe room to the guest quarters. That's where Blake stayed during his visits. Dwight could traverse between the two undetected by the staff or guards. After I arrived, he would disguise himself as me and exchange places with me from time to time. He enjoyed fooling the guards when they came to take him for the scheduled late evening walk. That night happened to be one of those times, and he wanted to see for himself what was taking place down at the dock. I'm sure he was surprised when the SEALs showed up instead of his guards that night."

Directing his next question at Rodriguez, Alex said, "I want to know how you figured it out so quickly that it was Dwight and not your husband."

She glanced up at her spouse of eighteen years with a twinkle in her eye, "Carl is from Calgary and has never mastered the pronunciation of my first name correctly due to his Canuck accent. The dead giveaway was when Dwight said my name and stated the *r* perfectly in Maria. Plus, Carl tore his left ACL playing hockey in college and, as you can see, walks with a slight limp. Dwight made the mistake of favoring the wrong leg as he approached me."

Alex smiled. "Remind me never to attempt to bamboozle you." Addressing the professor, he said, "Brian told me your wife was the one who found you locked inside the hidden closet."

"Correct. Dwight was unhinged by the time he came to get me. The weather, the invasion of the castaways, and the delayed shipment of a stolen drone had him so rattled that he didn't realize he had left his satellite phone behind. When he didn't come back within the normal time-span, I grew restless and started poking around. It was at that moment I caught sight of the phone peeking out from beneath his discarded clothing lying on the floor." The professor put an arm around Rodriguez's shoulder and drew her closer. "I texted the one number I know by heart, and she was the first one through the door."

Switching topics, Alex said, "What became of Blake's son-in-law, the lawyer?"

Rodriguez began clearing their dishes. "We've got Paul Dyer on tax evasion and money laundering. All his assets—along with Blake's, including the mansion and Dyer's house in Charleston—were seized. Blake's wife and daughter had to relocate to a townhouse. Fortunately for them, a few of Blake's investments were actually in his wife's name. They'll be able to live comfortably, though not in the same affluent lifestyle they were accustomed to in the past."

Favoring his right arm, Alex used his left to snag a piece of garlic bread before she wrapped it up. "What's the latest regarding Dwight?"

The professor was the first to respond. "I'm helping the Feds interrogate him. Some of the IT stuff is even beyond their scope of intellect. He's brilliant but so screwed up. It's a shame."

"As you've witnessed, my husband is far more forgiving than I am," Rodriguez said with a scowl. "By the way, Agent Fillmore plans to drop by tomorrow to debrief you. Unfortunately, you won't be here."

"Really? Where am I going to be?"

"Dr. Newman has located a good facility in Raleigh where you're able to rehab and get your strength back. Plus, you have some friends there who are missing you. Bishop has commandeered a friend's private jet to fly you home. An ambulance will be here first thing in the morning to pick you up and take you to the airport."

She finished packing up the food and handed the containers to her husband. "Be a dear and go ask the nurse to warm some of these leftovers for Alex later. I'm sure he'll be hungry again soon. I'll catch up with you at the elevators."

The professor shifted the carryout bags to his left hand while extending his right to shake with Alex. "Captain, I'm eternally grateful for all you've done for my wife. We're both very grateful. I pray you'll have a speedy recovery, and please keep in touch."

"Thank you; I promise I will."

As the door closed, Rodriguez straightened the rumpled bedding, repositioned the bedside table, and stepped to the side of the bed. Raising her hand, she stroked the month's growth of whiskers on Alex's chin and cheek. "It's a shame you'll have to shave it off when you put the uniform back on. There's a touch of gray in it, and it's coming in nicely. Looks good on you."

He reached up and took her hand in his as their eyes met.

Clearing her throat, she said, "So, Captain, I suppose you'll be stepping back into the cockpit as soon as they allow it. How do you think that will feel after working for the FBI?"

Alex smiled. "I have to admit it may not be as action-packed, but I believe I've had enough excitement for a while."

Fighting back the tears of gratitude, she flippantly said, "If you come to your senses and change your mind, you know how to find me."

She leaned in, and they hugged. "I'm so glad you woke up. I was afraid I would never have the chance to thank you for being there for me. You always said the right thing at the right time, even if I didn't want to hear it."

"Well, you can be stubborn at times."

They both laughed as she withdrew.

"Maria, thank you for dragging me into this mess. I wouldn't have had it any other way."

"Oh, I almost forgot. I have a present for you." She stepped to the end of the bed and reached for a long, narrow box leaning against the bed frame. Placing it on his lap, she said, "I saw it sitting in the corner of Richard's cabin when I was his unwilling guest and had it sent to forensics. Your fingerprints were on it plus traces of hair and tissue from when he clobbered you. I thought you might want it back."

Alex tore open the box and stared in disbelief at his missing bat. "This day just keeps getting better and better."

CHAPTER FIFTY-EIGHT

TALL CORNSTALKS AND INTERMITTENT crops of wheat, painted golden by the morning light, danced in the breeze on both sides of the country road leading to Highway 41. Off in the distance, orange pumpkins ready for harvesting lay scattered in an open field. The heat and humidity of summer had surrendered to cold nights and the crisp, invigorating days of autumn.

At the edge of Sanford, Alex merged onto Highway 1, thus turning north toward Raleigh. Traffic was light today, and in less than an hour, he swung left off the main road and entered Oakwood Cemetery. Both of the Bishops' grown children had been laid to rest here in the company of sixteen hundred North Carolina soldiers from the Civil War, state politicians, and family members with political or historical lineage. So much had happened since the day he had traveled this same route in May with Jim Bishop.

He pulled the Silverado to a stop, climbed out, and slipped on his uniform coat and hat with the captain's embroidered gold leaves. It remained a mystery as to who his visitor was the night everything changed for the better. When he awoke from the coma the next morning, Alex inquired as to the man's name and learned he had had no visitors the previous evening.

The shooting and month-long coma took a toll on his body. However, the physical therapy and his determination to get back in the air paid off. Alex rotated his right shoulder and flexed his fingers. The arm was stronger than before he was shot, and gone were the headaches, along with the nightmares. He didn't miss them, though he did miss the mystical presence of Marcus and Caroline. If it weren't for the events as they unfolded, Alex would've believed the sightings of the Bishop children were hallucinations attributed to his PTSD.

He planned to continue the sessions with the psychiatrist, Dr. Fletcher, even though the anxiety attacks no longer plagued him, having receded into the dark corners of his mind, for good, he hoped.

The team of physicians treating him unanimously agreed it was a miracle that Alex had experienced no side-effects from the trauma to his head. Not only did his wounds heal quickly, but his motor skills tested perfect, as did his hearing and vision. He was officially released for duty, effective today. However, he wanted to visit the cemetery first, prior to driving to the Greensboro Airport.

He retrieved a graveside spray of flowers in bright autumn colors from the backseat and walked up the grassy knoll to where two modest grave markers sat side by side. A large maple tree lay a few feet beyond; its fall foliage blanketed the ground in a kaleidoscope of orange, red, and brown leaves. He noticed another picturesque tree off to his right—half of it cloaked in bright red leaves and the other half in emerald green—with a sculpted bench stationed beneath it.

His attention was drawn to the two engraved markers. He removed his hat, placed the flowers on the ground between them, then stepped back, giving himself some space.

"Marcus . . . Caroline, you two nearly sent me over the edge with your haunting dreams and those crazy cryptic messages from beyond. I'm glad you didn't give up on me, and—and—" The next few words caught in his throat, but he needed to say them. "Thank you for saving my life time and again."

Sensing a change in the atmosphere, the hair on the back of his neck bristled, and the crown of his head tingled as if ants were parading across his scalp. The autumn air grew colder as a slight breeze stirred the leaves on the ground at his feet. The adult Bishop children materialized in front of the tree. Caroline, silhouetted in an elusive radiant light, stood next to her brother, Marcus, whose image was noticeably sharper than hers.

"Hello, sir," Marcus said. "We're eternally grateful for what you did for our parents, and it's been an honor knowing you."

"I'm so glad you're both here." Alex's tone reflected the sense of awe he was experiencing. "I have so many questions I want to ask you."

The iridescent light surrounding them grew in intensity, and Marcus slowly shook his head. "It's time for us to go."

Alex looked at Caroline, and she greeted him with a smile. The degree of unconditional love radiating from her reminded him of the day she had appeared in the rearview mirror of his truck.

"Wait. Before you do, I have to ask, why me? Why did you pick me to help you?"

"Oh yes, about that," Caroline said. "The truth of the matter is this was a team effort."

As their images faded, they were replaced by Alex's father and his wife.

"Dad! Sarah!"

The leaves rustling in the trees overhead went unnoticed, as did the red cardinal singing to its mate. As far as Alex was concerned, the world had ceased to exist beyond those who appeared just beyond his reach.

His father beamed, the smile reaching the older man's eyes.

"Son, I'm so proud of you. So many have benefited from your efforts and your help - the Bishops, Agent Rodriguez and her husband, even those in Côte d'Ivoire."

"I miss you guys," Alex said, a sob catching in his throat.

"We're always with you, son. Once someone occupies a place in a person's heart, they're never really gone."

Alex's eyes met Sarah's, and he knew it was true.

"I have a special message for you from God," his father said as he continued. "Do you remember the time you came home during your senior year of high school and announced that you had changed your mind and weren't going to college? You said performing in the air shows was your true destiny."

"I remember," Alex admitted, ashamed of the memory now.

"I always supported you in whatever life choices you made, yet that was one time I couldn't. You needed to go on to college. You were angry, and two weeks passed until you spoke to me again. Eventually, you came to the right decision on your own. I loved you even more during those difficult days you shut me out. Now you understand how God has felt these past few years."

Alex's throat constricted as he fought back the tears.

"There may be times in our lives when we may turn our backs on God," his father said. "But He never turns away from us. On a soul level, He's always there and couldn't love you any less or more than He does in this moment or any other given time."

"I miss you so much, Dad."

"Oh, one more thing. Tell your mother there was never a day I regretted giving up the sea for her. She was my safe harbor."

"I will," he promised.

Sarah remained behind as his father's image faded. As she spoke, the memory of her voice came flooding back and filled his heart.

"I was worried about you for a while; now, I know you are going to be okay. I'm so proud of you, darling."

"My life's been unbearably empty without you."

"I understand." She paused briefly, then continued. "I want you to know you'll always be a hero in my eyes. I love you." And she was gone.

For a second time, Alex felt as if his heart took flight with her parting, leaving behind an empty shell of a man. His strength gave way, and he collapsed to his knees, sobbing. Heart-wrenching pain spilled forth as he bent over and pressed his forehead to the ground.

He cried for the loss of his father and close friend and wingman, Chris. He cried for all the victims and their families from past wars, current ones, and those in the future. Finally, he wept for the loss of the most precious thing in his life, Sarah.

In time, the tears subsided. With a big sigh, Alex released the heaviness that had lived within his chest for so long. Knowing Sarah, along with the others, was in Heaven with God, and Jesus filled him with a sense of peace.

Sitting back on his heels, he reached for a handkerchief and dried his eyes. "Thank you, God, for never giving up on me."

Rising to his feet, he teetered momentarily prior to getting his footing. Alex stared at the area where the four spirits once stood, wishing they would reappear, before accepting the fact that they were gone for good.

He doubted he could fully explain what had just happened. In any case, he would share what just transpired with Robert, Dr. Newman, and Agent Rodriguez.

Bending down, he picked up his hat, which had fallen to the ground, and brushed grass cuttings from his pant legs. As he straightened, Alex sensed someone was watching him. Glancing to his right, he noticed Suzanne, Marcus's fiancée, sitting on the bench underneath the maple tree. A gentle smile graced her face.

"Have you been there long?" he said, embarrassed.

"Not long, really." Her eyes gave nothing away.

He determined that she wasn't being totally honest and made up his mind to let it pass. "May I join you?"

"Please do." She slid over, making room for him on the bench. Once he was seated, a questioning expression mirrored her next words. "You look vaguely familiar. Have we met before?"

"In truth, this is the third time we've crossed paths. We first met at Caroline's funeral. The second time was when you spilled coffee on me in Starbucks at the Crabtree Mall."

"That was you! Oh, dear. I had to leave and didn't get the chance to apologize, although Jim said afterward that you were okay."

He began to laugh and didn't want to stop. How long had it been since he had laughed, really laughed? "I promise the pain of the experience was minimal," he said, trying to suppress another outburst. He couldn't help it. It was such a quirky thing running into her after all this time.

She tilted her head. "Are you okay now? You seemed upset earlier."

Her words sobered him a bit, and he addressed the question. "I guess you were sitting here longer than a few minutes?"

"Maybe." Her expression changed to one of surprise. "I just realized you're the Galaxy captain who worked with the FBI in apprehending Dwight Sanders." Her eyes glistened with tears, and she reached into her purse for a tissue. "You helped solve the murder of my fiancé. Captain Decker, how can I ever thank you enough?"

"I appreciate your words. And I'm grateful that everything worked out the way it did."

Once she collected herself, he added, "My first name is Alex. It's a pleasure running into you again, Suzanne, especially since there's no coffee in sight."

His words caused her to chuckle lightly in response.

"I've grown fond of the Bishops," he admitted. "They're extraordinary people."

"I couldn't agree more. We have dinner together after church each week. Would you like to join us sometime?"

"Thank you, but if it's not imposing, I would like to do both church and dinner."

"Why yes, that would be wonderful."

Noticing the time, Alex said he needed to get to work. As he walked Suzanne to her car, a thought crossed his mind. "Have you ever flown in an antique biplane?"

"No, I can honestly say I haven't."

"Saturday is predicted to be another beautiful day. Could I interest you in taking a spin in my new airplane?

"Is it safe?"

"Safer than the trip you're about to take in this earthbound vehicle," he said as he opened the driver's door for her.

"In that case, I accept your invitation, Captain."

AUTHORS NOTE

I thought you might enjoy the following tidbit of information.

English: Chimera Spanish: Quimera
   Pronounced: ki-mira
   • (in Greek mythology) A fire-breathing female monster
     with a lion's head, a goat's body, and a serpent's tail.
   • A thing that is hoped or wished for but in fact, is illusory
     or impossible to achieve.
   "the economic sovereignty you claim to defend is a chimera."

synonyms: illusion, fantasy, delusion, dream, daydream, pipe
dream, a figment of the/one's imagination, castle in the air,
mirage
"is this great love of hers merely a chimera?"
http://cathleendunn.com/what-is-a-chimera/

https://translate.google.com/#view=home&op=translate&sl=en
&tl=es&text=chimeras

Made in the USA
Middletown, DE
28 December 2025

26302043R00177